Sweet Hawaii 2

Stella Preissler

.... **Chapter 1** ....

Waikiki Wahine 1970

"I want to nail *that girl*," Duke Haku said out loud. Duke was standing outdoors on the lanai at the Waikiki Outrigger Bar and Grill restaurant. He'd been watching *that girl* on the beach for the last half an hour. His eyes glued to her bronzed, tanned, playboy body in that black bikini. Stunning, with beautiful legs that seemed to go on forever and her long wavy honey brown hair was the color of a fine blended whiskey with golden highlights. She was enchanting, bewitching, and very sexy, he thought.

As a local boy, Duke had a thing for *haole* (Caucasian) girls. He was drawn to them, like these tourists were to the Hawaiian sunshine. They were so different from the local island girls he'd grown up with on the big island of Hawaii. And *that girl* was in a class all of her own, he mused.

Duke was the food and beverage director at the Outrigger Surf Hotel located right in the heart of Waikiki. The outdoor grill was packed with tourists enjoying happy hour, *pupus* (appetizers), and tropical drinks. It was abuzz with activity and loud animated voices. There was Hawaiian music in the background along with the sounds of people, and their drink glasses clinking in the spirit of aloha. Good, he thought, not much of a chance that anyone heard his words about wanting to nail *that girl*.

He ran his hand through his well-groomed, thick black hair, and then adjusted his aviator sunglasses. Who was she? Did she live here? He'd find out soon; but for now, he just wanted to watch her a little longer and bask in the titillating high that she provoked in him. He sat down at the bar and ordered a Coke. He'd ask around about her before checking on the banquet staff for the evening. One of the benefits of being food and beverage director was that he could pretty much write his own ticket and do what he wanted, just floating around checking on the bars and restaurants within the hotel. Staff perked up when they knew he was near. It was just another thing he loved to do, strut his stuff and give orders, he mused, with a smile as he continued to be fascinated by *that girl*.

She was with a girlfriend, they were talking. Too far away for him to hear what they were saying, fifty yards down the beach. They were soaking up the sun, sprawled out on their beach mats. He took a swallow of his Coke deciding that when he was done, he'd stroll over and introduce himself. But for now, he would just sit back observe, and wait for the right moment.

◆◆◆

"Brandi, are you ready for a swim?" Donna, my roommate asked, while wiggling her toes in the hot sand and sitting up. She adjusted her baseball cap and pushed a strand of her long dark hair behind one ear.

"Not yet, I'm content to just sit here a little longer. It's so breathtakingly beautiful," I replied. But the truth was I was in a melancholy mood today, reminiscing about my past navy submarine boyfriend, who had left the island three months ago for additional nuclear sub training back stateside...without me. Skip had stolen my heart and soul from the first time I had met him. I had never been so in love with a man as I had been with him or so devastated in the end, leaving me without a promise or commitment.

I had been living on the island of Oahu for a year now. At twenty-one years old I had bravely left the bleakness of Seattle last December and headed for Honolulu, Hawaii. I was desperate for change and new adventures. Skip, my navy man, had definitely given me that, I thought, even though he had shattered my heart when he chose to return stateside for more naval training. The letters I'd received since he'd left for New London, Connecticut only indicated that he really missed me, but it didn't mention that he couldn't live without me.

They were vague and newsy, leaving me with little hope. Snap out of it, quit pining for him, it's a lost cause, my inner voice said.

I stretched out on my bamboo beach mat and glanced around. Ah...Hawaii. This was my favorite spot in front of the Outrigger Hotel. How many days had I spent hanging out here this past year? Too many to count. It was Sunday and Donna and I had the day off.

Waikiki Beach was packed with tourists and families. People watching was one of our favorite pastimes. I glanced over at Donna, who was now sprawled out on her back with her baseball hat pulled over her face. Her skimpy blue bikini and tan skin glistened with small beads of perspiration, evidence of the intense Hawaiian heat, even in early December.

The sun shone brightly with big white puffy clouds overhead and the trade winds blew softly, as the palm trees swayed gently in the tropical breeze. Out beyond the beach, the ocean was littered with a couple dozen surfboarders catching waves. A catamaran filled with tourists sailed effortlessly beyond the reef, as if it were motorized with its sails fully blossomed by the trade winds.

Taking a deep breath, I thought about how much I loved living here in paradise, even without my Skip. I reached for my Coppertone sunscreen, poured out a handful massaging it into my tan legs, arms, and midriff as I looked over once again at Donna.

"You want some Coppertone, Donna?"

"Nah, I'm good, thanks, Brandi."

"Okay," I replied, thinking that I could lie here all day if I wanted because I had the evening off, too.

I was now working at the Hilton Hawaiian Village at the north end of Waikiki strip. It was my second home and where I did everything from hostessing, waitressing, bartending, and working banquets. I worked the swing shift, which was perfect because it enabled me to hang out at the beach during the day. Then I could either walk down *Kalakaua* Avenue or hop the metro bus for a mile and a half ride to the Hilton Hawaiian Village.

Turning up the volume on my pocket-sized transistor radio, a Beatles song, "Yesterday" came on and Donna started singing along happily. Loneliness swept through me. It was such a struggle learning how to live without Skip in my life. At least I had two groovy roommates, Donna and Sherry, for best friends, I thought, while staring at the sparkling blue ocean in front of me wishing that Skip were here.

Donna sat up eyeballing me. "Are you thinking about Skip again?" she questioned, looking pathetically at me.

"Yeah, I miss him so much," I said, while putting my long honey colored hair in a ponytail and then adjusting my sunglasses and visor.

"Brandi, for God's sake, I think Skip would have asked you to be with him by now. It's been three months since he left," Donna said with an impatient tone.

"Yeah, I know, but it's so hard to move on," I responded. The song, "Can't Get No Satisfaction" by the Stones, played on my transistor radio and echoed in my ears making me even more nostalgic. That seemed to be my MO these days. No satisfaction in sight.

"I know, Donna, I really need to stop clinging to hope and move on," I said, slumping back down while letting the sun toast the front of my already bronzed body.

"Brandi," Donna said, turning to face me. "You're only twenty-one. Trust me, I'm close to thirty. You will get past this no matter what. Skip's not the only guy that will float your boat and set your hormones on fire. And there are certainly a lot of good looking local boys around. You need to date again, girlfriend," she stated with conviction, as she slipped off her baseball hat and sunglasses. "I'm hot; I'm going for a swim. Join me when you're ready." She stood up and ran down to the beach like she couldn't get there fast enough.

"Yeah, okay, I will in a little while," I yelled after her.

Settling into a reclining position, I closed my eyes. Donna was right; I should date again. A vivid picture of Skip with his sandy blond hair, those deep blue eyes, cute cleft chin, and that sexy Midwestern Nebraskan drawl in his voice, seemed to haunt me.

The song, "I've Been Lonely Too Long" by the Young Rascals, now played. I had been lonely for too long. Disgusted with myself, I turned off my transistor radio thinking that I had to stop this pining for Skip once and for all.

God, I needed to go for a swim. Grabbing my beach bag with my money in it, I decided to leave it at the Outrigger pool towel shack for safety reasons. My friend, Tonklin, was working there today as a guard. He was a local and a full-time firefighter with the Honolulu Fire Department. Like many locals, he worked a second job, hence the Outrigger pool guard.

I got up, ran quickly barefoot across the scorching sand, and stepped up to the pool deck stairs. "Hey, Brandi girl, how you be?" Tonklin asked, as I neared the towel shack.

"I'm okay, Tonklin, lonely without my Skip, but I'm going to move on." I looked at his tall, muscular, oiled, brown skinned body. Tonklin was so cute with dark black soft eyes and a sweet genuine smile. We were such good beach friends.

"How's that new baby girl, Tonklin?"

"Ah, she so good," he replied, with a big Hawaiian smile. "I so happy, yeah."

"I'm happy for you. Can you watch my bag while I go for a swim?"

"Brandi girl, anything for you." He reached for my beach bag and stuffed it into a shelf behind him in the towel shack.

"Okay, thanks, Tonklin," I said and headed down the beach. I waded out to my waist and then dove into the ocean. Swimming always helped center me. I'd been a competitive all American swimmer during my teen life. Endless hours of pool training, but open water swimming was so different. No laps, no sets, and no flip turns. Oh wow, the cool salt water against my heated skin; it felt so good. Heading out past the reefs, I swam like a dolphin, doing freestyle and some butterfly. I pushed myself to get a good long open water workout in, while letting my thoughts drift like the easy moving current.

◆◆◆

Duke didn't miss the exchange between Tonklin and *that girl*. He left the Outrigger Bar and Grill and headed to the pool towel shack. He'd ask Tonklin about *that girl*, who piqued his interest beyond anyone he'd seen in a long time. He liked the way she moved. She had a grace about her along with a killer body, long beautiful legs, and a rack of bodacious tatas that aroused his appetite even more. He couldn't take his eyes off her as she headed out into the surf. And then, he'd watched her swim. He knew instinctively that she'd been a competitive swimmer. Not many girls could swim like that, he surmised. Beautiful freestyle stroke and fly. His kind of girl, athletic and sexy as hell in that little black bikini. God damn, he had to find out more about her before she left the beach. Determined to get with her, he headed over to Tonklin.

"Hey Tonklin, how's it going?" Duke asked, as he reached the towel shack with one objective in mind.

"Hey Duke, it be good and you?" Tonklin responded, thinking that Duke looked the part of a food and beverage director wearing white cotton pants, white shoes, and a blue print aloha shirt. His black hair was swept behind his ears and shagged in the back, reaching below his neckline. Tonklin thought that Duke could be a real prick at times. Hot shot, a lot of employees called him. Someone you didn't want to mess with, arrogant, cocky, and a womanizer. Duke had fired people right and left when he took over three months ago as food and beverage director. Luckily, Tonklin thought, he didn't have to report to him.

Relaxing, Duke rested his elbow on the towel shack bar. He pointed out to the open water. "Who's that gorgeous *haole* girl in the black bikini that you were talking to?"

Tonklin raised an eyebrow. "Yeah, she be gorgeous for sure. Her name, Brandi. Brandi McGraw. Real nice girl. She be here a year from Seattle."

"She have a boyfriend?" Duke asked, knowing that it wouldn't matter to him even if she did. He had a way of charming the ladies into whatever he wanted and screwing over boyfriends that got in the way.

"Not now. Navy guy broke her heart. Gone stateside. She be so in love with him still. Why? You interested?"

"Who wouldn't be, with a sexy thing like that," Duke stated with a wide grin, while adjusting his aviator sunglasses. "You know where she works?"

Tonklin folded some clean towels and put them away. He wasn't sure if he should tell Duke. He didn't like guys like Duke, bossy, overconfident, and a player. "Yeah, she work at Hilton Hawaiian Village," he replied reluctantly.

"Really?" Duke asked, with amusement and couldn't believe his good luck.

"What does she do there?"

"Oh, she waitress, hostess, and works banquets, just about everything," Tonklin stated, glancing at the pool, watching some kids dunking under and playing pool games.

"Tonklin, I'm leaving this hotel in a week, going to be the new food and beverage director at the Hilton Hawaiian Village. I guess she'll be working for me then," Duke stated with a devious grin. He wanted to wine and dine *that girl*, Brandi. And that wasn't all he had plans to do. He'd use his new position to spend time with her, mentor her along and stoke her fires until she was putty in his hands. He'd make her forget about that navy guy.

"How old is she?" Duke questioned.

"She be twenty-one. Too young for you, Duke. What you be, thirty-two or so?"

"Yeah, thirty-two," he lied. He wasn't about to tell anyone he was really thirty-six. That might really scare Brandi off. His Polynesian skin never seemed to age. He could easily pass for younger. Plus, he lifted weights every day to keep his body muscled and firm.

"By the way, Tonklin, she's not too young for me," Duke added sarcastically, thinking that he liked his women in the early twenties.

"She friend of mine, nice *haole* girl. You stay away from her," Tonklin threatened.

"That's not up to you, Tonklin," Duke said smugly as he turned and walked away. What were the chances that he'd be working at the same hotel that this Brandi McGraw worked at? He shook his head in disbelief. Coincidence or fate? Whatever it was, he intended to work his magic on her. He always got what he wanted, no matter what. And he wanted *that girl*, Brandi...wanted her badly. Wanted to make her his in every way. And like the constant flowing tide, Brandi wouldn't even know what hit her until it was too late. However, he intended to spoil her and make damn sure she loved the ride with him while it lasted.

Time slipped by when I was out there swimming in the open water. When I came back in, I was totally refreshed and determined not to think about Skip. I stopped at the Outrigger outdoor shower, rinsed off the salt water, and then made my way toward the pool towel shack.

"Hey, Brandi girl, you sure swim good."

"Thanks, Tonklin. It makes me feel so renewed. Can I have my beach bag, please?" I asked, while using a towel to dry off.

"Oh, sure." Tonklin handed me the bag.

"Well, I better get back to my girlfriend, Donna. I'll see you around, my friend."

"See you around, yeah. You stay sweet Brandi girl. Watch out for bad guys."

"I will. Thanks again," I said, heading down the beach and wondering why Tonklin would tell me to watch out for bad guys.

◆◆◆

Donna was packing up her gear. "You ready to go Brandi?"

"Yeah, I had a great swim out there and talked with Tonklin." We rolled up our beach mats, slipped on our flip flops, put on our beach cover-ups, and then headed to the street sidewalk.

We walked past the bronze Duke Kahanamoku statue that graced the beach walkway. It stood about nine feet high displaying the strength and dignity of this Hawaiian legendary Olympic champion swimmer from 1912 thru 1922. He is also known as the father of international surfing. Tourists stop at the statue and place their leis around the Duke's arms and at his feet to honor him. Today, it had over a dozen colorful purple and white leis draped on it. I didn't have a lei to hang on it, but I stopped and placed my hand on his leg and whispered a prayer of thankfulness, grateful for living here in Hawaii.

◆◆◆

My two roommates, Donna and Sherry, and I lived at the *Makaleka* apartments on the backside of the Ala Wai Canal in the *Kapahulu* district, primarily a Korean neighborhood about a mile and half from Waikiki.

As we walked, I recalled the history of the Ala Wai Canal. It is an artificial waterway that serves as the northern boundary of the tourist district of Waikiki. It was built in 1928 for the purpose of draining the rice paddies, wetlands, and swamps that were considered unsanitary. The dredging of the canal's soil resulted in the building of the Waikiki area, where new construction back in the 1930s had to be above sea level. It's being used today by many outrigger canoe clubs to practice and compete. However, it is not safe to swim in due to high levels of bacteria, but it is a landmark that I walk past almost every day to and from Waikiki. Just past it was one of my favorite spots to eat.

Donna and I stopped at the Rainbow Drive-In on the way back home from the beach. I was treating myself to a Loco Moco plate lunch for my dinner. It was a local favorite dish consisting of your choice of beef or chicken or a slab of Spam, rice, and a fried egg, topped with gravy for only $1.50. I had the beef. Donna ordered a teriyaki chicken plate with two scoops of rice and macaroni salad. I had some extra tip money from last night so I sprang for Donna's.

The sun was starting to set and the sky was cast in pink and orange hues. Traffic buzzed by as we sat at a picnic table eating our plate lunches. A dozen local boys took up several other tables, chatting away in their broken sing-song *pidgin* English.

"Well, it's back to work tomorrow," Donna commented.

Lucky her, I mused. She worked an eight-to-five job with weekends off as a recreational manager at the YMCA. Donna was from California with a degree in recreation. My other roommate, Sherry, was from Chicago, a middle school math teacher. They had been my roommates for a year now. Both were family to me. We were *haole* sisters in paradise. We were taking that leap, learning how to live on our own, being self-supporting.

"Yeah, it's back to work tomorrow and we have a new food and beverage director starting later this week. I hope he's better than the last one and doesn't come in and fire everyone," I remarked. "Not sure what it is about those food and beverage guys, but they think they own the place, at least the last one did."

"Maybe this one will be cool Brandi," Donna replied, while scooping the last forkful of white rice into her mouth.

"Yeah, maybe he won't be a dickhead," I said, laughing as we got up, cleaned our area, and then headed down *Kapahulu* Street towards our apartment complex. Christmas decorations adorned the windows of stores and shops. It was a couple of weeks away.

Tonight, we girls were going to watch a new comedy hit show called *M*A*S*H*. It was set in South Korea during the Korean War at a United States mobile army surgical hospital, referred to as a

M*A*S*H unit. It was the latest rage with off-the-wall characters, including one army doctor, Hawkeye Pierce, who we girls drooled over. A glass of wine and watching *M*A*S*H* with Donna and Sherry would be a great way to end the weekend before starting the work grind again. As we turned onto Date Street, two blocks from our apartment, I once again couldn't help but wonder who our new food and beverage director would be. I said a silent prayer asking for someone more professional and not some arrogant jerk.

Chapter 2

E Komo Mai (Welcome)

I was walking through the Hilton Hawaiian Village heading to the employees' uniform shop to get ready for work on this Thursday afternoon. It was *Kona* weather today, hot and humid, when the trade winds stop and the wind blows from the south. My skin felt sticky and damp. I couldn't help but admire the scenery surrounding me. A feeling of love for this beautiful hotel setting swam through me.

Originally, the Hilton Hawaiian Village boasted two towers known as the Village Tower and the Diamond Head Tower with a five acre man-made lagoon fronting the village. The legendary hotelier, Conrad Hilton, purchased the village for $21.5 million in 1961, one of the biggest hotel transactions of the times, including eighteen acres of property and an additional three acres of adjacent property.

I glanced to my right remembering that two years ago, in 1968, the famed new Rainbow Tower had been completed and opened. I loved the mosaic tile design which spanned 286 feet high by 26 feet wide. Both side walls of the tower hotel had 16,000 brilliant colorful tiles that completed the mosaic display. It was the village's signature, as well as the numerous koi fish ponds throughout the grounds. In the Japanese culture koi represents tranquility and happiness. The koi ponds were a wonderful testament of the mixed Hawaiian and Japanese spirit.

Also on the grounds was a man-made beach lagoon perfect for families to swim and play in without a strong current. The whole village was stunning. Truly another perfect reflection of Hawaiian paradise, I surmised.

The open-air lobby which I was walking through was enormous. It spanned a couple of blocks in square footage. Decorative brown and white large tile floors in the main lobby, numerous comfortable alcoves with rattan furniture of brown, white, and green bamboo print cushions that beckoned you to sit and relax. Several open-air bars and cafes along with at least three outdoor tropical grotto swimming pools added to the village's allure.

In addition, there were forty new ethnic shops being built. At the entrance was a Thai temple, a replica of a red and gold Japanese pagoda that had been shipped from Japan. Besides all this beauty, the entire lobby was graced with magnificent local floral displays. Flowers I had never seen until moving here a year ago. Giant bouquets of bird-of-paradise, red, blue, and white crepe ginger flowers, bamboo orchids, Chinese hibiscus, and plumeria filled the lobby with brilliant bright colors. The island beauty, the tropical weather, the aqua ocean; it never ceased to amaze me, I thought, as I continued towards the employees' uniform shop.

◆◆◆

Our new food and beverage director had started yesterday; however, I had not met him yet. Maybe I would tonight. Rumor had it that he was a gorgeous dark skinned local man and that he came across as charismatic and charming with a side of arrogance.

This week I was the hostess in the upscale *Makaha* dining room, off the main lobby. It was one of four restaurants within the hotel and the most expensive. It boasted full service dining with a maitre d' , a wine steward, and twelve male waiters that made for an excellent dining experience.

I'd never been a guest or had the privilege of dining in a formal setting like the *Makaha* room. But I found that I fit in nicely and I loved the class of customers that patronized it. Not only was the food outstanding, but it offered tableside prepared Caesar salads, flamed entrées, and desserts. Everything was first class and it made me feel very classy. With its sweeping panoramic view of the horizon, it offered spectacular ocean views and Hawaiian sunsets.

I left the Holiday Inn in Waikiki two months ago and came back to the Hilton Hawaiian Village, where I had my first island job back in December 1969. Waiting tables, hostessing, cocktailing floor shows, and doing banquets here offered me more money. Things were going well, except that my navy man, Skip, wasn't in Hawaii anymore. Donna was right. I needed to move on, date again, but I wasn't willing to give my heart away like I had with Skip. Would I ever feel that kind of all consuming love again?

It was time to switch gears though and get into work mode. I stepped up to the uniform shop open-air window. Java, the lady that ran the shop, was the sweetest local person, short and big boned with long black hair and dark bronzed skin. Samoan, I think.

"Java, I need the long hostess dress for the *Makaha* room tonight. Size ten, please," I said, leaning over the open counter.

"Okay, Miss Brandi, here you be." She handed me the beautifully designed hostess dress. I loved this outfit; it fit me perfectly. It was a long sculptured black dress, with a high Mandarin style collar. Edged in gold trim, it was designed with cut-in sleeveless shoulders and a side slit running up the right leg to mid-thigh. It was stunning with my gold heels. Every time I got to wear it, I felt like Hawaiian royalty.

I took the dress and headed behind the counter to the changing rooms. Once there, I slipped into it while admiring how beautifully it fit. Reaching up, I did a high ponytail with my long golden brown hair, leaving a few flowing strands at the nape of my neck and in front to frame my face. I freshened up my makeup, slipped into my gold heels, and then stepped back out into the interior of the uniform shop.

Standing there outside of the uniform shop was a really good looking local man. "Wow!" he said. "You look stunning." He extended his hand. "Hi, I'm Duke Haku, the new food and beverage director here," he stated, with a dynamic smile that lit up his entire face.

Oh God, I was staring at him! This was going to be my new boss? Holy cow! He was way too...too gorgeous. His dark black hair was swept behind his ears in a groomed shag cut that hung to the middle of his neck. I couldn't tell if he was Polynesian, Hawaiian or Asian. Maybe a combination of all three, but he definitely reeked of confidence as well as raw male sexuality with a muscular athletic body. Standing about five feet nine inches tall, he had a handsome round Asian face, high cheek bones, and almond shaped black eyes. He continued to smile mischievously at me. Those inquiring black eyes, I felt, probably hid lots of secrets. It was unnerving as though he were reading my mind.

I cleared my throat and smiled back. "Oh, hi, I'm Brandi. Brandi McGraw. *E Komo Mai"* (welcome) I said as I shook his hand. He gripped mine with a slightly forceful yet commanding shake. I felt an instant buzz of energy shoot through me. Something I hadn't felt since...since my navy man, Skip.

Duke's smile brightened with my local greeting. "It's nice to meet you, too, Brandi. I understand that you kind of do a little bit of everything around here?" he questioned, while his piercing, black eyes raked over me once again with approval and something else that seemed to throw me off balance.

"Ah...yeah, I guess I do. I'm hostessing in the *Makaha* dining room tonight and the rest of the week."

"So I see and a very pretty hostess, too," he added, with another brilliant smile. "I'm headed that way myself. Why don't I walk you there?" he asked, opening the exit door from the uniform shop.

Man he thought, she looked just as good up close as she did in that black bikini he'd seen her in last week at the Outrigger Hotel beachfront. Big brown bedroom eyes, straight nose, tall and slim, full busted, and a golden bronzed body, shit...it put his imagination in overdrive. He'd had a lot of women in his thirty-six years, but not one in a very long time that had aroused him like this.

"Um...okay," I replied as I stood next to him. His pleasure of escorting me didn't go unnoticed. I felt his hand press on the small of my back as he guided me forward toward the main lobby. The heat that blossomed in my body from his touch didn't go unnoticed either. Was he hitting on me? I wondered how old he was. Probably early thirties. His unspoken mannerisms said that he was a man used to getting his way professionally and probably with the ladies, too.

My heart was racing like the pounding surf from the attraction I felt. Oh God, I thought, he'd be watching and evaluating me as I worked tonight. If he was coming on to me, I wasn't sure how to handle it. I took a deep steadying breath thinking that tonight I would just be myself, friendly and professional to all, and try not to think about how good looking my new boss was.

Duke pushed open the dining room doors allowing Brandi to enter before him. She sure fit the part as a classy hostess. The gentle sway of her sweet *okole* (ass) moved with a grace he hadn't seen in someone so young for a very long time. Her sultry voice took his breath away, low and throaty. Bedroom eyes and a bedroom voice, he mused, thinking that in time he would have her in his bedroom, right where he wanted her. However, he had to play this out with patience. She'd had her heart broken by some navy guy, the pool guard had told him.

A navy guy...what a waste, he thought. She'll forget about him. I'll wine and dine her. She deserves someone like me with class, who's able to give her more than some navy guy. He smiled, thinking that yes, she was already his. She just didn't know it yet.

♦♦♦

The *Makaha* dining room had a single lit candle on each of the thirty tables. White table napkins folded into a pleated fan in front of each place setting, along with white tablecloths. A small floral display of orchids and delicate white ginger flowers graced all the tables as well. I just loved the simple elegant beauty of this room.

When Duke and I entered the dining room, I moved ahead of him, but I was acutely aware that his piercing dark eyes were watching me as I made my way to the hostess stand. My body burned from the feel of his lingering eyes that seemed to penetrate heat into my skin.

"You fit this room beautifully, Brandi," Duke stated, as he stood beside me at my station. "I'll leave you to get ready while I check on the staff and our chefs, but I'll be here most of the evening. If you need anything, please ask me," he said, with a nod as he headed to the kitchen.

I watched him stroll towards the kitchen. I had to admit that he did have a very appealing backside. Sexy with that fit muscular body which spoke boldly of his athleticism. I wondered if he lifted weights or what he did to stay in such good physical shape. I reached for a stack of menus and began attaching tonight's chef specials to each one. However, my focus shifted to Duke. Get a grip, I told myself. He's too old for you, he's your boss for God's sake, I thought, as the aroma of sautéed garlic butter from the kitchen wafted in the air making my mouth water. Baked mahi-mahi in a delicate white cream sauce, flavored with soy, ginger, shallots, and macadamia nuts along with Hawaiian fried rice and stir-fry vegetables. I knew what I was having later for my dinner, if it was okay with my new intriguing boss, Duke.

.... **Chapter 3** ....

Brandy Manhattan

The dinner rush floated by this evening like a swift catamaran skimming across the open waters. Only the most experienced waiters and staff worked this prestigious *Makaha* dining room. Soft Hawaiian ukulele music from the far corner of the room echoed in the background. Our local Samoan, Puna, was a regular musician here that the staff loved. He made our working hours disappear with the sounds of his alluring voice and ukulele serenades.

I smiled at him as I was stacking the dinner menus and putting them away at my hostess stand. He was a big heavy-bellied man with dark skin, a ponytail of thick black curly hair and a winning smile. Tonight, around his neck was a strand of kohio black nut beads that rested on a green and brown aloha shirt, accompanied by white pants and flip flops. We all teased Puna relentlessly because he had what we called *"luau feet,"* which were big flat feet. It was all in fun. We were like family here, but I noticed a shift in his body language as Duke approached from the kitchen.

Dinner service was coming to an end and this was Puna's last song, "Tiny Bubbles." I hummed along thinking that for such a big man he had an incredibly enchanting, gentle voice and I loved listening to him. He had become my trusted friend.

That song, "Tiny Bubbles," made me feel like a soft tropical breeze had kissed my heart and soul. I was so grateful for my job and many new local friends here on Oahu. Waking up to sunshine every day and blue skies, it was like summer all year long. No bleak gray or continual rain like back home in Seattle. Hawaii filled me with so much brightness and love, except that I missed my navy man Skip, more than I thought possible. Did he have another girl in his life after being gone for three months? I didn't know, his letters were vague. I took a deep breath, resolved not to pine.

Puna finished his song and he started packing up. He waved just as Duke came strolling towards me from across the room. A look of concern crossed his chubby, chocolate face again, like the way a father might react to someone he didn't want his daughter hanging around. I wondered if Puna knew Duke before he came on as food and beverage director. I would have to remember to ask Puna later. I smiled and waved goodbye to him and then focused my attentions on the approaching Duke.

He walked with an air of authority, confidence, and purpose. He grinned at me as he neared. That award winning smile could melt icebergs, I admitted. His dark cocoa skin made his teeth look brilliant white. I noticed that when he smiled at me his black eyes danced with amusement and something else that I couldn't quite put my finger on. Intention? He made me uneasy.

Those black pants and that white aloha shirt did look striking on him, I thought. He played the part of a food and beverage director with great aloha pride and poise. He seemed like he'd be okay as a boss and not a jerk like the last director had been.

Throughout the evening, I had watched Duke work the floor directing and managing the flow of things and stepping in to help when needed. I noticed that he personified the aloha spirit with a charm that seeped out of him like the sweet floral perfume of the island air. It seemed to pique the customers' appetites for more of the Hawaiian mystique. Duke's Polynesian look and his enchanting Hawaiian warmth seemed to make him the star of the show, but unfortunately, I felt he knew it, too.

I sensed a certain kind of smugness and conceit about him as if he'd been raised with money. Privileged. A cut above the rest of the staff personnel, I surmised. He didn't even speak *pidgin* English like most locals, but had more of a refined English cadence.

He calmly strolled over to me. "Brandi, I was impressed with you tonight," he said with admiration. "You bring a touch of class to the room," he commented, with seductive eyes that raked over me from head to toe. It made me feel flattered, but also guarded. I swallowed hard, pausing before replying.

"Oh...oh, thank you, that's nice of you to say, Duke. I do love working in the *Makaha* dining room," I said, wondering if his comment was a line or if he truly meant it.

He planted himself directly in front of my hostess stand. He looked me straight in the eyes. "I have some things I'd like to talk over with you. How about you join me for an after work drink before you leave tonight? I'll be at the Schooner Bar."

I bit my lower lip and let my eyes rove around the dining room. Only the wait staff was still around. Assistant waiters were clearing off the used white tablecloths and replacing them with new ones. I could hear the kitchen help talking in the background. The smell of garlic and teriyaki sauces wafted in the air. My stomach growled. I was starving. I wanted to head to the staff kitchen for a plate of whatever the chefs were serving us.

He sighed impatiently. "It won't take long, Brandi. I'll expect you in fifteen minutes. Get something to eat and I'll see you there soon," he stated, with an air of authority.

What the heck did he need to talk to me about? My mind was buzzing with conflicting possibilities and concerns as I watched him walk away. And then...my eyes lingered on his backside.

Once again, I shouldn't have been looking at his sweet *okole*, but I did. He looked good...real good, I had to admit. Firm, tight athletic build with broad shoulders and slim hips. Stop it, I told myself admitting that I was attracted to him. What could he possibly need to discuss with me tonight? Couldn't it wait until tomorrow? Was this business? Or did he have an ulterior motive? He was my boss, after all; I couldn't decline, could I?

◆◆◆

The Schooner Bar was crowded with hotel guests, tourists, and a few military men this time of night. It was dark inside the bar and smoky. I stopped at the entrance letting my eyes adjust to the dimness. There were red candles on each of the dozen and a half tables that occupied the room. I glanced at the old naval clock on the side wall. It read 11:00 p.m., but that was bar time, so it was really 10:50 p.m.

I looked around, but I didn't see Duke. He should have been here by now. I hoped I didn't have to wait long. I liked this bar. It had some sweet memories of when my navy man Skip, met me here several evenings for drinks. I took a deep breath remembering the sweetness of Skip while admiring the decor.

The room was shaped like the bow of a large schooner. The customers' bar had wooden edges that circled the counter frame, giving the illusion of sitting in the bow of an old sailing vessel. Inside the bar, where the bartenders worked, was a metal bow-shaped frame suspended from the ceiling. There were many different kinds of liquor bottles and glasses that hung on display from the metal frame. Surrounding the bar were at least a dozen barstools.

Kona was bartending. He was a short, stout, local boy from the big island, hence his nickname Kona. He was wearing the hotel uniform, a green and black print aloha shirt with black pants. Behind the bar, he was working his magic, adding a flare to mixing tropical drink orders and creating colorful Hawaiian specialty drinks topped with pretty orchids and pineapple wedges. He was swamped at the moment. I found a vacant stool at the bar and sat down with a heavy sigh.

"Hey Brandi, what it be, girl?" Kona asked, as he placed a coaster in front of me.

"I'll have a rum and Coke, please, Kona. Have you seen our new food and beverage director, Duke?" I questioned, while looking around in the dark smoky bar.

"No, he not be in tonight. Why?" he responded, wiping the counter down with a bar towel.

"I'm supposed to meet him here. Apparently, he wants to discuss some things and I haven't a clue as to what that might be." Nervously, I brushed a long strand of my hair behind one ear. I had changed my clothes and let my hair fall loose around my shoulders. I checked my watch. Just after eleven. Where is he?

"Here you go, Brandi," Kona said, placing my rum and Coke in front of me.

"Thanks, Kona," I replied and took a hefty swallow while letting the rum mellow my nerves.

For the next fifteen minutes, I sat there nursing my drink and waiting for Duke. One thing about living in Hawaii, the locals are never on time. It's called Hawaiian time and it looked like Duke was on Hawaiian time. Geez, I'm so tired, I just want to go home and go to bed, I thought wearily.

Moments later, Duke came strutting into the bar looking very handsome and sporting a wide grin when he saw me. A zing of attraction buzzed through me as he came and stood next to me.

"What are you drinking?" he asked, with raised eyebrows and dark eyes that commanded attention. Eyes that seemed to boldly caress mine.

"Umm, just a rum and Coke," I replied with a smile.

Duke shook his head. "Kona, please make us two brandy manhattans, straight up," he said, with a wave of his hand. The barstool next to me was empty so he slid into it. I felt his thigh touch mine. Heat rolled through me like a slow breaking wave. This can't be happening. My heart belongs to Skip.

What was it that my roommate, Donna, had said recently? *Skip's not the only man that will rock your boat and set your hormones on fire.* Hmm...here it is only three months after Skip had left me for New London, Connecticut, broke my heart without any promises, and now I feel this kind of undeniable heat from Duke? Impossible. I wasn't even sure if I liked or trusted him yet. Geez, he's my boss for God's sake! I took another deep breath before replying.

"Really Duke, I'm good with a rum and Coke," I challenged.

"Have you ever had a brandy manhattan, Brandi?" he asked with a wide grin.

"No, but I..."

"Then you need to try one," he stated convincingly and placed his arm around my shoulder. "I bet there are a lot of things you haven't tried," he whispered in my ear, as Kona placed our drinks in front of us. "To you, Brandi," he toasted, raised his glass, and then took a slow deliberate swallow.

I bet there are a lot of things you haven't tried. What did he mean by that? Definitely a sexual connotation, I contemplated. Yes, there were a lot of things that were new to me here in Hawaii, especially when it came to figuring out men. He was definitely hitting on me, but I wasn't about to give him the go ahead and flirt with him. Play dumb, I told myself and remember he is your boss. Besides, he had to be at least ten years older than me, probably late twenties or early thirties. Way too old for me, I calculated, as I cleared my throat with a little cough.

"Okay then, thank you, Duke," I said, while taking my first taste of this drink. It was served in a stemmed martini glass. It was pretty to look at, the color of copper brown, and a stemmed cherry resting at the bottom of the glass. I took a tentative sip, savoring its tart strong taste. "Wow, it's strong, but pleasantly smooth! Very nice, Duke. I think I like it," I said with sincerity.

"Ah, yes, strong and pleasantly smooth, just like you, I think," he said, with a hint of intrigue in those dark, piercing, almond shaped eyes.

I wasn't sure how to respond to that comment. I shifted my position and changed the subject. "So Duke, what is it you wanted to talk to me about anyway?"

"Well, first I wanted to know a little bit more about you, Brandi. Like what brought you to the islands?" he questioned, with a look of interest.

"Oh, well, I was tired of living in rainy Seattle. I needed a change. I love the sun and the beaches. I couldn't see the end of the tunnel with college. So, I decided to be adventurous and move to Hawaii. I've been here a year now and I love it," I commented with enthusiasm, while crossing my bare legs and sitting up straighter.

"That takes courage to branch out on your own. I heard you once managed the Windjammer Cafe at the Holiday Inn down the strip. Why'd you step down from manager to waiting tables and hostessing?" he asked over the noise, music, and chatter around us.

I wondered how he knew about that. He must have looked at my résumé. "Oh, well, I kind of talked my way into managing there with little experience. It was a lot of long hours. I found out that I could make more money waiting tables. You know, with tips. So I asked to step down from managing. Later, a friend of mine told me about openings here. This place is ten times more beautiful than the Holiday Inn. The tips are far better, too," I admitted, before taking another sip of my brandy manhattan.

Duke nodded his head. "So you buffaloed your way into managing there?" he questioned with a laugh. "A girl with spunk and gutsiness. I like that about you. I think we'll keep you around." He lifted his glass with a flirtatious wink. "By the way, Brandi, I saw you this past week long before I met you."

"You did? Where?" I asked with surprise.

"You were swimming out in front of the Outrigger Hotel. I used to work there before starting here. I asked Tonklin the pool guard about you. You must have been a competitive swimmer; at least it looked like it from what I could see. Impressive fly and freestyle you have there."

"Oh thanks, yeah, I spent a lot of time in the pool training. It became a full-time commitment when I was a teenager."

"Well, it shows. By the way, I really like that little black bikini you were sporting," he said with a salacious grin. "Once again, impressive, Brandi. Very impressive."

I swallowed hard. I reached for my glass. Hmm...he was flirting with me. And he saw me in my itsy bitsy bikini. Yikes! "Uh...was there anything else you wanted, Duke?" I asked, feeling a deep blush swim across my entire face.

"No, mainly I wanted to just get to know you a little better. You rotate around here at the hotel and I'd like to keep it that way. Is that what you like?"

"Yeah, I like roving around to different jobs. Keeps it interesting and I meet a lot of employees that way." I ran my hand through my hair feeling a little unnerved as I finished off my drink. "How about you, Duke? Did you grow up here in the islands?" I questioned.

"Yes, on the big island. We have some royal blood in our background," he boasted.

"Oh, royal blood. Really? That's very cool," I marveled, wondering if that was really true, but then why would he make up a story like that?

"I've been in San Francisco, Oregon, Colorado, all over the place with my food and beverage director career. I've moved around a lot," he countered.

I wondered why that was, but didn't want to dwell on it. "Well, Duke, if there is nothing else, I better be heading home, I'm beat." I stood up and reached for my purse.

"How are you getting home?" he asked standing up, with a questioning look in those big dark mysterious eyes.

"Oh, I'll take the bus. I'm not far from here, just up the road about five miles in the *Kapahulu* district."

"Well, you're not taking the bus at this late hour. I'll drive you home, Brandi."

"Uh...uh...that's nice of you, Duke, but you don't have to. I'm used to taking the bus."

"It's no trouble, besides, I want to," he grinned easily, and placed his hand on the small of my back leading me towards the exit. "And

I promise, I won't bite you," he whispered close to my ear. Another unexpected jolt of electricity swam through my veins, making me acutely aware of his bold pretentious touch. Was this just his charm or a liberty he took with all women? I was pondering that when I suddenly remembered something. "Oh, I forgot to pay for my first drink," I said with alarm.

He laughed. "It's on the house, sweet Brandi. Perks of my job."

"Oh," I said with surprise. "You have a lot of perks then?"

"Yes I do," he stated, thinking that he'd use his hotel expense account on dinner and drinks with her very soon. She exited a few steps ahead of him. He couldn't help but notice that black mini skirt she was wearing. Those beautiful long, sexy, bare legs, slim hips, a rack to shout about, and her long golden hair. She made him hot all over.

A young *haole* goddess, he thought. She was just the love interest he needed and was looking for. He was so glad he had called it quits with Darla last week. She'd been way too needy, constantly asking him if he was going to marry her. Jesus, he'd only been sleeping with her for a month. Married...that would be the day. It had never been in his repertoire, nor would it ever be. At thirty-six, he intended to always live the carefree single bachelor life. Monogamy was not his thing.

♦♦♦

The drive home was quick and short, thank goodness. However, I did have about ten minutes to ask Duke some more questions. I was curious about his job as food and beverage manager.

"So Duke, what does a food and beverage manager do?" I asked, as we pulled out of the hotel parking lot in his big red 1964 Ford Galaxie convertible. A muscle car if ever there was one. Strange, most locals drove small compact cars here in the islands. This big thing stuck out like a beached whale, not too practical, I thought. However, I did like driving around in a convertible with the sweet tropical air dusting my skin. And it was roomy with red leather bench seats up front and in the back. It reminded me of a drive-in movie make-out car. It suits Duke's personality, I thought. Bold and visible.

Duke ran his hand through his shaggy thick black hair and grinned. "Well, to answer your question. I'm responsible for the overall operations of all restaurants, bars, and staff. I oversee all managers and chefs as well as purchasing of food and stock. Plus, scheduling, hiring, firing, and training of staff, along with kitchen safety and health standards. Basically, I run the show on anything related to food, beverage, and banquets. It's more than a full-time job. Most of the time I kind of work around the clock. Long hours, but I'm very good at it. I have a lot of hotel perks," he boasted.

"Yeah, like what?" I questioned, as we turned off of *Kalakaua* Avenue and headed past the Ali Wai Canal on *Kapahulu* Street.

The lights of Waikiki's high-rise hotels twinkled behind us like the dark star-filled sky. It was warm and balmy, probably around seventy degrees. Traffic was still busy even at eleven forty-five at night and the tourists seemed to be nocturnal. Even the sidewalks were still crowded with people clipping along as if late for a party.

Christmas was only two weeks away. It was tinsel town in Hawaii, I reflected, as we passed by apartment lanai balconies where colorful lights were strung everywhere you looked. Fake Christmas trees in the windows stood out like a tourist with a bad sunburn. I found myself thinking about the beautiful fresh Pacific Northwest evergreen trees that were a highlight of my holidays. In Seattle, most homes had real trees that said Christmas. That fresh piney scent was one thing I really missed here in Hawaii. What was Duke saying? I turned my attentions back to him.

"Yes, I have a great many perks like an expense account. And I can write off dinners for myself and guests. I even have access to a hotel room if I need it," he stated, with a tone of insinuation. "Sometimes it's just too late to go home, so I crash there."

"Really? Well, your job sounds like a lot of responsibility," I replied. "Oh, Duke, turn left onto Date Street a mile up."

"Okay. And yes, Brandi, it is a lot of responsibility, but I like the prestige, the challenge, and even the long hours," he claimed.

"Here's Date Street," I pointed out.

"Okay," he said and turned left.

"Go another half mile and turn right onto *Makaleka* Street. It's the second apartment complex on the left."

"Got it," he responded as he continued on.

"Did you go to college on the mainland?"

"Yes, I went to a college in San Francisco, majored in hotel hospitality right after high school. I've been in the food and beverage business for the last ten years."

The last ten years, I thought. So that would make him about thirty-two or so, way too old for me.

"I did some time in Vietnam, too," he casually mentioned.

"You did? What branch of the military were you in?" I asked with surprise.

"Air Force. Trained as a pilot after college. I was in for four years and flew in Operation Rolling Thunder in '65. It was a top secret strategic bombing campaign against the North Vietnamese," he divulged. "Stuff I shouldn't talk about...classified, but it was a method of deterring the North Vietcong politically by fear and increased bombardment of selected targets, like industrial bases and transportation networks."

"Wow! I didn't know you had served in the Air Force or in this ongoing insane Vietnam War."

"Well, there's a lot you don't know about me, Brandi. I loved the F-105 aircraft I piloted," he lied, thinking that girls loved that story. It drew them in like an undertow they couldn't resist. "Bombing missions were hellish! When my military stint was up, I got the hell out and came back to Hawaii," he said, with conviction as we stopped at a stop light.

Silence pursued while my mind was calculating his story. Something seemed a little bit off. If he went to college right after high school and graduated at twenty-one, how had he done military service and training as a pilot in the Air Force in 1965? Food and beverage work for the last ten years? Pilot of an F-105?

"How old are you, Duke?"

"Thirty-two," he lied again as the song, "Games People Play" came on the radio.

Hmm...I knew that Skip had a friend that was an Air Force pilot. It required that you have a bachelor's degree, go through officer training school, be tested for flight school or have graduated from the Air Force Academy just to get into the program, and another couple of years to become a certified pilot.

I sat there in his car as we approached my apartment building wondering about all that. My dad had been a B-17 fighter pilot during World War II. He dropped out of college to enlist in the Army Air Corps. Boot camp and several months of pilot training, before he could even become a co-pilot. He flew twelve bombing missions over Germany as co-pilot and then twenty-one missions as the captain. The average B-17 bomber lasted about six weeks in combat. My dad beat the odds and lived to tell about it. My hero.

Duke said he enlisted for four years, which would make him older than thirty-two. Maybe thirty-five or more. Was he telling me a made up story or the truth? It felt twisted. However, I wasn't about to question him further. He seemed to know a lot about Operation Rolling Thunder, which I also remembered hearing about on the news during the Lyndon Johnson presidency in 1965. Who knows... so I let it drop and changed the subject.

"So where do you live now, Duke?"

"Oh, a couple of miles from here. I have a house with two girls."

"You live with two girls?"

He stopped the car and pulled into a reserved parking spot. "Yes, I find girls are much better roommates than guys. Nicer and way easier to manage," he said, while looking into Brandi's big chocolate brown eyes. God, he wanted to get lost in those bedroom eyes. That long honey colored hair of hers was begging to be touched. Instinctively, he reached forward taking a loose strand of it in his fingers. "You have the prettiest golden hair that I think I have ever seen...silky, too," he whispered.

Oh God, he was touching my hair. Was he going to try and kiss me? Panicked, I quickly turned to open the door. I stepped out of the car and turned around. "Well, thanks again for the ride, Duke," I said, feeling unsure of his motives along with my conflicting feelings of attraction.

"It's been delightful getting to know you. I'll see you tomorrow night at work," he promised, with amusement in his voice. "Sleep well, sweet Brandi."

Walking across the courtyard, I headed up the stairs to my apartment. I didn't hear his car start. He didn't drive off right away. I had the distinct feeling that his eyes followed my every move, but I didn't turn around to look. God, now he knew where I lived. Was that a plus or a minus? I wasn't sure. Was he going to want to drive me home all the time? And he had taken the liberty of touching my hair. An intimate gesture for sure. Nevertheless, there was something alluring and commanding about him that stirred my senses. I liked assertive men, but he...he made me nervous. I wondered what he meant about living with girls, that they were easier to control.

Just like the red flags displayed for high dangerous surf, my red flags were on alert, but I couldn't deny the strong current that was surfing between us.

Muumuu Girl Time

I opened the front door to my apartment and a little green gecko scampered across my flip flops. I was getting used to these little island creatures; they were always around. In Hawaii, if you saw one in your house, it meant good luck. A smile crossed my face; these geckos were harmless and cute.

Leaving my flip flops in the hallway, I heard the TV on and laughter from my two roommates, Donna and Sherry. Our apartment had a large living room furnished with a rattan bamboo framed sofa, and two single chairs of the same kind. The cushions were a Hawaiian print of palm trees, with bamboo sticks running diagonally across in a pattern.

Off the front room, we had a good sized lanai with sliding glass doors. It was open. A cooling late night tropical breeze drifted in blowing the white curtains around. A sweet floral scent from our huge plumeria tree, beneath our lanai, made me breathe deeply. Its fragrance, a Hawaiian love of mine, seemed to linger in the outside air turning the entire island into a wave of subtle sweetness.

"Hi all," I said, entering the front room. Donna was sitting on the floor drinking a Coke and wearing a purple floral muumuu. Sherry was lounging on the sofa with a colorful orange and yellow print muumuu, eating popcorn. *The Flip Wilson Show* was on and Flip was doing some crazy ass skit that they were laughing over.

"I'll slip into my muumuu and join you in a minute. It's been a long evening. I'm pooped. I could use some girl time. Plus, I need to talk."

"Okay, sure Brandi," Sherry answered. "The show is almost over." She brushed a strand of her short blond hair behind one ear.

"Wonder what's going on?" Donna said to Sherry.

"Don't know, but I'm willing to bet it's boy trouble. You know how Brandi is missing Skip and all," Sherry replied, while pulling her muumuu down over her chubby knees. She lit a cigarette and blew smoke into the air.

I strolled back into the room. *The Flip Wilson Show* ended and a commercial came on.

"What's up, Brandi? Missing Skip again?" Sherry asked, as I sat down on the sofa with her. I adjusted my blue print muumuu over my bare legs and got comfortable. "Pass the popcorn please," I said. "And yes, I am always missing Skip, but no, it's something else." I reached up and started twirling my hair, an old habit of mine when I was tired.

"It's our new food and beverage director, Duke. I think he's coming on to me. He insisted we have a drink together tonight after work in the Schooner Bar, and then, he wouldn't let me take the bus and drove me home."

"Sounds like a gentlemen to me, Brandi," Donna remarked.

"Well, he is that, but...but..."

"But what?" Sherry asked. "Is he cute? Is he local? How old is he?"

"Yeah, he's cute, he's local, and he says he's thirty-two, but I think he may be older than that. Some of his stories just don't add up. And geez, he's my boss!" I cried with exasperation. "I'm not ready for this yet, but...but I am kind of attracted to him. And that scares the crap out of me," I said, while I took a handful of popcorn.

"He has this air of superiority and he speaks perfect English, not *pidgin*. He's very commanding and...and intimidating. He makes me nervous like he sees right through me." I turned and looked out the sliding glass door as I munched on my popcorn.

The hillside was sprinkled with Christmas lights from the surrounding apartments and houses, giving the illusion of a cluster of beautiful twinkling stars. I loved this view with the gentle tropical breeze drifting into our front room and the rustle of nearby bamboo trees outside. If only Skip were here, I found myself thinking again. Christmas was going to be so different this time. I wouldn't be cooking a big turkey dinner for twenty navy submarine guys like I did last year. God, my heart felt empty and sad over that, but I was choosing to work on Christmas for time and a half pay.

"So did Duke ask you out when he drove you home?" Donna questioned.

I turned around. "No, but he made a move," I said, bringing my attentions back to my roommates. "He...he took a strand of my hair and ran it though his fingers. He then told me how silky it felt. An intimate gesture, don't you think?"

Sherry shifted her position sitting up straighter. "Yeah, it is, but you said you're attracted to him, right, Brandi?"

"I hate to admit it, but yes, in a strange way. I feel this underlying current, but my heart belongs to Skip," I sighed heavily. "Besides, he's so much older than me and he's my boss."

"Oh God, Brandi," Donna said with exasperation. "Skip left you hanging. He's five thousand miles away in New London, Connecticut. If Duke asks you out, go out with him. Stop sitting around waiting for Skip, he's history. That's my advice. It doesn't matter if Duke is your boss. It's up to you and it's nobody's business but yours." She rose from the floor and stood. "I have to go into work early tomorrow, so I'm going to hit the rack. Goodnight, you all," she said and drifted down the hallway to her private master bedroom.

Sherry patted my shoulder. "She can be so direct sometimes, but I do think Donna is right, Brandi. You once told me to move on when Ben broke my heart and married Mai Lei. I know I moved home to Chicago for awhile, but I came back to Hawaii because I love it here. I have moved on and you can do the same. Date someone else, have some fun again." She smiled softly and patted my shoulder again. "Come on, let's get some sleep, too."

"Okay," I said, as I rose from the sofa with a heavy heart still mooning over Skip. However, I wondered what I'd say if Duke did ask me out. I hadn't been out with a man since early September. Maybe it was time to move on, but with Duke? I wasn't sure about that. Nevertheless, there was no denying the slow burn of attraction that was messing with my head and body.

Chapter 5

Poolside *Tapa* Bar

A week passed since Duke had driven me home from work. I was glad that he didn't take that gesture as his opening to spend more time with me. However, he had been in the *Makaha* dining room every night since and had made hints that he'd like to take me out. So far, I had put him off.

Lately, I had been feeling sorry for myself and really missing my navy man, Skip. Puna's soft romantic ukulele music which played throughout this evening didn't help. It made me melancholy and reminded me of those romantic times with Skip. What was it that Skip had last said to me at the airport before he boarded the plane for stateside? Oh yeah, *that he'd get things set up and see how things went*. What was that supposed to mean, I wondered again for the hundredth time.

Nevertheless, tonight I found that I couldn't take my eyes off of Duke as he worked the dining room like a pro. He made a point of stopping at all the tables and chatting with the tourists. That Hawaiian charm that I found so tempting. That muscular body, broad shoulders, slim hips, cocoa brown skin, and his dynamic smile made him burning with island male sexuality.

Both my roommates were asleep at midnight as I entered my apartment. They had normal day jobs. Wearily, I climbed into bed thinking of Skip until my thoughts shifted to Duke. To Duke? What would it be like with him? I drifted off to sleep remembering his appealing dark chocolate skin and his captivating smile.

♦♦♦

The following day and the rest of the week I was working the *Tapa* poolside cafe from noon to 6 p.m. I loved working outside, waitressing and cocktailing. Tips were always good and it was just fun being by the pool and talking with all the tourists. My tray was loaded with half a dozen tall tropical drinks, decorated with pineapple spears and purple orchid flowers. Mai tais were always popular, especially during happy hour. I needed one of those, I thought. Sighing deeply, my body felt like I'd been in a sauna all day. Hot, sticky, and damp.

Today had been very busy with a lunch rush around 1 p.m. I had been running my legs off serving meals and drinks ever since. It was happy hour now with free *pupus,* consisting of teriyaki chicken bites and deep fried calamari strips served with a zesty hot dipping sauce. My stomach growled. I hadn't had a break or a snack all day. One hour to go, and then I would have their signature *tapa* burger, topped with pineapple and teriyaki sauce and an extra large Coke. It would be just what I needed, I thought, as I glanced around admiring the setting and collecting some dirty dishes and glasses.

The grotto pool was the biggest of the three pools on the grounds of the Hilton Hawaiian Village. It was a huge kidney shaped pool that sported a waterslide, a grotto waterfall, and a splash pool for the little ones. Everywhere there were blue and white striped lounge chairs lined up side-by-side, spanning the entire pool area, as well as small side tables for drinks and food. Those little gray doves roamed the pool grounds cooing softly and looking for crumbs of food.

The pool water sparkled with the sun beaming on it. Kids played Marco Polo in the water, their voices echoing throughout. Parents were sprawled out on the lounge chairs sipping their tropical drinks and indulging in free *pupus.* All my customers were taken care of now. A small local musical group consisting of three ukulele players stepped up to the tiny poolside stage. Shaded from the sun, a large cabana which looked like a grass shack provided a cover for the musicians. Oceanside music of sweet romantic Hawaiian songs began, which lifted my mood and filled me with the spirit of aloha. How lucky was I? It was paradise living here.

This magical, spiritual place of the Hawaiian Islands was laced with a past history of love and violence among its ancient tribes. Currently, their economy depended on the flow of tourism. I dearly loved living in a resort community. It was so alive and full of activity. Waikiki was always buzzing with night clubs open all night. However, it had been a long time since I had been to a night club. After three long months of not dating, maybe it was time to open that door again. Take the leap. Skip certainly hadn't asked me to join him in New London. Would he ever? Give it up, I told myself again. Move on, girl.

It was nearing the end of my shift and the musicians were playing a Christmas song, *"Mele Kalikimaka"* (Merry Christmas), since it was only a week away. It was weird seeing Christmas decorations throughout the village with the brilliant sunshine and tropical weather, unlike the dark wet winter Christmases back home. It just didn't feel like Christmas, when it felt like summer outside.

Out of the corner of my eye, I saw Duke approaching the *Tapa* Bar. God, he was so sexy looking. That dark skin and muscular body, wow! He was sweet on the eyes. Delivering the last of all my orders, I sat down on the empty bar stool next to him.

"Hey Brandi," Duke said.

"Hey Duke."

"You sure look good in that mini skirt, but then you have those long beautiful tan legs to go with it," Duke stated, with a captivating grin. Yeah, he thought, long sexy legs that he'd like to have wrapped around his bare body. Patience, he reminded himself. He hadn't missed the fact that Brandi had been watching him last night in the *Makaha* dining room. Hell, she couldn't take her eyes off of him. That thought made his ego soar.

Man, she was so young at twenty-one. Was she ready to have some local boy fun with him? Three months without a man was a long time in his damn book for a young thing like her to go without some good lovin'. This week he would make sure to ask her out for dinner and begin his plan of seduction.

"Oh," I said, feeling a little awkward that he was looking at my legs. I was wearing the *Tapa* Bar poolside employee outfit. It was a black and brown *tapa* print mini skirt and a brown tank top that showed my cleavage. My hair was pulled back into a high ponytail that helped to keep me cool. Was he stepping over the line talking about my mini skirt and my legs? He was flirting with me. However, I had to admit that I liked his attention and the slow burn he was creating in me. Nevertheless, I reminded myself again that he was my boss.

"It looks like it was busy today," he commented, running his hand through his groomed black hair.

"Yeah, it was a very busy day," I replied. "I'm almost off, then I'm going to head home and crash on the couch. My feet are killing me," I said with a sigh. "At least I get to wear tennis shoes. Plus, tips were great today and that makes it worth it," I stated, with a satisfied smile.

"Well, good for you, Brandi. I like to see my employees happy. I've got to go and check on a private banquet this evening, but I'll make sure to see you tomorrow." He stood up. "Maybe I'll have lunch poolside so we can chat," he beamed. "I've been so busy this week that I haven't had time to catch up with you," he said, with an endearing smile. "I'll see you tomorrow then, Brandi, around lunchtime."

"Okay, Duke, I'd like that," I replied with enthusiasm.

"You would, would you?" he asked with raised eyebrows, thinking that she was so sweet. He couldn't wait to be able to taste and kiss those sexy *haole* lips. This past week, he'd found himself thinking about her all the time. He felt like he was being reeled in like a marlin, unable to resist the pull of the line. However, he reminded himself that she would just be a savored fling for as long as he wanted. Or would she? Why was she running through his mind all the time? He never got hung up on one girl. He shook his head with confusion and then turned and waved. "Have a nice night, Brandi."

"Thanks, I will." Tomorrow, I thought, as I once again couldn't take my eyes off his sweet *okole* and that confident stride he sported.

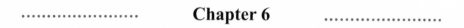

Chapter 6

Cock-a-Doodle

The sky was a soft pinkish hue, another beautiful sunset on the horizon as I looked back across the beachfront. It was 6 p.m. when I walked out of the Hilton Hawaiian Village after my shift ended. It had been a little unnerving chatting with Duke earlier with his suggestive comments. I pushed it aside. I was dog tired. I just wanted to get home and relax.

Christmas decorations were everywhere, strung up like tinsel town. Tourists crowded *Kalakaua* Avenue as I neared the bus stop. Traffic was a zoo. According to my watch, I'd have a twenty minute wait for the next bus. With that thought, I neared a corner and stuck my thumb out. I wasn't in the mood to wait twenty more minutes. Hitchhiking was pretty common here. I'd done it a few times during the daytime and never had any problems. It was still light out so I'd be fine. Wouldn't I?

A white sedan rounded the corner nearby. The car slowed down as it approached me. The driver, a Caucasian man, probably in his forties, asked if I wanted a ride. I hesitated...but then said, "Yes." Something inside me shifted...a warning? A jolt in my gut hit me as I opened the door and got in.

"Where are you headed?" he asked nicely and adjusted his sunglasses.

"Oh, up about five miles in the *Kapahulu* district," I replied and settled into the passenger's seat while adjusting my black mini skirt and crossing my legs.

"I'm going that way, too," he stated with a crusty voice. "It's your lucky day," he said, with a tone of...of sarcasm and a wicked grin. My red flags immediately went up. A sense of uncertainty and concern shot through me again. I rolled my window down as we drove a few blocks while making uncomfortable small talk. I glanced out my side window.

Looking at the aqua waters of Waikiki, I noted that they were dotted with a few surfers trying to catch that perfect wave before it got dark. Beach goers had retreated to their respective hotels leaving the beach almost vacant. However, sailboats skimmed the horizon; a perfect breeze tonight for sailing, I thought.

The Waikiki strip was abuzz with activity; outside restaurants were packed with tourists having dinner. Gaiety everywhere, but somehow I didn't feel that way. Something sounded strange inside the car like a slapping noise. What was that? I turned to look at the man driving.

Oh my God! Oh my God! He had unzipped his pants! He had *IT* in his hand. He was slapping *IT* and stroking *IT* and moaning. Panic and fear shot through me. I quickly turned my eyes away. Looking straight ahead, I pretended that I didn't see what he was doing. Oh God! What if he reached over and locked my door! What if he took me somewhere and beat and raped me? I had to get out! That fight and flight instinct crashed through me like a fifty foot wave. "Get out! Get out," my inner voice yelled.

We were going about thirty miles an hour, too fast for me to jump out without getting hurt. I could see from my peripheral vision that he was looking at me with a sick wicked grin. "You want some of this?" he laughed, while stroking himself harder. Suddenly, he slowed down for a red light.

Red light! Red light! Terrified, I jerked opened the door. I jumped out! I stumbled momentarily, but somehow my feet hit the ground. In a panic, I stood and ran.

There was a crowd of people standing on the pavement waiting at a bus stop, which was near *Kapiolani* Park. Among the bus riders, I lost myself in the middle of the group and ducked down so as not to be seen. The stoplight turned green. He drove off slowly. I watched as his car kept going. Thank God he didn't turn around. Shaking, I tried to catch my breath. My legs like noodles hardly able to support me.

A city bus pulled up to the stop. Gingerly, I climbed aboard. I didn't know if it was my bus; it didn't matter. I just wanted to feel safe, ride this bus wherever it was going. Finding an empty seat, I collapsed into it. Sucking in a deep breath, I tried to stop shaking as the bus pulled out into traffic.

For the next hour, I stared out the window unaware of what I was seeing. Everything was a blur. I was afraid to get off the bus. So I just kept riding around. Visions of what just happened kept flashing before my eyes again and again. I couldn't believe there were men like that. Creepy men that got their kicks out of scaring young girls or worse, kidnapping and raping them.

I considered myself lucky to have escaped without physical harm. However, the emotional scar would haunt me for a lifetime. Tears stung my eyes. I was so mad at myself. How could I put myself in a position like that? Stupid girl. I promised myself right then that I would never, ever hitchhike again. An hour later, I cautiously stepped off the bus a block from my apartment. I kept looking over my shoulder praying that I didn't see that white car.

It wasn't until I stepped into my apartment that I heaved a sigh of relief. Sherry and Donna were eating dinner while watching a local news channel about the Vietnam War. I was sick of hearing and seeing Vietnam War stories. I felt that way right now, sick to my stomach.

I dropped my purse on the nearest chair and leaned against the kitchen counter. A soothing evening breeze drifted in from the open lanai door, but did little to calm my shattered nerves. Reaching for a glass, I filled it with cold water. My mouth tasting like bile. Rinsing it, I spit into the sink, and then I splashed cold water on my face.

"Hey Brandi, you look awfully pale. Are you okay?" Sherry asked, while scooping a forkful of white rice into her mouth.

"Yeah, you do," Donna concurred. "We thought you'd be home an hour ago."

"So did I, but...but something horrible happened on my way home," I replied, using a hand towel to dry my face.

"Like what?" Sherry questioned. "Here, sit down with us. You want some dinner? There's plenty of chicken and rice."

"No, but thanks, I couldn't eat if I tried." I pulled out one of the chairs and sat down next to Donna.

"So what happened?" Donna asked.

"God, you aren't going to believe this. I hitchhiked home and the driver he...he pulled *IT* out."

"Pulled IT out, what do you mean?" Sherry asked, with a blank look on her face.

"You know, IT!" I said loudly.

"You mean his...his..."

"Yes, Sherry, IT.!"

"Oh my God!" Donna and Sherry both said at the same time. Donna placed her hand over mine. "What did you do?"

"I was in shock. I turned away quickly, pretending not to notice. Yuck, he was stroking himself and moaning. As soon as he slowed for a red light, I jumped out. I lost myself in a crowd waiting at the bus stop. When the bus came, I got on. I must have ridden it for over an hour. I was so afraid that he might be following the bus and waiting for me to get off. I didn't want him to know where I lived. God, I'm still shaking. He scared me so much," I said with a shaky voice.

Sherry got up and put her arms around me. "Well, you're safe now. You didn't see his car when you got off the bus did you?"

"No, thank God."

"What a creep," Donna said, as she took her empty plate to the dishwasher. "Was he old or young?"

"Does it make a difference?"

"Well no, but what a pervert!" Donna cringed.

"He was old, probably in his mid-forties. Geez, I'm never going to get that obscene picture out of my head. It was just gross!"

Sherry and Donna started to laugh. "It's not funny, you guys," I cried.

"I know, but you have to agree it's a cock-a-doodle of a story. Pardon my pun," Sherry giggled. "I'm just glad it didn't happen to me. God, I hitchhike all the time into Waikiki."

"I don't," Donna stated. "It's just not safe."

"Yeah, that's for sure. I never will hitchhike again, ever," I said, standing up and heading into the comfort of the front room. The big rattan sofa with its yellow and beige cushions beckoned me to stretch out and try to relax. The *Ko'olau* mountain range out beyond our lanai windows was dotted with houses decorated with colorful Christmas lights that twinkled in the twilight. Christmas was only a couple of days away. No Skip, no tree, no feast this year and I was working both Christmas Eve and Christmas Day. I suddenly felt exhausted and full of self pity.

"Come on, Brandi, *M*A*S*H* is almost on TV. That show always makes you laugh," Donna stated. "Although I'm sure you will probably have nightmares over what happened to you tonight."

"Nightmares for years to come, I'm afraid. Lesson learned, my friends. I consider myself lucky to be home safe and sound," I stated, as I flopped down on the sofa thinking that I had two wonderful roommates. I loved them both, but I so wished I had my Skip here so I could rest my weary head on his shoulder and he could comfort me throughout the night. Those deep blue eyes, cleft chin, sexy smile, and that soft Midwestern drawl; it made me ache to hear his voice once again. Tonight as I sank down on the sofa, I would just dream about him and how beautiful he always made me feel.

"By the way Brandi, there's a letter on the counter for you from Skip," Donna said, coming into the front room to join me with a smoke in her hand.

"A letter from Skip!" I jumped up. Just what I needed to help change the tide of events. Would he tell me how much he missed me and loved me? Hope sang in my heart for the first time. His letter would for sure lift my spirits...wouldn't it?

◆◆◆

The letter was dated from a week ago. Mail took so long to get delivered from the east coast to Hawaii. By the time you received a letter it was old news. I didn't want to read it in front of my roommates, so I went to the privacy of my bedroom. Taking a deep breath, I opened it with hope and trepidation.

Dear Brandi,   *Dec. 16th*

My sweet island girl, I miss you so much. More than I ever thought possible. You are always on my mind. Three months is a long time to be without you. I'll be honest with you though, I am struggling with what to do about us. I left you without any promises. By now you are probably seeing someone else? Which brings me to a rumor I heard. It's going around that you are with another guy? You know how rumors get started and travel fast in this navy community. This has been my greatest fear that you will find someone else. Is this true? Again, I can't blame you if you are with someone else. I left you hanging on a thin line. I will tell you that I have been going out, dating other girls, but no one can replace you. So here I am once again still stuck on you, but not knowing what to do about it. Would you even leave Hawaii if I asked or leave the guy you are supposedly with?

Okay, enough. Just let me know where you stand with us. Life here in New London is busy what with the boat going through conversion to the Poseidon Weapons Systems. The boat is being totally overhauled, but I am not part of the technical crew that is involved with that. I may be looking at applying for officer training in Virginia Beach. I'm not sure about that yet, but it is something I am thinking about.

I love hearing from you and miss you by my side, no matter what. Don't stop writing me. Christmas won't be the same this year without you. And that Christmas dinner you cooked for all my navy buddies last year, well, nothing can measure up to that. Last Christmas is branded into my memory forever. How can you top that Christmas when we made love for the first time. You can't!

Be good my sweet Brandi. You are in my dreams always.

Mele Kalikimaka,

Love, Skip

◆◆◆

With another guy? Who would tell him that? It wasn't true and it hurt. No wonder he hadn't written in several weeks. What a...a bag of mixed messages. Misses me and dreams about me, but won't commit to anything. Same old, same old. Not sure what he wants. My transistor radio was on and the perfect song, "You Keep Me Hanging On" by the Supremes echoed in the background. Boy, did that song say it all. There's just no easy way to deal with a long distance relationship when no promises are made. Just no easy way, I surmised, as I put the letter under my pillow feeling even more upset and discontent than ever. Was there even an "us" anymore? He was like sand slipping through my fingers, lost in the sea of distance between us.

Sitting on my bed, my grandma's words came back to me as I remembered her saying something like, *it's all about the timing when you meet and marry a man.* I didn't understand that as a teenager, but I sure did now. Timing was everything and our timing was way off. With the passage of time and distance, Skip was dating again.

Distance makes the heart grow fonder? Who believes in that? I wasn't sure anymore. Was he dating because he had heard a rumor that I was with some other guy? Or was he just trying to see if he could replace me with another girl that stoked his fires more than me?

Frustrated and disillusioned, I joined my roommates in the front room to watch *M*A*S*H*. Maybe for the next half hour I could try to forget my complicated, no strings attached, and burning love for Skip. Don't leave me this way Skip, I pleaded to myself. Ask me for a commitment. God, I needed some sweet lovin' tonight more than ever. I wanted Skip to know that the rumor wasn't true, but as strange as it was, I didn't feel like writing him back right away. I was hurt and mad, stuck in the middle again, and trying to make sense of it all.

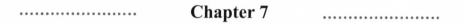

Chapter 7

Hawaiian Arms

The following day at the *Tapa* poolside bar, Duke didn't come in at lunchtime like he had said he would. My shift was almost over. It was close to 6 p.m. when he strolled into the cafe bar area. He parked himself at a table and motioned for me to come over.

"Hey Duke, what can I get you?" I asked, without much enthusiasm and stifled a yawn. I was trying to shake the image of what had happened last night when I had hitchhiked home. And also Skip's letter that had me troubled and upset. Seeing someone else! Didn't Skip know that I had been true since he'd left? However, now I was beginning to wonder why? Indignation sullied my mood.

Duke squinted up at Brandi while blocking his eyes from the sun. Was she upset? Something in her voice seemed off. "Yes, I'll have the chicken teriyaki burger, no fries, a green salad with ranch dressing, and a Coke, Brandi. I'll just sit here and look at how pretty you are," he grinned, hoping to raise a smile out of her, but she didn't smile back.

"Sure, I'll put your order in and get you your Coke. Be right back," I replied, not acknowledging his compliment or giving him an inch as I headed towards the kitchen grilling station. I should have been more pleasant; he is my boss after all, I mused.

Hmm...Duke thought. Her body language and demeanor were definitely down today. She wasn't her usual bubbly self. Maybe she was just tired like he was. He'd been running since 6 a.m. this morning, problem solving, putting out fires, managing employees, and getting the private banquet ready for tonight.

A conference of a hundred Japanese businessmen was scheduled for a cocktail hour and a banquet dinner. He had one and a half hours to kill before needing to be at the affair to manage it. A quick bite to eat and relax for a spell was all he needed to recharge...and some time with Brandi before her shift was over.

Looking around, he admired the striking gold and pinks that painted the horizon. Another gorgeous Hawaiian sunset. Surfers and sailboats sprinkled the aqua blue waters along with people bobbing in the surf. It made him want to get out there for a cool refreshing swim. He hadn't done that in a while. Open water swimming was a passion of his.

"Here's your Coke, Duke," I placed it in front of him. "Your food should be right up," I stated, with a little more enthusiasm in my voice.

"Great, are you almost off?" he questioned.

"Yeah, about fifteen more minutes," I answered with a sigh.

"You look a little strung out. Is something wrong?" he asked with concern.

"Just really tired. I'm ready to catch the bus and go home."

"I have some free time. Let me drive you home," he pleaded, hoping she would say yes. He really wanted to get her to talk, open up with what was troubling her.

"Oh...that would be so nice, Duke, but you don't have to. I can catch the bus," I replied, thinking that it was good of him to offer. I just wanted to get home, take a shower, and watch some mind numbing TV.

"I know I don't have to, but let me drive you anyway. I have to be back here for a banquet shortly. It will only take twenty minutes round trip," he grinned. "Please, Brandi, let me do this. You seem kind of depressed."

"Okay, I am really tired. Oh...I see your order is up. I'll be right back," I said, feeling relieved that I didn't have to wait for the bus tonight.

♦♦♦

Duke watched Brandi walk away. He couldn't help but dwell on the sweet sway of her hips and those long sexy legs. She sure looked good in that mini skirt. He wondered if she would tell him what was bothering her. For some odd reason he wanted to be that person that she could confide in. Another way to build the trust he needed to make his move on her.

"Here you go, Duke. Enjoy, it looks good. I'm going to clean up around here and then I'll change my clothes. Shall I meet you in the front lobby where you can drive up?"

"Yes, I'll bring my car around. Give me fifteen minutes to eat and I'll meet you there."

"Okay, and thanks, I really appreciate it," I said, with a slight smile.

"My pleasure, Brandi. It will give me a chance to catch up with you," he beamed. "Go do your thing and I'll see you in fifteen minutes."

"Okay," I replied, thinking that he was really good looking. I loved that dark skin and that brilliant smile increased my attraction that I kept denying. It was sweet of him to offer to drive me home and I was content to let him do just that.

♦♦♦

I changed clothes quickly into a pair of hot pants, a tank top, and flip flops, and then headed to the main hotel lobby pickup and drop off area. The bell hops hustled between cars and taxis pulling up and tourists arriving. Luggage was stacked here and there as suitcases were loaded and unloaded. The usual sweet floral scented air was mixed with gas fumes from cars waiting and engines running. That unpleasant scent assaulted my senses. Traffic at the hotel pickup area was a zoo just like it was in Waikiki this time of the evening. I took a seat on one of the rattan sofas and waited for Duke in the open-air lobby.

Minutes later, he pulled up in his big red '64 Ford Galaxie convertible. He waved and I stood up making my way to the passenger's side of the car. I opened the door and slipped into the comfy red leather bench seat. Once again, I laughed thinking that these big bench seats were made for heavy necking and drive-in movies, unlike the bucket seats that the newer model cars sported these days. I leaned back fully into the seat, enjoying the feel of the plush leather, the roominess; glad to be off my aching feet and not having to wait for the bus.

We pulled out into the busy noisy traffic. A cool evening breeze washed over me refreshing my sticky skin as we headed towards the backside of the Ali Wai Canal, away from the Waikiki rush. Good, I mused, he's taking the longer route through the local neighborhoods, fewer traffic lights, more tree shade, and not so noisy.

Even though I felt relief to be driven home, my head was still spinning with thoughts of last night's horrible incident. It was hard to get that sick picture and panicky feeling out of my head. I wasn't in a talkative mood. Duke must have sensed my distance and preoccupation. He glanced over at me with concern.

"So Brandi, do you want to tell me what's troubling you? You're really not yourself today. I'm a good listener," he stated, as we came to a red light and stopped.

"I...I am not feeling well today," I said, wondering if I should confide in him. The light turned green, but he took an unexpected turn and pulled over to a neighborhood side road next to a sprawling fragrant plumeria tree. Its white blossoms filling the branches in small groups of bouquets that made me think of how lush the island was with all its natural floral beauty everywhere. But why was he stopping here?

Duke turned off the engine. He turned to face me with his arm flung over the back of the bench seat. "Brandi, I'm pretty good at reading people. Tell me what's bothering you. Maybe I can help." He wondered if she was just lonely and missing that navy boyfriend he'd heard about. "Talk to me."

I looked straight ahead. Oh God, I hardly knew Duke and yet, for some reason I did want to tell him what happened last night. I took a deep breath and turned to face him. "Okay, last night I hitched a ride home. The driver was an older Caucasian man. He...he exposed himself in the car. He was playing with *IT* right in front of me. Oh God, Duke...I...I was so scared! It all happened so fast. It was all I could do to look straight ahead and pretend not to see what he was doing. Somehow, I managed to get out of the car when he slowed for a red light," I said, with a trembling voice and my body started to shake all over again.

Instinctively, Duke reached over and pulled me into his arms. "Oh sweetheart, I'm so sorry. No man should ever do that," he declared, while my head rested on his shoulder. He ran his hand over my upper back stroking me softly.

The subtle vanilla scent of her hair and skin stirred his senses and his attraction even more. She felt so good in his arms just like he knew she would. Soft, feminine, and vulnerable. Tenderness moved through him. Suddenly, he felt a voracious feeling of protectiveness. Protectiveness? That was new. Why did he feel so protective of her? Because, he told himself, he had strong feelings for her, and not just sexual feelings either. God, he hadn't even slept with her yet...and yet she was drawing emotions out of him that he had never let surface before and it scared the crap out of him.

"It's okay, Brandi," he whispered and kissed the top of my head. "I wish I knew who the guy was. I'd give him a piece of my mind and make it so he couldn't walk for days." Anger surged through him. It pissed him off, that someone would scare her like that. "Thanks for telling me. It means a lot. Now, let's get you home so you can relax and chill out." He broke the hug, but those lingering, strange protective feelings stayed with him.

"Thanks, Duke, for listening and the hug, too," I responded, thinking that he had strong Hawaiian arms that felt good around me. It had been a long time since I'd had a man hug me. A comfort that I admitted I deeply missed and liked. However, it was the concern that I saw in his dark black eyes as he dropped me off at my apartment that had touched me. He had made me feel like a pearl inside a shell... safe.

◆◆◆

Later that night, before I went to sleep, I wrote Skip a letter:

Dear Skip,　　　　　　　　　　　　　　　　*Dec. 21, 1970*

Hey there navy man, I just got your letter and read it. I have missed you more than I did while you were on patrol. At least on patrol, I knew you were coming back to Hawaii and were not five thousand miles away and stationed in New London. By the time you get this, Christmas will be over. It won't be the same without you, but I hope you have a wonderful Christmas! You will be in my thoughts and heart.

I really don't know where we stand. Is there even an "us" to hope for? I don't know who you get your information from or who started the rumor about me being with another guy, it isn't true. It hurts Skip, that people would say things about me that are lies. Who told you that? I am still living with Donna and Sherry at Makaleka apartments. Dating? Really...I haven't made the time. I cling to hope and wonder if some day we will be together again. My roommates tell me to move on, that you left me hanging, and I should get over you. But alas, my heart still belongs to you.

The only thing that has changed is that I am now back working at the Hilton Hawaiian Village instead of the Waikiki Holiday Inn. I'm a floater there, so I do poolside waitressing, cocktailing, hostess evenings sometimes in the Makaha dining room, and private banquets. The tips are so much better there and the setting is ten times more beautiful, and I love it!

You said that you are kind of dating. I'm not sure what that means. Are you seeing someone else? Someone that might replace me? If you are seeing other girls...then I'm going to date as well. I will admit that I am very lonely without a man in my life here, but I've been busy working my sweet okole off. Honestly, Skip, I don't think I can keep living on hope. You are five thousand miles away. Do we just keep writing, trying to keep us alive while we see other people? You said you would see how things go, get things set up back there. I just don't know what you expect of me. But you will always be in my heart, no matter what, Skip.

Love always, your island girl, Brandi

Sealing the envelope, I addressed it, and put it in my purse. I didn't tell him about the hitchhiking thing. He wasn't here to comfort me like Duke had done. Besides, I was tired and still emotional over everything, including Skip's letter and the rumor. Snuggling under the sheet, I closed my eyes and found myself remembering how comforting Duke's hug had felt.

.... **Chapter 8** ....

Slow Wave

As Duke drove back to the Hilton Hawaiian Village, his thoughts ran rampant. There was no doubt that he wanted to take Brandi to bed. But for some reason he didn't want to just do his usual dinner out and then sex. He seldom spent much personal time with his women other than bedding them. He scratched his head confused with the unsettling thoughts. She was so down to earth, so sweet, and so young at twenty-one.

What he'd like to do is spend a full day with her first. A full day? That was odd, he admitted. Maybe a day with her at *Hanauma* Bay where they could swim around the point to the blow hole and picnic; now that would be fun. It might be a first for Brandi. For reasons he chose not to dwell on, he wanted to do something with her that perhaps she had never done before. Strange. Why was that important to him?

He reached over and turned up the radio. "I've Been Lonely Too Long" by the Young Rascals, blared and its lyrics made him acutely aware that he had been lonely for a long time. Well, he wasn't going to analyze that right now; instead he found himself thinking that if any girl could make that *Hanauma* Bay swim, Brandi could. She had a strong competitive swimming background that he admired.

Swimming around the point would be a challenging endeavor because of the erratic tidal changes, which take place offshore and can create dangerous currents called the *Molokai Express*. This current can often drag swimmers out to sea where their struggles can become their death sentence, but he had done it many times.

Smiling as he drove on, he concluded that he'd never found a girl that could even come close to doing the swim. Brandi would probably be ahead of him most of the way. Her endurance would come in handy once in the open water. On windy days when the tide is high, the ocean breeze can make the current difficult. Somehow, he felt confident that Brandi would love to do the blow hole, too. The only way to get to it was to swim a half mile around the point.

Duke had experienced the blow hole several times. It's a cave-like rock hole that shoots sea spray high into the air. The water drains out and comes rushing back in, plummeting people a few feet into the middle of the sea spray. A rush that always thrilled him even though it was extremely dangerous and people had been seriously hurt doing it. He was a risk taker in life, he didn't believe in sitting back.

♦♦♦

As he got closer to the hotel, Duke grinned, thinking that he'd love to see Brandi in that black bikini again, but she'd probably wear a Speedo for the swim around to the blow hole. Very few women he'd been with had been as athletic as Brandi. He found it so appealing, refreshing, and even a bit intimidating as he thought about which day might work for them to go.

He remembered that they were both working Christmas Eve and Christmas Day this week. Two long days, so maybe the day after Christmas at *Hanauma* Bay would work and a beach picnic as well. A day date would make it seem less of a real date and put Brandi more at ease. So it was settled; that's what he would do.

Twenty minutes later, he turned into the hotel village parking lot. Brandi was still on his mind. She was dredging up emotions that he'd kept buried for the last decade. The last thing he needed was a long term relationship with this young sexy Brandi; he couldn't deny the fierce attraction. But would she date her boss? He suspected it would be uncharted waters for her. However, he would just not accept no for an answer. Brandi was going to be his, no matter what. There was just too much of a sexual current swimming between them. He felt sure Brandi would not be able to resist his undeniable charms.

If he played his cards right, spoiled her, soon she would be his. At thirty-six years old, it was the chase and the conquest of a woman that drove him like a rutting bull. Ride her for as long as he could until the kick was gone. That was his past history with women and he wasn't about to change his habits, no matter what.

However, strange as it was, he didn't think this infatuation with Brandi would fizzle out quickly. Perhaps she would continue to enchant him longer than the multitude of past flings. It would fizzle out at some point. They always did. However, like the song now on the radio, "Hooked on a Feeling" by B.J. Thomas, he couldn't deny that he felt those old familiar feelings of early infatuation once again.

Nevertheless, he knew that Brandi had been bitten by the shark of love and left to fend for herself with a broken heart. He would sweep her off her feet. Spoil her with fancy dinners and smother her with attention. He was good at doing just that. Charming the ladies. But he'd never had one that was still in love with another man. He put the car in park and turned off the engine. Ready or not, he would possess her and make her need *him* instead of that navy man stationed five thousand miles away.

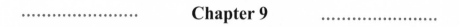

Chapter 9

Tropical Snorkeling

Christmas came and went without much fanfare and 1971 was rapidly approaching. Loneliness swept through me as I entered my apartment late on Christmas Day evening around 11 p.m. I had pulled a double shift cocktailing and waiting tables all day at the *Tapa* poolside bar, and then hostessing at the *Makaha* dining room for the dinner shift. My body felt like it had been smashed by a rogue wave giving me a pounding headache.

Sherry was still up and in her Hawaiian print muumuu watching *The Johnny Carson Show*. Her cigarette smoke drifted around the front room like a ghostly mist. The lanai door was open and the balmy night breeze feathered through the worn flimsy white curtains, but it did little to dispel the smoke haze. Thank God, I had quit that stinky habit after Skip had shipped out, but I was really only a party smoker so it was easy to quit. It seemed like all the military guys and everyone else smoked these days. It was becoming harder to live with smokers as roommates, but I reconciled the fact that I wasn't home that much anyway.

Glancing around our living room, I noted that we had no Christmas tree or decorations this year. Neither of us girls wanted to spend the money and Donna had gone back to the mainland for Christmas with her family. I plopped myself down on the sofa next to Sherry and kicked off my flip flops.

"You look beat, Brandi," she commented, while crushing out her cigarette.

"Yeah, I am. Double shift, but I made over a hundred dollars in tips, so I guess it was worth it," I replied with a yawn. "How was dinner at your teacher friend's house?"

"Oh, it was good, lots of little *keikis* (kids) running around full of the Christmas spirit and sugar. Remind me never to have kids, but the food was delicious. I got home about two hours ago. You're off tomorrow, right?" she asked, pushing a loose strand of her blond hair behind one ear.

"Yep, and I'm going to *Hanauma* Bay with Duke for the whole day. We're going to swim around the point to the blow hole, so I need to get some rest." I stood up and stretched my arms above my head.

"The blow hole? Well, be really careful. There are dangerous currents out there. I know you are a really good swimmer, but be sure you have fins, a snorkel, and a mask. You'll need them, especially if the winds are up and the tide is high."

"Yeah, Duke said he would bring me a set of all that."

"Well, okay then. Hey, I'm glad you are finally going to go out with Duke."

"It's not a date, Sherry...it's just a day at the beach with him," I shrugged my shoulders in response.

"Call it what you want, but it's a date, girl," she grinned. "Go to bed. I'll see you in the morning. What time are you leaving?"

"Around 11 a.m. If I'm not up by nine, please wake me," I said, dragging my tired *okole* down the hallway and wondering what a day with Duke would be like. I couldn't help but visualize what he would look like in swim trunks. If what he looked like in street clothes was any indication, then I pictured a bare muscular chest and tight abs. Oh, and let's not forget that sexy dark skin. Yum...yum. Stop that, I told myself. He's your boss, remember that girl. And you're not sure about some of his stories that just don't add up.

However, I couldn't stop the feeling of how good his strong arms had felt around me when he had hugged me the other night. Alas, my dark Hawaiian prince, one that was there to comfort me when I had needed it the most.

◆◆◆

Duke picked me up the following morning. The day promised to be a typical Hawaiian weather day of blue skies, balmy trade winds, and lots of sunshine. We headed out in his big red muscle car, the '64 Ford Galaxie, with the top down. My ponytail was blowing in the breeze and Duke was humming along to the song, "Magic Carpet Ride" by Steppenwolf, which buoyed my appetite for more fun today.

Driving from my *Kapahulu* neighborhood, we caught Highway 72 with Diamond Head Crater behind us. We drove around Koko Head and then past the Koko Marina where boats littered the inland bay, bobbing in the sparkling current while some made their way out to deeper waters.

We passed through the Hawaii Kai residential area with a variety of shops. The neighborhood was like a colorful arboretum where bushes of natural flowers grew in abundance surrounding the yards. Everywhere I looked I saw gently swaying palm trees, bird-of-paradise plants, pink and white shelled ginger, and plumeria bushes. All those beautiful vibrant colors never ceased to amaze me. Colors that were so rich against the blue sky that it made me aware of God's amazing beauty and the wonder of creation.

There was a local park that we passed, which was already filled with families staking out their spots for a day at the beach. Even though it was only around 11:30 a.m., tangy smells of teriyaki chicken and beef grilling on hibachis seeped into the air. Families were already preparing their feasts to indulge in throughout the day. I wondered what Duke had packed for food and drinks. He had said he would take care of everything. I was beginning to feel spoiled since all I had to do was be his partner for the day.

"Have you ever swum around the point to the blow hole, Brandi?" he questioned, as we slowed to round a curve and the glorious blue ocean waters beckoned beyond.

"I've been to *Hanauma* Bay snorkeling, but no, I've not swum around the point. I hear that it can be really dangerous though," I replied with concern.

"Yes, it can be," Duke stated. "The current and the winds can make it a difficult swim for the novice, but with your swimming background hell, I doubt that you will have any trouble navigating it," he said grinning at me. "In fact Brandi, I will probably be trying to keep up with you," he raised an eyebrow and laughed.

"Well, I was a nationally ranked distance swimmer, Duke. So I'll try not to leave you behind," I teased.

"Please don't, sweetheart, I might get scared or worse lonely out there by myself," he countered, with a tilt of his head.

Did he just call me *sweetheart* again? Didn't he use that word the other night when he held me in his arms? Endearing, I thought. Does he think of me already as his sweetheart? How did I feel about that? Hmm...I wasn't sure, but it did have a nice ring and warmth to it. It made me feel enamored.

Once at *Hanauma* Bay parking lot, we walked down the steep paved half mile stretch to the beach. Located on the southeast coast of Oahu in the Hawaii Kai area, the marine bay looks like a huge tuff ring. A giant horseshoe shaped bay. It's both a nature preserve and a marine life conservation district. Because it has over four hundred species of fish and beautiful coral reefs, it's one of the most popular tourist attractions on the island. Shallow waters of four to five feet in depth occupy the inner part of the bay, but once crossing the reefs, it becomes very deep with the dangerous *Molokai Express* currents. These currents can drag you all the way to the island of Molokai, some sixty-six miles away, which is the closest island to Oahu from the southeast coast.

"Here's your gear, *sweetheart*," Duke said, handing me my fins, snorkel, and mask.

Hmm...there's that word again, *sweetheart.* I couldn't resist smiling at him though, as he laid our bamboo beach mats in the shade along with the cooler.

I glanced over at him. He really looked good in his black and red Hawaiian print swim trunks. Well-defined muscular legs like a runner would have. And then he slipped off his T-shirt. Whoa! He had chest muscles that looked like he pumped iron in the gym. Taut, firm, very masculine, and sexy. Tough like a firefighter's body. He grinned at me with a look that said, *come and get it, baby.* Was my tongue hanging out? I felt sure it was. I could only stare. And that dark skin with the sun shining on it, he had me panting before I knew what hit me. I swallowed hard. My breath caught in my throat.

"I've got some sunscreen. I'll put some on you, if you'll lather me up, too!" he said, with a sensuous implication. "Did you wear that sexy black bikini today? The one I saw you in when I first spotted you at the Outrigger Hotel?"

"Oh no, I didn't because it isn't good for open water swimming; the top doesn't stay on very well," I replied, feeling a blush rush to my face and thinking of the visual I just gave him.

"Doesn't stay on well, huh?" he teased, with a big deliberate smile. "I'd like to see that," he added with cockiness.

"Hmm...I bet you would. But, I'm wearing a two-piece red Speedo instead. It's made for this kind of endurance swimming." I lifted off my beach cover-up and suddenly felt shy.

A slow grin fanned his face. His dark black eyes raked over me. "A two-piece Speedo. That's new. Wow! Red hot! Has anyone ever told you, Brandi, that you have an incredible body?" He shook his head, thinking that she could be a playboy bunny with those long sexy legs, slim hips, full luscious rack she sported, and that long honey colored hair. His thoughts blistered into overdrive. Easy, Duke, he told himself. Timing is everything with this one; remember she had her heart broken recently.

He walked up to me with a tube of sunscreen. "Can you do my back?" he asked grinning, while longing to feel her hands on his skin.

"Uh...sure, Duke." I reached for the lotion. I squeezed a good portion out into my hand and then I gently rubbed it all over his muscular back. My pulse sizzled. His skin was smooth and dark. Muscles that I wanted to touch over and over again, but I had to stop or he might think I was overdoing it.

"Your turn," I beamed, as I handed him the tube and turned around so he could do my back. His hands were gentle as he massaged the lotion into my skin like a massage therapist. Expert in motion. Hmm...I could get used to this. A man with a soft touch. Very sensuous and tempting, I realized, while enjoying his touch a little too much.

◆◆◆

Beautiful, silky tan skin, Duke thought, as he lingered longer than necessary smoothing the sun lotion on her back. He didn't think he'd ever been with a young woman that had such defined trapezoid and upper back muscles. Years of competitive swimming training that was for sure, but it wasn't masculine in any way. In fact, he found it extremely appealing and left him aching to touch her all over.

"I love your swimming muscles and your soft skin. I'd be glad to do your front and legs, too," he teased, handing me the lotion.

"Yeah, I bet you would, Duke. But...but I think I can handle that part."

"Damn, can't blame me for trying, Brandi," he laughed. "Finish up and let's head out to snorkel for a bit, then cross over the reefs, my red hot *Wahine*," he laughed. However, he didn't miss the blush that crept across Brandi's pretty face and the twinkle in her big brown eyes. She'd be in his bed by the end of the week; he had no doubts about that.

◆◆◆

We snorkeled together in the shallow part of the bay for over a half an hour. Duke pointing out the array of different fish to me. Side-by-side we drifted, enjoying the exotic beauty of the sea life and coral. We spotted *opakapaka,* a Hawaiian pink snapper, along with the vast schools of reef fish like the yellow tang, bluestripe snapper, and the famous Hawaiian state fish, the yellow and black striped *humuhumunukunukuapua'a.* Hard to pronounce, but breaking it into two syllables at a time was the only way to say it correctly, and I always had fun trying to say it, such a tongue twister.

We fed the fish little green peas that Duke had brought along. They were so friendly they ate right out of our hands. Giant sea turtles swam around us, too, spanning three feet or more in an elegant dance of movements that seemed effortless. We skimmed along in the crystal clear blue waters, as if we were a part of this school of tropical fish.

The gentle ebb and flow of the current in the sheltered reef bay was easy to navigate. It wasn't too crowded because it was the day after Christmas. This bay could get so overpopulated with families and tourists that it could spoil the fun. But today, it was like our own private aquarium. I noted that Duke was very comfortable in the water, a good swimmer. With our fins on, we held hands and just kicked together snorkeling as one. I was lost in the brilliant colors of sea life and its tranquil majestic beauty. It was an infinite universe of unending life that left me in awe, just like Duke was making me feel.

.... **Chapter 10** ....

Sunkissed

When we crossed over the shallow coral reefs, it was another story all together. The wind kicked up. It was deep open water and the waves became choppy. The current was tugging at us, ready to pull us further out to sea. I stayed next to Duke since I hadn't done this swim before. However, even though swimming with him was a slower pace for me, I loved the challenge and I loved being out there with a man that could do this. I had never done this with my past navy lover, Skip. Had Duke been a competitive swimmer or lifeguard? He had a strong freestyle stroke. I'd have to remember to ask him later.

My thoughts drifted as we swam along in the vast open ocean. I wondered what Duke was thinking as we stayed stroke-for-stroke making our way toward the blow hole around the rocky cliff point. A good half mile swim at best.

Duke couldn't believe how easily Brandi kept up with him with her easy crawl stroke. He marveled at her smoothness and endurance. What a remarkable girl, he thought. No fear, just ready for the challenge of this open water long swim. She was probably not even tired, he contemplated, thinking that he'd never done this with any girl. Impressive. It just made his attraction to her even stronger.

Once reaching the blow hole, Duke was out of breath. He glanced over at Brandi; she wasn't even winded as they climbed up the rocks and removed their gear. "Let me catch my breath, Brandi, before we jump into the blow hole."

"Oh, are you out of breath, Duke?" I teased with a sly grin.

"Just a little, but I see you're not," he said, taking a deep breath while sizing her up. "Man, you sure can swim girl. I'm so impressed."

"Thanks, Duke. It's known that I am part fish. At least, that's what my dad says," I laughed with a teasing smile. I was beginning to like flirting with him.

"A beautiful mermaid is more like it," he shot back. Moving to stand behind her, he wrapped his arms around her waist in a big Hawaiian hug. It was the first time he'd felt her pressed up against him. Loving the feel, he rocked her gently against his pelvis. Their wet bodies touching skin-to-skin while the hot sunshine dried them off. The heat between them escalated like a spiked fever in Duke's body. He kissed the back of her neck. She tasted of fresh salty sea water, but her skin was soft and silky.

Duke's arms felt just as good around me as they had the night in his car, when he first hugged and comforted me. I was acutely aware of the want that my body was responding to, especially with the subtle kiss he had gently placed on the back of my neck. A much older man, my boss to boot. My handsome, dark, sexy Hawaiian prince wanted me; that I knew for sure.

"You make my head spin," he whispered in my ear, and turned me around facing him. Placing his hands on my hips, he pulled me in close. We swayed together with the trade winds brushing against our bare skin. Duke teased me with a gentle *hula* rocking motion. The sun glistened off Duke's dark, chocolate skin as he suddenly kissed my lips with a sizzle that pulled me in like a strong current... betraying my guarded heart. I'd been sunkissed and was trying to swim against the undertow...breathless and weak from the shear power of his kiss.

"God, I've wanted to kiss you from the first time I saw you on the beach in front of the Outrigger Hotel," he said with conviction. "And damn, you kiss good, too!"

"Kiss me again, Duke," I said, wrapping my arms around his neck and throwing caution to the trade winds, and he did just that.

A long exploring kiss that lingered with the promise of more, if I wanted.

Pulling away, I said, "I have a mermaid's heart, Duke, but it's been broken recently. I'm not looking for any kind of commitments, just a good ride and some fun," I challenged.

He tossed his head back and laughed loudly. "Well, Brandi, I can promise you that I'm not the committed kind and I can definitely give you a good ride and a lot of fun," he boasted. He planted a quick kiss on my lips before breaking the hold around my waist. "Speaking of fun, are you ready to get flushed, girl?"

"Flushed?"

"Yes, flushed." He pointed to the cave-like blow hole. "See how the water quickly drains out of that deep cavern?"

I looked down into the cavernous six foot by ten foot wide hole. "Yeah, the water is now only about a foot deep." Duke came around to my side and took my hand in his with a gentle squeeze that sent sunshine radiating through me.

"Watch now, in a moment or two, it will come gushing back in and spill over the sides like a huge geyser. Here it comes," he pointed at the wall of water rushing into the hole from a small tunnel, flooding the ground floor.

Within seconds, the water level rose with a gigantic rush of sea water and white foam that sprayed into the air like Old Faithful at Yellowstone Park, but not nearly as high or big.

"Are you ready? I'll keep hold of your hand. We'll jump in as the water starts to recede. Then we wait until it comes gushing back in. It will toss us airbound like high surf, but once it starts to recede, swim back to the rocks and climb out with me."

"Are you sure this is safe?" I frowned.

"No, but it's a thrill and a rush. Don't disappoint me, Brandi. You can do this. Trust me." He squeezed my hand tighter for reassurance.

I took a deep breath to calm my nervousness. "Okay, Duke. I'll try it, but don't let go of my hand." I silently prayed that I would live to tell about this.

We stood there waiting. The sun beating down on us. Timing it just right, we jumped into the hole, holding hands as the high water started to recede. Gradually, the water seeped out through the cavernous tunnel until we stood a foot deep in water. Moments ticked by. My heart pounding in my chest like drums at a luau.

"Hold on. It's coming back, Brandi," Duke hollered, as an explosion of water jolted us several feet into the air. I screamed. I laughed. We were floating on foam and tons of swift sea water, tossed around as if in a blender. A rush like you felt on a roller coaster. As the geyser started to recede, we somehow managed to climb onto the rocks to safety.

Thrilled to the bone and breathless, we rested on the rocks. "Wow! Can we do it again? What a rush," I cried, sitting next to Duke.

He leaned back and chuckled heartily. "Yeah, a couple more times, but we need to get back to shore before that wind kicks up even more." He pointed out to the increasing swells and white caps.

◆◆◆

We did the blow hole flush three more times before getting our snorkeling gear on. "I'm glad you are a strong swimmer because it will be a bit more challenging swimming back now," Duke advised with concern.

"I think we'll be okay. With our snorkels we don't have to fight the chop to catch a breath, but let's increase our pace a bit. Do you think you can keep up with me, Duke?" I challenged, nudging him gently in the side.

"I'll try, my mermaid of the sea," he winked at me. "Don't leave me behind. I intend to stick to you like glue and not just during the swim either," he responded, with a commanding tone. He placed his mask and snorkel on as we headed down the rocky cliff to the water's edge.

Stick to me like glue? That would be completely the opposite of my past navy love, Skip, who often reeled me in and then cast me out. It might be endearing to have a man stick to me like glue for a while, even if he wasn't interested in a long term relationship, I thought. We slipped our gear on and dove into the open water.

I was glad we had fins on because the current was strong, choppy, and challenging. And I was happy that Duke was with me. I wouldn't want to swim alone out here in this chop and white caps. Even the best of swimmers could get in trouble with this *Molokai Express* current.

Once we reached the coral reef, we crossed over into the shallower calmer marine life bay. This time I was out of breath. I was humbled to even be able to manage the return swim, grateful for my swimming skills, and thrilled that Duke believed in me enough to know that I could handle it.

♦♦♦

"I'm starved," Duke sang out, as we made our way to our shady picnic spot. He dropped his gear in the sand and opened the cooler up. "Are you hungry?"

"Famished! What did you bring us?"

"I cooked up some teriyaki beef strips and chicken wings last night and some *poke* salad (Hawaiian seafood salad)," he beamed. "Oh, and some fresh cut pineapple." I sat down on my beach mat, while he dished me up a plate and handed me an ice cold Coke. "Here you go."

"Yum, it looks delicious. You cooked this?" I asked, with a raised eyebrow.

Duke sat down on my mat next to me and crossed his legs Indian style. "I did, just another of the many things that I am really good at doing. Food is my business Brandi," he declared with confidence, taking a bite of beef and *poke* salad.

I dug in. "God, this is really good, Duke. I'm impressed."

"Good, I want you to be impressed," he affirmed, raking his hand through his damp, thick, black hair. I'm going to spoil you, wine and dine you, and that's not all."

I looked him in the eye again. "Really? What else are you good at besides swimming and cooking?" I teased with a grin.

He reached over and played with my wet ponytail. "Well, that's for you to find out and me to show you," he grinned. "But I am very good at tennis and downhill skiing. I lived in Oregon for a while with a food and beverage job, took ski lessons and got really good, became an instructor. Imagine an island boy on skis," he chuckled. "Growing up here I was on the tennis team in high school, state champ. Did a little summer swim team, too."

"Wow, again I'm impressed." He lived in Oregon? I wondered when that fit into his age timeline that still was questionable.

"Do you ski or play tennis?" he asked, while taking a drink of his Coke.

"Nah, I was always training for swimming. Pretty tunneled into that one sport. I competed at Nationals a handful of times."

"See, now I'm impressed. I'll teach you tennis. *Kapiolani* Park has public courts and night lights. I've got extra rackets. We can begin later this week at night."

"I'd love that, Duke. I've always wanted to learn tennis."

"Well, with your athletic abilities, I think you'll catch on really quickly," he praised, as he inhaled another bite of *poke* salad. "Eat up, *love,* and let's head back. I've got to check in at the hotel for a private evening cocktail party."

"You have to work tonight?" I asked between bites, thinking that he called me *love* this time. Hmm, I liked that, too.

"I'm always working, unless I take time off to spend with a sexy girl like you, which I intend to do regularly from now on," he declared, as the sun sank lower on the horizon and my pulse did a series of flip flops.

"You're going to dinner with me tomorrow," he said flat out. "And I won't take no for an answer. I know you are off then, so be ready at 7 p.m. And wear your beautiful hair loose and down. I love it that way."

I blinked. I guess I was going out on a date with him tomorrow evening. "Okay, are there any other requests?"

He ran his hand up my thigh. "Yes, wear something sexy with a lot of your beautiful skin showing."

I finished up my plate of food thinking that he certainly was forceful and hard to say no to. Yikes, he was telling me how to wear my hair and dress. Was that a good thing or problematic? He really was fun to spend a day with. I could only imagine what dinner out with him would be like...romantic, I was sure, based on his kisses today. However, like the slowly sinking sun, I wondered if being with Duke would float my boat or eventually sink it.

Chapter 11

New *Haole* Roommate

Sherry and I spent the next day hanging around our apartment and getting to know our new roommate, Jenny, who had moved in this afternoon. Donna was returning today from Christmas on the mainland.

Our *Makaleka* apartment had three bedrooms. Donna had the master with her own bathroom. Sherry and I shared a larger bedroom with two twin beds. The third bedroom was really a studio room, very small with an accordion door that separated it from the living room. Not very private. That room had been empty for several months.

The cool thing was that each bedroom had a different rent rate. Mine was only $100.00 a month. Luckily, you were only responsible for your personal rent. So if someone moved out, their rent was absorbed by management until they filled the vacancy. The downside was that management moved people in at their own discretion, which meant that you could end up with a girl you might not like.

Jenny was from Minnesota, a college grad with a teaching degree in home economics, fresh out of school. She was scouting out Hawaii for possible job opportunities, but mostly she was on an extended paid vacation from her parents as a graduation gift. How lucky was she? Spoiled, I gathered.

Sherry and I were in the kitchen talking with her before I needed to get ready for my dinner date. Sherry was cooking Jenny some stir-fry shrimp and vegetables in a sweet soy sauce with sticky white rice on the side. Jenny adjusted her sunglasses on top of her head. She was petite, around five foot four with hazel green eyes, long, thick, fiery red hair, lily white skin, and caramel freckles that covered her entire face and body. She'd stick out on the beach like a red lobster, I thought. And probably burn that pale skin in less than twenty minutes, if she wasn't careful.

I shifted my stance against the kitchen counter. "Jenny, you really need to be careful here and not get sunburned. That Scandinavian skin of yours will burn within minutes," I warned her with concern. "People think they are okay to stay out in it longer than they should, but I see so many tourists burned to a crisp."

Jenny glanced out the window. "Yeah, I will. Thanks, Brandi, but I don't think I need to be mothered," she sassed back, with a tone of sarcasm.

"Oh...just saying, that's all," I replied with surprise. I turned and rolled my eyes at Sherry, who rolled her eyes back in silent agreement. Was this new roommate going to get along with the three of us? Time would tell. Four of us now, with a change in dynamics that could spoil our happy three musketeers' family.

Jenny continued to look out the kitchen window. "This place is sure packed with military guys. Don't you know?" she claimed, with a slight Nordic accent.

Sherry and I both grinned. "Yeah, we both know that. Always a party somewhere in the building," I said. "Mostly submariners, three months in port and then three months under the ocean on top secret deterrence nuclear patrols. This cold war with the Russians keeps our Pacific fleet busy. If you're smart, don't get involved with any of them. I did and he broke my heart," I warned.

"Yeah, me too," Sherry countered. "My navy guy ran off with my Polynesian girlfriend. He married her even though she is twenty years older than him. Broke my heart. You can go to their parties, but don't get hooked on one," Sherry said, while stirring the shrimp and vegetables in the soy sauce mixture.

"Really, well, I'll do as I want," Jenny grumbled with conviction. "But, thanks for the warning anyway," she tossed her flaming red hair in defiance.

"Hey," Sherry said, "don't take that the wrong way, just warning you, Jenny. Will you be looking for work soon?"

"Don't know, my parents gave me unlimited spending for a couple of months," she bragged.

"Oh, how nice for you." Sherry raised an eyebrow with a snort. "Almost ready. Grab a plate, Jenny."

"Okay, I don't think I've ever had shrimp and vegetable stir-fry." She wrinkled up her nose. "Let alone soy sauce."

"Well, get used to it. White rice and soy sauce are staples here," Sherry shot back, as she dished up their plates.

"Well, you two enjoy your dinner. I need to get ready for my date with Duke."

Jenny raised her eyebrows. "Who's Duke? Not a navy man!" she smirked.

I sighed deeply. "No, thank God. He's my...my boss at the Hilton Hawaiian Hotel, if you must know. The one I spent yesterday snorkeling with at *Hanauma* Bay."

"What! Your boss? Isn't that rather inappropriate? I mean, really, Brandi."

I put my hand on her shoulder like a mother would do. "It's none of your business, Jenny." I fumed. "Oh, and he's Polynesian with beautiful dark skin and he's at least ten years older than me, too." That ought to get her goat, I mused.

Her mouth fell open and she gasped. "Polynesian! How dark *is* he?"

"He's dark like...like Kahlua! Is there something wrong with that?" I countered, with a condescending tone.

"Uh...well...my parents would disown me if I dated someone of...of darker skin."

"Well, it's common place here, Jenny. There are a lot of mixed couples and marriages with beautiful *hapa haole* (half and half) kids," I clarified as I left her to ponder that.

Boy, was she totally out of her element or what? I strolled out of the kitchen and into the *lau* (bathroom) to take a shower. Our new roommate, Jenny, might prove to be a challenge for us. Secretly, I hoped she would decide to find another place to hang her beach hat. She ruffled my muumuu the wrong way!

Chapter 12

Royal Hawaiian Delight

Tucked inside the Royal Hawaiian Hotel, perched on the Waikiki beachfront, the Azure Restaurant was a bejeweled dining establishment that boasted exceptional service and delicious cuisine. I was impressed that Duke had reservations and that he was taking me to such a fine five-star restaurant.

The pretty, dark haired local hostess of the Azure Restaurant looked up with surprise and an expression of unease as we entered. "Mr. Haku, it's been a while, sir," she said, accentuating the sir with a tone of animosity. Did they have a history with each other? Had they been lovers once?

"I see you have reservations." She reached for two menus. "Right this way, please," she said. Her body language was guarded as she escorted us to a reserved oceanside table. However, Duke seemed unconcerned while his hand rested on the small of my back as we followed her. The heat it generated didn't go unnoticed and sent tingling vibes through me.

Nestled off to the side, against a black metal patio wall, tables were set with small, wooden pineapple candles that glowed in the shadowy sunset. Delicate woven table placemats of *tapa* print, fan-shaped folded white cloth napkins, and pristine table settings gave the restaurant a look of elegance and romance.

Duke pulled out my rattan chair for me. I slipped into the plush white, Hawaiian print, chair cushions. Soft and luxurious. Duke took his seat while smiling at me and practically ignored the hostess. "I love this place. The view is really something, don't you think?" he asked, taking the menu that was offered him.

"Thank you," I said to the hostess, while opening my menu. "Yes, it's stunning," I agreed, looking out at the beautiful soft pink and purple sunset that spanned across the vast horizon. Diamond Head Crater was off to my left with a profusion of white lights from hotel high-rises and apartment buildings that covered the skyline like brilliant stars.

"Your server tonight will be Chan. He'll be with you in a moment. Enjoy your evening with us, Mr. Haku," she stated, with another hint of scorn before leaving.

"She knows you?" I asked with raised eyebrows, thinking that at thirty-two, Duke had probably known a lot of ladies here and had many women in his bed. I wondered what their history was. It really wasn't my business, but she was obviously harboring some resentment.

"Yes, I've been here many times. I know a lot of people in the food and beverage industry," Duke said, with a bit of irritation. "I went out with her a few times. It was a bad break-up." God, he couldn't believe Leah worked here now. He'd slept with her a couple of times and hadn't bothered to return her persistent calls. Bitchy and possessive. Why did women think they owned you once you slept with them? He quickly diverted the subject back to the present moment.

"By the way, Brandi, you look especially exotic and beautiful in that red halter dress. Stunning. I can't take my eyes off you," he said, with flashing eyes as our waiter, Chan, approached and I blushed as red as my lipstick.

♦♦♦

Dusk was such a mystical time of day here. I could almost feel the spirits of the past watching over the land with a sense of protectiveness, pride, and ancestral knowledge that wrapped its arms around the islands. Doves and a variety of birds sang their songs of orchestrated chirping, their nightly ritual call to settle into the trees until dawn. My heart was glowing with the sheer beauty and magic of this tropical setting here at the Royal Hawaiian Azure Restaurant. Once again, I fell in love with living here.

"Aloha, Mr. Haku," Chan bowed slightly. "May I suggest the sashimi for an appetizer? It is the freshest you will ever taste," he acknowledged.

"Is it *ahi* with heart of palm, avocado crema, and that delicious sauce you serve with it?" Duke questioned.

"Yes sir, it is and the *ahi* is fresh, too. A most excellent sashimi dish," he beamed with another nod.

"Perfect, we'll start with that then and a bottle of your best Viognier."

"Excellent choice to complement the sashimi, sir. I'll be right back with your wine; please know that our house special tonight is *opakapaka* island style. It's today's fresh fish catch served with a crusted seasoning, flavored with sesame and chili oil, and *harmakua* mushrooms. Truly a must, Mr. Haku," he said before he left us.

"Wow, Mr. Haku, I'm impressed!" I teased. "You seem to know everyone and you ordered sashimi for me. I've never had a man do that before. Sashimi, it's raw fish, isn't it?" I wrinkled up my nose.

"Yes, but trust me, the *ahi* sashimi will melt in your mouth. It's cut and sliced for maximum tenderness. You won't even know it's fish," he reassured me.

I wasn't sure about that, but I didn't argue as our waiter returned with our wine. He poured for Duke, who completed the smell and swirl test before tasting and approving it. A ceremony that I enjoyed watching, thinking that Duke knew his way around wines and how to impress a young woman like me. I couldn't tell an expensive wine from a cheap wine, but I guessed I was going to learn, if I stuck with Duke. He seemed so worldly, and had expensive taste without a concern for cost.

I had limited experience with actual dining at such an upscale place, mostly because it was expensive and I didn't have that kind of money. It was one thing to work in an expensive dining room and quite another to be a paying customer, I surmised.

"It's perfect. Dry and full bodied. Lovely tangerine bouquet," Duke said, as he swirled his glass. "Nice legs on it," he commented. "Thank you," he declared, while Chan poured both of us a glass and left the bottle in an ice bucket tableside.

"To you, my beautiful mermaid," Duke said, as he raised his glass with an expectant smile and his dark black eyes met mine with a flirtatious gleam.

"To you, Duke, my...my handsome Hawaiian prince," I added, adoring his dark skin and his rakish full head of black hair. He was very hard to resist and very charming, I thought. That white short sleeve shirt against his dark skin made him stand out like a Hawaiian male model. He was spoiling me with an expensive dinner and wine and I loved it!

◆◆◆

I tried the sashimi. It did melt in my mouth and didn't even taste like fish. Smooth and succulent. I was always willing to try something new. Do like the locals do, I thought, as we indulged ourselves and continued to talk.

"Did you know this place is known as the Pink Palace of the Pacific?"

"I didn't know that, Duke," I replied, taking a sip of my wine as a warm tropical breeze washed over my bare skin.

"Well, I'll give you a little history lesson then. It's made of pink concrete stucco and it's about ninety years old. The architecture is a Spanish/Moorish style. It's one of the oldest, most luxurious and famous hotels in Hawaii."

"Is it haunted, too, like the old *Moana* Hotel next door?"

He laughed and leaned back. "Oh, so you know that tale, do you?"

"Yes I do. Some rich old lady from California was supposedly murdered there at the turn of the century, and that her ghost haunts the hotel halls at night or so the story goes."

He leaned forward. "And her murderer has never been found. There are lots of stories like that throughout the islands, Brandi. It's said that their spirits appear as guides or ghosts. Friendly or not so friendly according to the locals. I happen to believe the folklore," he said, finishing up the sashimi.

"Ghosts." I felt goosebumps on my bare skin, "I don't much believe in that, but spiritual guides and angels, yes. My grandmother told me about some experiences she had confirming that they do exist and I believe her," I said, as our Asian waiter came and cleared the appetizer plates.

"Mr. Haku, what would you and the lady like for your dinner tonight?"

"We'll have your house ocean salad and the *opakapaka* chef's special that you recommended, Chan, and another bottle of wine with dinner please," Duke stated.

"Ah...yes, very good, sir. The fish is, of course, fresh today and bought early this morning at the pier auction market," he stated, and then refilled our wine glasses before leaving.

"They catch the fish fresh daily?" I asked with surprise.

"Well, the fish buyer for the hotel bids on what the local fishermen bring in to auction at the pier. Each morning at 5:30 a.m. the ringing of a brass bell starts the bidding. It's quite the scene with buyers from all over the island trying to get the best deal. That's why the fish served here is called Hawaiian style...fresh from the ocean and succulent to the palate. It's a delicate white fish that will melt in your mouth. Trust me again, you will love it," he grinned boldly.

I sat back with my second glass of wine in hand and sighed deeply. The sun sank and darkness swept in, as the sound of a *conch* shell blew loudly throughout the grounds. Appearing out of nowhere, a Polynesian man, wearing only a long *tapa* sarong tied around his waist, ran through the grounds holding a lit *tiki* torch. Strong arms and a bare chest, he stopped and lit over a dozen *tiki* lanterns that graced the Royal Hawaiian Hotel beachfront.

Fire from the lanterns burned into the night air making everything appear surreal and creating an ambiance of Hawaiian beauty. My heart and soul danced with the romance of it all...and Duke. I'd never been out with someone as commanding, assertive, confident, worldly, and so much older than me.

◆◆◆

Our ocean salad was served. It was beautifully plated. "What's in the salad, Duke? It looks scrumptious!" I said, picking up my salad fork.

"It's Kona lobster, prawns, scallops, avocado, Dungeness crab, baby lettuce, and it's seasoned with tarragon and crème fraiche dressing. It's a favorite of mine," he smiled with pleasure.

I took a bite. "It's delicious, Duke. I love the creamy dressing. It's just so...so yummy. Seafood is one of my favorite foods."

"I'm glad you like it, Brandi, and I'm very happy that you are here with me." He raised his glass. "You're so sweet."

"Ah...thank you, Duke," I blushed as we continued to eat and talk until our main course was served.

The chef's special of *opakapaka* fish blew me away. It was the best white fish I had ever tasted and to think that I grew up eating fresh salmon and steelhead back home in Seattle, what with my dad being an avid fisherman. However, this island style fish was in a class all its own. It was delicate with a melt in your mouth deliciousness, served with Hawaiian fried rice and slices of fresh *guava* on the side. And the white wine, Viognier, complemented it beautifully.

I have to say that the dreamy night atmosphere, the Waikiki lights surrounding us, the gentle lapping sounds of the ocean, and the wine made for the most romantic dinner ever. And our constant flirting boosted my lonesome ego. Out with a much older man, one with a lot of culture and prestige. It made my heart sing with royal Hawaiian delight.

Chapter 13

Under the Stars

The legendary beachfront bar at the Royal Hawaiian Hotel was our after dinner place of choice for a nightcap. Duke insisted that we dance under the stars. Located just steps away from Waikiki Beach this oceanfront bar offered nightly *mele* (songs) performed by some of the island's most talented musicians.

Tonight my old friend, Puna that I knew from the Hilton Hawaiian Village was the sole entertainer. Duke and I sat close, side-by-side at the bar. Puna nodded at me, but a frown appeared on his face as he recognized who I was with. Once again, I wondered what it was that he didn't like about Duke. I dismissed the thought as his ukulele love songs and his soft, soulful voice filled the outside bar with pure Hawaiian romance.

Palm trees graced the outside area with large pink sun umbrellas situated for shade during the day and early evening hours. All the chairs had soft pink cushions with black metal frames. Tables were smoked glass with an indented marbled texture, along with similar black frames. In the darkness, candles on each table glowed and *tiki* lanterns burned throughout the beachfront grounds, casting their spell of Hawaiian exoticness.

"Have you ever had Kahlua?" Duke asked, while planting a soft kiss on my cheek.

"No," I answered, feeling a little awestruck. I watched several couples slow dancing under strands of white hanging lights, which encompassed the dance floor area.

"Well, then you are in for another treat. It's a coffee-flavored liqueur from Mexico and the perfect after dinner sipping drink. I like it over the rocks with a splash of cream." He waved the bartender over.

"Two Kahluas on the rocks with cream, please," Duke said to the bartender, and casually slipped his arm around my bare shoulders. God, her skin was so soft, he thought. Her long golden hair smelled like coconut mixed with vanilla. A scent that drove him mad with want.

This evening with Brandi had been such a pleasant change from other women he'd dated. Brandi was so unpretentious, so natural, and down to earth. He liked that about her and...her youth. Unspoiled. Sincere and gracious. She was still a little naive about the real world. Not to mention that she was sexy as all get out. He didn't miss the looks from the wait staff and men as he walked into the bar with Brandi on his arm.

"Two Kahluas on the rocks," the bartender clarified, as he placed the drinks in front of us with a pineapple shaped coaster underneath.

"Thanks," Duke replied. "To us, Brandi! To many more fabulous Hawaiian nights together," he beamed.

I raised my rock glass. "To us!" I agreed. "This has been such a fantastic evening, Duke. I am just so impressed," I said, taking a swallow of the Kahlua and cream. I licked my lips. "This is yummy!" I crossed my bare legs and Duke placed his hand on my knee with a gentle massaging touch. Sparks and heat sizzled through me.

Duke laughed. "You're yummy." He took a couple sips of his drink and I laughed as we continued to chat. When we had finished our drinks, Duke said, "Come on," reaching for my hand. "Let's dance."

He led me to the dance floor. It wasn't crowded. A few couples only. Puna's ukulele strummed the song, "Somewhere Over the Rainbow" Hawaiian style, as he sang along in his soft tenor voice.

Duke's hand hugged my lower spine firmly. His other hand grasped mine gently in a possessive hold, letting me know that he knew how to lead a woman on the dance floor. Oh...God, he could dance! Smooth and easy to follow. Was there anything he didn't do well? He moved me easily with the measured rhythm of the tender music. Being about the same height, we danced cheek-to-cheek.

He had this way of pausing in between several steps. He would pull me tightly into his body, press his pelvis into mine, and pause holding that position. It was extremely sexual and provocative. I had never slow danced with any man like this! It was like making love on the dance floor.

If he moved this good, what would he be like if I slept with him? Could I even do that? I was still mooning over my past navy lover, Skip. What if I got involved with Duke, and then Skip called and wanted me to come to New London to be with him? How would I explain myself? I sighed deeply, thinking that it was probably over with Skip anyway. He'd left me without any promises. I was tired of waiting and hoping. Tonight, I was having a wonderful time with Duke.

We danced the next song, "Pearly Shells" written by Don Ho, a local Hawaiian singer. It echoed in my ears, as well as Duke's tempting seductive words, "Come home with me, *love*. Let me rock your world," he whispered.

I felt myself giving into the mood and the wanting to be held, adored, and made love to throughout the rest of the evening. We danced and danced under the stars until midnight. Maybe it was just the wine and drink, but it had been three long months of abstinence. At twenty-one my hormones were in raging overtime. Should I go home with him? My heart said no. However, when his lips met mine in a provocative slow kiss, it teased my senses and left my body burning to say yes!

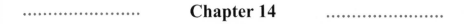

Chapter 14

Island *Hula* Lover

The midnight tropical air dusted my skin with its coolness. Duke and I walked the beachfront barefoot in the moonlight. We held hands as if we were lovers. The soft sounding surf seemed to silence my nerves and anticipation of what was to come. Approaching the Outrigger Surf Hotel, where Duke had once worked, we headed up the beach steps and into the open-air lobby.

"Let's stay here tonight, Brandi. I won't have to drive home or disturb my roommates. And I'd like to share the sunrise on the lanai with you. Have you ever stayed overnight in Waikiki?"

"No, that would be a first for me. But, I...I'm not sure I'm really ready to spend the night with you, even though I want to."

He stopped and pulled me into his arms. "Well, let me reassure you then. I want you tonight and you want me, too," he stated with conviction. "I know you think you're in love with that navy guy, but he's gone, Brandi. He left you here...alone. I want you now," he stated emphatically, and planted a deep thrusting kiss on my lips that left me aching for more.

"Okay, Duke," I said breathlessly as the kiss ended. He ran his hands through my long golden hair.

"Good, now let me get us a room that faces the ocean. I'll be right back," he replied, with a quick teasing pat on my *okole*.

At this time of night, the subtle lighting, gentle Hawaiian background music, and limited staff created a serene setting. Beautiful huge displays of vibrant local flowers and varieties of small, gently swaying palms graced the open-air lobby. Comfortable, soft sofas and side tables offered places to relax. I'd been here so many times hanging out at the Outrigger pool sun tanning, but I'd never spent the night here.

I watched as Duke approached the front desk with a self-assured stride. An older local woman wearing a long colorful muumuu and a plumeria flower tucked behind one ear greeted him, but I was too far away to hear their conversation.

"Uh...Mr. Duke, you want a room, eh? Pretty lady you have," she grinned knowingly, looking directly at me.

"Yes, she is that. You know me too well, Lee," he grinned.

"I give you room you like, eh? Ocean view just for you, Mr. Duke."

"You're too good to me, Lee," he responded with a wink, handed her a twenty, and took the room key.

Turning, he headed toward me with a spark in his eyes, buoyancy in his step, and a glowing grin as big as the ocean. I couldn't help but return that grin with a playful laugh, as he took my hand and we rode the elevator up to the 10th floor.

◆◆◆

Across the dark ocean of Waikiki, the moonlight created silver strands of light on the waters. We stood on the lanai, side-by-side, swaying in the gentle breeze like a slow *hula*. The dark sky was filled with stars that painted a canvas of artwork against the vastness of the universe.

"Pretty isn't it?" he said.

"Yes, very pretty."

"Just like you." Duke turned and wrapped his arms around me in a hug that spoke a thousand words of intimacy yet to come. "My sweet, darling, Brandi," he said, as he took my hand leading me back into the hotel bedroom. Dim lights and a queen size bed filled the room. Before I knew it, Duke had slipped off my red halter dress leaving me with only my red lace bikini underwear on. "Good God, woman," he marveled as he stripped down. "You're so damn sexy," he uttered, with a low seductive voice, which left me gazing at him with admiration.

He was gorgeous with that dark skin and chest muscles that were ripped with definition. My body ached for his undivided attentions. He wrapped me in his arms and kissed me with an eagerness that left me more than ready. At the moment, I wanted nothing more than to give myself to this island *hula* lover all night long.

◆◆◆

Spending the night with Duke was blissful and exciting. He was an experienced lover, fun, playful, but he didn't have my heart like Skip did. There was such a big difference between making love with someone you are in love with and someone you are not in love with. I knew that Duke was too old for me, but I liked his charm, assertiveness, and worldly ways. I wondered where this would lead as he snuggled up next to me, face-to- face.

"Good morning, my sweet Brandi. What fun you were last night," he joked, with a heated look in his dark black eyes. Then, he rolled on top of me eager to play once again. I sighed sleepily, but was soon as willing to please as he was.

◆◆◆

The morning sun and a soft breeze drifted into the hotel bedroom through the open lanai door. Duke reached for the phone and ordered room service with fresh *Kona* coffee. Meanwhile, I showered and slipped on a fluffy white hotel bathrobe before stepping out onto the lanai.

Diamond Head off to my left and down the beach on my right I could see the Hilton Hawaiian Village. The warm tropical sun kissed my face with the aloha spirit. The aqua waters, the puffy white clouds, the endless blue sky, and the cooing of pigeons nearby made it feel like I was on a honeymoon. Delightful and dreamy.

Waikiki Beach was already showing signs of life with early beach walkers and people getting in a morning swim. I wished I had my Speedo with me; I could use a good open water swim before heading back home this morning. It might help wash away the tinge of guilt I was now feeling after sleeping with Duke.

My thoughts drifted to Skip, my past navy lover. The one I was crazy in love with. Had he slept with someone else yet? He'd been gone three months. God, would I ever get over him? Would I always be comparing him to every man I might be with? In the background, on the radio the song, "These Eyes" by the Guess Who, filled my senses with nostalgia. I inhaled deeply, thinking that it wasn't fair to Duke when my heart belonged to Skip, but then Duke wasn't looking for a long term relationship, nor was I.

. A knock on the door and room service was delivered. Taking a seat at the small circular lanai table for two, I waited as Duke carried our plates out, put them on the table, and then lifted the plastic lid covers that were keeping our breakfast warm.

"Ah...fried eggs, rice, and Spam. Perfect!" he beamed, while sitting down and pouring us both a cup of *Kona* coffee.

That first sip of rich black coffee made my taste buds come alive. I still couldn't get used to the idea that Spam seemed to be an island staple. The locals loved it and apparently so did Duke.

"I'm famished, Brandi," he grinned. "Thank you for spending the night with me, you were incredible!" he sighed, while taking a bite of his eggs. "I take it you had fun, too?"

I lifted my fork and took a bite of rice mixed with egg. "Umm... yes, Duke, you are...are very skilled," I teased back, thinking that I hadn't felt this physically satisfied in three months.

"Good, then we shall make a point of being together again soon for New Year's Eve," he stated, with confidence and took a sip of his coffee. "By the way, I have to fly over to Kauai this afternoon. I'll be back later tonight," he said.

"Kauai, why are you going there?" I asked, with raised eyebrows as the song, "The Beat Goes On" by Sunny & Cher, played on the clock radio. What an appropriate song, I thought. The beat does go on, no matter what. Time to live a little again.

"A business opportunity has come up. I have an interview with the Coco Palms Hotel."

"An interview? But you've only been at the Hilton for a month. Are you planning to leave?" I questioned.

"I always have my options open, Brandi. People in this business move around a lot. A better deal comes up and I grab it, but don't worry, I intend to keep seeing you," he said assuredly. "I don't intend to leave you hanging like your navy man did, unattended, that's for damn sure!" he vowed.

"Oh," I said, feeling a little stunned. *He didn't intend to leave me unattended?* What did that mean? I didn't want to be committed to him. I liked him, but I wasn't in love with him.

I swallowed hard. "I thought we were just going to have fun, no strings attached, Duke."

"Me too, Brandi. But a girl like you, well...I've changed my mind after sleeping with you. You need to be wined and dined and swept off your feet. And I'm just the man to do that," he insisted and leaned over to kiss me on the cheek. "Besides, if I get this food and beverage position on Kauai, I'd have my own beach house as an added perk. No rent. Wouldn't you love to come visit me every other week on Kauai? It would be like a honeymoon each time you are there. I'd wine and dine you the whole time. You need that kind of attention," he said, taking another bite of his Spam and eggs.

I looked over at him a little surprised and continued to eat my rice and eggs. "Well, Duke, I'm not sure about all of that. I don't know if I could afford the airfare a couple of times a month," I stated emphatically.

Turning, I glanced out at the ocean water, sparkling like beads of silver sequins. The surf was up and a half dozen surfers were out there catching the morning waves. The sun heated up the lanai, but I was left with a chill of concern. Duke might be leaving me? Did I want to have boyfriend miles away, where I had to fly to see him?

"If you get the Kauai position, I wouldn't see you that often," I said with an apprehensive smile.

"Well, I would fly you over on your days off, Brandi. You'd get to attend a lot of private cocktail parties with me. And I know you would love that. You're the type of woman that needs to be shown off. Rest assured that I would buy you some beautiful evening wear," he confirmed. "Let's just see what happens first though," Duke said, thinking that it would be the best of both worlds. Having Brandi come visit for romantic stays and leaving him free to pursue other women when she wasn't there. Brandi could be his main squeeze, but those one night stands he loved; they were always available to a man like him.

"Yeah, it would be fun to fly over, and you do spoil me," I said, finishing up my breakfast. Wow, he would pay my way to come visit him. Was that okay to let him do that? "Well, I'll get dressed and be on my way and see you later at work then," I said, rising from the table and heading inside. I wasn't sure I could say no to him right now. After all, he is my boss...I remembered. God, I'm sleeping with my boss! And he's at least ten years my senior or more. I still wasn't sure what his age really was.

"You are officially mine now, Brandi." he boasted, with a tone of arrogance and conceit. "You have to admit, it was a beautiful evening from the start of dinner to this morning, wasn't it?"

I paused for a moment and turned back to face him on the lanai. "Yes, it was. It was...a very romantic evening," I said, with a tender tone, thinking that it really was just that. The dinner, the dancing under the stars, having a hotel room, sleeping with him; it was a truly beautiful evening. I could get used to being spoiled like this, wined and dined like royalty. But...*officially mine now?* Did he think he could own me? Maybe it would be a blessing if he did move to Kauai and I just visited him now and then.

I had to admit that Duke was very classy, charming, and sexy in bed. I changed into my clothes, and then left the hotel room as the song, "A Beautiful Morning" by the Rascals, played and danced in my head. It was a beautiful morning; I couldn't deny that, and last night was the best night I'd had in three long months.

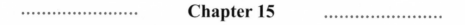

Chapter 15

Volcanic Alert

The walk home from the Outrigger Hotel was just what I needed after spending the night with Duke. Time by myself. Time to just reflect. Traffic rushed by me, but I hardly noticed the sounds of honking horns, cars, and tourists. Instead, I simply focused on the beauty of Hawaii. It never ceased to amaze me that it could be this warm so close to New Year's Eve. The ocean as my backyard and the continuous sunny blue skies, all the mixed cultures, and my new friends; it gave me an intense passion and love for the islands.

Heading down *Kalakaua* Avenue, I passed the International Market Place, which was already open to the tourists. It sported little shack-like shops selling all kinds of Hawaiian things from pick-a-pearl-in-an-oyster-shell to island aloha wear. My thoughts turned back to Duke and last night. He was so charming and experienced, but there was something about his morning comment about being *"officially mine"* which nagged at me. However, I couldn't deny the attraction I felt, even though my heart still ached for Skip.

Stop comparing, I told myself. Just enjoy Duke. Let him spoil you. So what if some things he'd told you don't seem to add up, like the Vietnam pilot thing. It's not like you are going to be with him forever, I conceded, especially if he moves to Kauai.

Turning left near the *Kapiolani* Zoo, I headed up a mile to the *Kapahulu* district, my neighborhood. A gentle morning breeze washed over me; however, it didn't erase my guilty feelings of sleeping with someone other than Skip. I forced myself to put that thought out of my mind as I approached my apartment building.

Once inside the apartment, I heard crying and my roommates' soft spoken concerned voices. My gut tightened. Something was not right. A strange feeling of remorse swept through me. It was only about 10 a.m. Donna should have been at work by now. What was she still doing home?

Cigarette smoke permeated the living room like a dark rain cloud. Sherry and Donna were sitting on the sofa next to Jenny, our new roommate. She sat in her bathrobe with a look of shock. Her face bruised and swollen. I stopped dead in my tracks. "What's going on? What happened to you, Jenny?" I questioned with trepidation.

Jenny put her head in her hands. She bent down sobbing uncontrollably as if she needed air or was going to faint. Her long, tangled, red hair splayed over her face.

"Brandi," Sherry said, "Jenny was beat up and raped last night."

"What!" I cried in disbelief. "Oh my God, Jenny!" I rushed to her side and placed my hand on her shoulder. "I'm so sorry." I turned and asked my roommates, "How'd this happen?"

Donna was in her work clothes, but obviously was taking the morning off. She crushed out her smoke. "She was walking home from Waikiki around midnight last night. Some guy along the Ala Wai Canal offered to walk with her since it was so late. She said he seemed nice. They talked along the way. When they got here, he forced her behind the gated pool area. The next thing Jenny knew he was hitting her in the face, knocked her to the ground and raped her."

"Oh, my God, that's horrible!" I shrieked, putting my hand over my mouth.

"Yeah, it is," said Sherry. "And she won't call the police."

Donna cringed. "She didn't even wake us! We just found all this out about an hour ago. She's blaming herself and just wants to fly home and never come back here."

"I can't say that I blame her for wanting to go home," Sherry added. "I'd probably do the same thing."

"God, she's only been here what...a couple of days?" I stammered. Poor girl, I didn't much like her, but this kind of violence should never happen to anyone.

Jenny looked up. "I...I need to call my parents. I'm going back home as soon as I can get a flight. I can't stay, I just can't stay here!" she cried helplessly.

Donna put her arm around her. "You do what you need to do, Jenny. We're here for you, but we understand why you want to go home. You really should report this to the police," she stated with concern.

"No!" Jenny screamed. "It was stupid of me to let a strange man walk me home. It's my fault!" she said, with deep sorrow in her voice. "I'm going to call home now, then pack, and get the hell off this island, hopefully by tomorrow." She stood up and slowly walked to the phone in the kitchen, as if her body had been run over by a semi truck. My heart was heavier, when I heard her crying on the phone to her mom.

"I can't believe she won't call the police," I whispered, looking at both Donna and Sherry.

Donna rose from the sofa. "I get it. The police will put the blame on her and make her feel like shit as if she led the creep on. She'd have to go through questioning and relive the whole despicable act again," Donna shook her head in disbelief. "I've got to get to work. You two stick close to her today and help her, okay?"

Sherry and I both nodded. "Of course," I said, "we'll do whatever she needs us to do."

"Okay," Donna said, while grabbing her purse and car keys. "I'll see you all later then."

I looked at Sherry with tears in my eyes and sadness in my heart for Jenny. It wasn't always paradise in Hawaii. A big city like Honolulu had a high rate of violent crimes, including gun shootings, murders, and unfortunately rapes. I was reminded once again of my hitchhiking incident. Boy had I been lucky, to escape that, and not end up like poor Jenny. It made me spitting mad that these kind of rape crimes often went unreported, because of fear and guilt, which resulted in letting the predator get away with it.

◆◆◆

The following morning I awoke around 6:30 a.m. to the sounds of muffled voices and feet shuffling. Sherry had risen and was in the shower. I heard Donna saying goodbye to Jenny when she headed off to work.

Rising, I wondered if Jenny would change her mind and stay here in Hawaii. I still couldn't believe that she had been beaten up and raped, and that she refused to report it to the police.

Barefoot, I padded down the hallway into the living room. The lanai door was open and a warm soft morning breeze drifted across the room, but it did little to comfort my thoughts. The radio was on and the song, "I Say a Little Prayer" by Aretha Franklin filled the room. I stopped and listened to the words of the song. Silently, I said a little prayer for Jenny.

◆◆◆

In the kitchen, drinking a cup of coffee, stood Jenny with a pained expression on her bruised face. I reached over and put my hand on her shoulder. "Can I do anything for you?" I asked with sympathy.

She took a swallow of her coffee. "No, I'm packed and just waiting for the taxi to arrive. I have a 9 a.m. flight this morning. My parents want me to come home," she said with conviction.

"Oh God, Jenny, I hope you can find a way to move past this. Don't let this destroy you. I don't know you that well, but I think you are a strong woman and you can survive this. Will you write us?"

She looked out the kitchen window. A horn honked. "No, I won't. I want to forget that I was ever here. My taxi just pulled up. Goodbye," she said, without a second look and then disappeared through the door. Once again, I hoped that by returning home Jenny would find God's grace and courage to move past the anger, fear, and guilt that overwhelmed her.

Chapter 16

Laie **Beach**

It had been only a day since our roommate, Jenny, had left the island. I hoped being home with her parents would help ease her pain from the rape. I wondered how she would fare in the months to come, but life went on. I couldn't dwell on it. Yesterday, I had told Duke all about it and once again he comforted me with a hug and kind words. Today, he was taking me body surfing at *Laie* Beach on the west side of Oahu.

Duke's big red Ford Galaxie convertible pulled into the building parking lot at 9 a.m. We were leaving early because we both had to work a late shift this evening. If we timed it right, we could be back by 4 p.m., plenty of time for me to shower and get ready for work.

Duke honked his horn and waved as I looked out the kitchen window. Scurrying, I gathered my beach bag, hurried out the door, and ran down the stairs.

"Hey, sweetheart," he called, as I opened the passenger's door and slid into the plush red leather bench seat. I tossed my beach bag into the back, crossed my bare legs, adjusted my beach cover-up, and tightened my ponytail.

"Hey Duke, I'm looking forward to body surfing and you teaching me," I chatted, thinking that he'd be surprised when he learned that I already knew how to do it, but I'd let him think he was teaching a beginner just for the fun of it.

He laughed. "That's not all I'm going to teach you," he teased and leaned over planting a quick kiss on my lips. "I've missed you. Have you missed me?"

"Only just a little, besides, I just saw you yesterday at work," I teased back.

"You know what I mean," he challenged, with a fiery look in his dark eyes.

I leaned back and laughed. "Oh that...yes, I believe I have missed you," I purred. He was so striking in his aviator sunglasses and his thick black hair, which was windblown from the top being down. Wearing a pair of jade colored beach trunks and a white tank shirt, I couldn't help but think how easily he could go from a classy sophisticated businessman to a sexy beach boy. Impressive.

A drive with the top down, this was going to be another fun day. I relaxed while the gentle tropical breeze blew my ponytail around and the sunshine kissed my skin with its warmth. The radio blasted out with "People Got to Be Free" by the Rascals. I sang along feeling happy to have part of the day off and spend it with Duke again. He was fun to do beach things with among other more romantic things, too, I mused.

"I thought we'd head over the *Pali* and connect with Highway 83, which will take us to *Laie* Beach. It's the best body surfing spot that isn't real dangerous with a sandy bottom and easy surfing waves."

"Sounds good to me. Drive on, Mr. Haku," I laughed. "You're the boss," I grinned, thinking that indeed he was the boss.

"Yes, I am the boss and don't forget it," he teased, while we drove along. I felt free and young at heart.

◆◆◆

The small village of *Laie* is located north of the famous Polynesian Cultural Center and south of *Kahuku* along the *Kamehameha* Highway on the windward side of Oahu. I hadn't been to the Polynesian Cultural Center even though I had lived here for a year now, nor had I spent any time in *Laie*.

"If you look to your right, Brandi, you will see the *Laie* Hawaiian Temple," Duke pointed out. "It's the fifth oldest Latter-day-Saints temple worldwide."

"Latter-day-Saints? I didn't know that there was a Mormon temple here? Is there a big Mormon population in *Laie*?" I questioned, as I glanced at the weathered white temple that was surrounded by tall sprawling palm trees, a water fountain, and a flagpole displaying the United States flag.

"Back around 1865," Duke said, "a lot of land was purchased by the president of the Hawaiian Mission of the Church of Latter-day-Saints. Members of the church living on Oahu were encouraged to move to *Laie*. Later, sugarcane plantations developed here. It provided economic growth and income for both the church and natives. Today, *Laie* is the home of Brigham Young University of Hawaii. So, yes, Brandi, there is a big Mormon population here," he confirmed.

"Oh wow, I never knew all of that, Duke. Thanks for the history lesson," I said, as he slowed down and turned onto a dirt road toward *Laie* Beach. He certainly knew his Hawaiian history.

Duke and I set our ice cooler in the shade, laid our beach mats in the sand, and stretched out side-by-side to soak up some rays before doing some body surfing.

"I love that black bikini, Brandi," he taunted, while rubbing Coppertone sun lotion on my back. "And I love your soft skin, too. If there weren't other people around, I'd take you right here on the beach," he joked. "God knows, I've missed you and your sexy body! It's been four days since I've had you in my bed."

I turned around grinning. "I'll admit I've missed you, too," I confirmed with a quick kiss, thinking that I wouldn't mind one bit if we did it right here on the beach.

"So, you've missed me. Good to know," he beamed. "Come on," he took my hand helping me to my feet.

He pulled me into his pelvis. He planted a big seductive kiss on my lips, cupped my *okole,* and groaned loudly. "We better give you some body surfing lessons before I can't walk and embarrass myself," he laughed.

Taking my hand in his and carrying our gear, we headed to the water's edge. Whitewash from breaking waves rolled into the shallow waters making the beach appear covered in foam. The waves were bigger than I thought they would be, probably about three to four feet high. We entered to our waist, put on our fins and hand paddles, and swam out past the break line.

Once out deep enough, we treaded water. "Okay, Brandi," Duke yelled. "When I say go, you kick hard with your fins and swim freestyle. Try to catch the wave right at the top as it begins to break and still has momentum. Once you are on it, you won't have to kick as hard, lift your head and steer through the breaking wave with your hand paddle. If you time it right, you'll get a great ride. If you want out of a wave, just tuck and turn backwards, but watch out for waves coming up behind you."

"Okay," I yelled, bobbing in the water next to him. This was going to be fun. I didn't tell Duke that I'd been body surfing a lot this past year and was pretty good at it. He was having so much fun thinking that he was teaching a novice. I'd tell him later or he'd realize it once he watched me ride.

Floating next to each other, we watched half a dozen swells build about fifty yards out from us. "They come in cycles, Brandi. Get ready, this next set building looks good," Duke yelled. "Take this one coming."

"Okay, I'm ready." We both started to swim fast as the wave mounted. I felt its force explode as I caught the crest of it. I lifted my head, riding with it, and steering with my hand paddle. Mounds of white water and foam broke out all around me. From the corner of my eye, I saw Duke pull out. He missed it! Laughing to myself, I totally enjoyed the ride all the way in. I stood up in the shallows.

White foam was all around my knees. I waded back out and dove under an incoming wave.

As I was swimming out to Duke, he gave me the *shaka* (way to go) sign. I gave it right back to him. "That was a cool ride!" Cool... just like Duke, I thought. We were bobbing together. Face-to-face. He was smiling at me with a surprised look in his eyes. He pulled me into a hug. His dark Hawaiian skin glistened in the sunshine. He wrapped his arms around my waist. I encircled his waist with my legs.

"You've body surfed before, haven't you?" he grinned with amusement. He pulled me tighter into him.

"A little yeah," I teased. "Actually, many times, but I just couldn't spoil your fun in teaching me." I licked my lips slowly, letting my tongue entice him. There were not many people out here in the surf near us; most were sunbathing on the beach.

"Well, I bet you've never done this before!" Suddenly, he slipped my black bikini bottom down to my knees. Before I knew it, he slipped his surfer shorts down to his knees and plunged himself into me with a force as strong as the wave I'd just ridden. My breath caught in my throat. My eyes widened in surprise. "No...uh...I...I've never done this before in the surf, Duke!"

"Good, you little tease," he taunted, as he pumped me hard and we bobbed up and down clinging to each other. Blinded by the sunlight and breathless, we were both captured in the moment of open water fucking fun. He was full of surprises, and I liked surprises...and his cockiness.

◆◆◆

We spent the next hour body surfing until exhaustion forced us back to the beach. "You are darn good at this body surfing, Brandi," he laughed. "So when I teach you tennis are you going to fake it? Let me think you don't know how to play, tease me?"

"Nah, I really don't know how to play tennis, Duke. Cross my heart," I said, as we rinsed off all the sand on our bodies under the outside showers, before heading back to our beach mats.

Reaching for my Coppertone sun lotion, I reapplied it to my entire body. I was going to comb my hair, but Duke took the comb. "Let me," he stated. Combing softly, he untangled my hair and ran his hands through it. "Your golden hair is such a turn-on. You don't see that color much here in the islands. Don't ever cut it. I love it long and I love running my hands through it, especially when it's dry and you're in my bed."

"Hmm...your bed. Are we going back to your apartment tonight? I've not seen it," I asked, with a raised eyebrow.

"No, I don't live there anymore. Those two girl roommates are too bitchy for me. I moved out yesterday," he said with indignation.

"You moved out?"

"Yeah, the girls claimed I didn't pay my rent for the last two months. I gave them cash last week, but they wanted me to leave anyway. They said they had another girl, who wanted to live there. I don't stay where I'm not wanted," he said crossly.

"But you were late with your rent money?"

"I paid what I owed them," he stated with anger. "They're not worth my time."

"So where are you living then?" I asked with puzzlement, thinking that I'd be pissed also if one of my roommates was late with their rent. I wondered if this was a bad habit of his or did he have a problem managing his money? I took the comb from him and then put my hair into a ponytail waiting for his reply.

"Right now, I have a room at the Hilton. Hotel perks, you know, but I won't be there for long. I got hired as the food and beverage director at the Kauai Coco Palms Resort. I start at the end of January," he gloated.

I sat up straighter. "The end of January?"

"Yes, and I get a rent free beach house, just a block away. You can come and visit as often as you like," he exclaimed, thinking that he wanted her in his bed as much as possible. Truth be told, he couldn't seem to get enough of her. She was definitely under his skin. However, he didn't want her to live with him. Having her full time on Kauai would cramp his player style. Having her visit was the best option, even though he would miss her as his regular bed partner, but he'd cross that bridge when he came to it, he decided.

He'd fly her over to Kauai at least twice a month and wine and dine her. Dance under the stars at the Coco Palms. Sweep her off her feet again, like their first dinner date at the Royal Hawaiian Hotel and their first night together at the Outrigger Hotel. He knew she was bowled over with the richness of those two evenings. A few more evenings like that on Kauai and she'd be begging to come visit as often as she could.

Smiling, he reached into the cooler taking out some sandwiches and drinks. He handed Brandi a chicken salad sandwich and turned up the transistor radio. Lyrics from the song, "I'm a Believer" by the Monkees, pumped its tune around in his head. He was a believer. Anything was possible when you had the skills, charm, and charisma to be persuasive.

◆◆◆

I took the offered sandwich thinking that I wouldn't be able to afford to fly to Kauai more than once a month. Duke was charming and fun, but I was beginning to feel that he was a master at manipulation and possibly someone who made up stories to gain your unquestioning adulation. Still...I couldn't deny how attracted I was to him. He was a rare kind of man. A man that commanded a presence when he entered a room. Cultured and polished in every area...including the bedroom. He was confident in wooing women off their feet. Could he be trusted? Did he have a posse of women wherever he went? I had the distinct feeling that he was sneaky about that. However, I wasn't looking for a long term relationship or a commitment from him.

"Well, Duke, I'll come visit you on Kauai, but I'm not sure how often that might be."

"Brandi, I still want to be with you and have you in my bed," he said. "I'll pay your airfare just to have you there. Plan on at least twice a month, okay?"

"Okay, I can do that," I appeased him, but would he pay my airfare? "Good sandwich," I said, changing the subject and chewing eagerly. "Oh, by the way, my parents are coming to visit later this week," I said, taking a swallow of my Pepsi.

"Really," he replied. "I hope I get to meet them. I'll take all of you to dinner at the Hilton and use my expense account," he bragged.

"But you're leaving the Hilton?" I questioned with concern.

"No one knows that yet. Don't say a thing."

"That's a little dishonest, don't you think, Duke?"

"Might as well take advantage of my perks while I can, Brandi," he grinned,

taking a bite of his sandwich.

I shrugged, thinking that he would do what he wanted to do, no matter what. "Well, if you're sure? I know my parents would love that. However, there might be another problem though. My dad, I'm not sure how he will react knowing that I am seeing you. I mean... you're not Caucasian and he can be bigoted and pig-headed about his daughter seeing someone of another race."

"You really think he'd be bothered by that? I mean, it is Hawaii after all."

I nodded my head. "Yeah, I do. I know you're not Japanese, but my dad fought in World War II and he may take one look at you and think...*Jap*. I'm sorry, but that's just how he is," I explained. "I'll call my mom and have her prepare him for the shock of me dating a Polynesian man," I assured him.

"You do that, and tell her what a great guy I am, too," he laughed. "Let's finish our lunch, pack it up, and head back, okay? I've got to check into a few things at the Hilton before working tonight."

"Sure," I agreed, reaching for my beach cover-up and gathering up our things.

"Why don't you plan on staying with me tomorrow after you finish your night shift? We can watch some of the New Year's Eve fireworks from my hotel lanai. Besides, I need you in my bed again, Brandi," he grinned, with a lusty gleam in his eyes.

"You mean stay at the Hilton with you? As an employee, isn't that against hotel rules, Duke?" I asked, thinking that I could lose my job if management found out.

"It is, but we'll keep it secret. I'll give you my room key, just be discreet. Makes it more taboo and exciting, don't you think?" He leaned over and planted a hot provocative kiss on my lips. My body stirred with sexual desire. Tomorrow night with Duke at the Hilton on New Year's Eve. How was I supposed to refuse that?

Loading up our gear, the early afternoon sunshine became shadowed by clouds. The wind picked up blowing dry sand in swirls. The surf had white caps out beyond the breakers, stirring up the waters like a warning of some kind of turbulence yet to come.

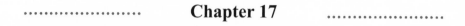

Chapter 17

Call Home

The next day at my apartment, I was fudging back and forth about calling my mom. I knew I had to give her a heads up about Duke before they arrived here. What would my dad think? Would he cause a scene or lecture me about dating a Polynesian man? Mom was the best smoother-over person I knew. Handling my dad after thirty some years of marriage was an art she had perfected.

With trepidation, I picked up the phone and dialed home. I had to make this quick since long distance phone calls were costly by the minute. I timed it so it was close to dinner time in Seattle, three o'clock Hawaiian time, five o'clock their time. Taking a deep breath, I heard the first ring, second ring, and then the third ring.

"Hello."

"Hi Mom, it's me, Brandi."

"Oh, Brandi, so good to hear your voice, honey. Is everything all right?" she asked with concern.

"Yeah, Mom, everything is good." I could just picture her starting dinner with her apron on, wearing a house dress. Her short, black and silver streaked hair neatly in place. Makeup on, red lipstick, and a smile in her twinkling green eyes. She was always so put together. A fetching woman with pin-up girl Betty Grable legs. However, unlike the famous Betty Grable who was only 5'4", my mom was 5'8" with long, shapely dancer's legs and a very sexy, curvaceous body to match. Needless to say, Mom had a pin-up photo in her glamorous rumba costume that ran a close second to Betty Grable's famous pin-up photo of the 1940s. Fortunately, my mom didn't smoke like

Betty had, up to four packs a day, who died at age fifty-six from lung cancer.

As a teenager, Mom danced at the famed Paramount Theater in downtown Seattle as one of the Barkley girls. These dancers were taught by the best Russian dance teachers in the area. When she was around my age, Mom moved to San Diego and lived there for several years. Working as a telephone operator for Ma Bell during the day. In the evenings, she danced at USO military bases in front of hundreds of marines shipping out to the war in the Pacific. I felt sure there were stories that I had never heard before and looked forward to hearing them when she visited.

Mom always looked fabulous in dresses and heels. I got my height from her. She was a picture of graceful poise, kindness, and understanding that I always admired. I remember her telling me to be proud of my height. *Stand up straight, wear heels, hats, and show off your tall beauty.* Now at age twenty-one, I had found the beauty in being tall and didn't feel embarrassed by it anymore. I took a deep breath, before continuing my conversation.

"Mom, I just needed to give you a heads up before you arrive here this week," I said, with a deep exhale. "I'm seeing a local man and he's Polynesian. I'm afraid Dad might not be happy about that?" I ran my hand through my long hair, pushing it back behind my ears. "Duke, that's his name, he wants to take all of us to dinner at the Hilton Hawaiian Hotel, where he's food and beverage director. I wanted to make sure that Dad would be okay with me seeing someone that isn't Caucasian."

"Oh," Mom said. "Well, you know how your father is, dear. Set in his ways and beliefs. He's very opposed to interracial couples, but, you say he's Polynesian...not Japanese?"

"Yeah, he's Polynesian and a very handsome man. He has beautiful dark cocoa skin, but he's not Japanese."

"Well, that's good because your father would disown you if he was a...*Jap.* I can't change that about him. Since the war that's what he calls them and probably always will." She paused briefly. "Is...is this serious with this man, sweetheart?"

"No Mom, I mean...he's fun and charming, but not someone I would ever consider marrying. You can tell Dad that, too, maybe it will ease the shock of it."

"You are on the pill, I hope, or taking precautions aren't you?"

"Yes, Mom, I'm on the pill. I have been for this past year."

"Oh good, I just had to ask. I don't want you getting pregnant. That would kill your father. You know, I am always here for you no matter what."

"I know that, Mom. I love that about you."

"Well, I've heard and seen it all over the years. Nothing can shock me. There are some stories about me, when I was your age, that you don't know about. You're old enough to understand now. Maybe we can have a beach day there when your dad goes deep sea fishing?"

"I'd love that, Mom! Just you and me, girl time," I exclaimed, while thinking that we had always been close. Mom always supported my competitive swimming career, always the one driving me daily to 6 a.m. and 8 p.m. workouts, always going to meets, encouraging me, but never pushy. She understood my devotion to my swimming career, just as she was devoted to her dancing career.

"Okay, I'll make sure and tell your dad that he is not Japanese. I'll have to work my magic on him though. Sweeten the pot. The old coot can be so bigoted and opinionated."

"Don't I know it. That's why I called ahead. I don't want any scenes when he meets Duke."

"Well, don't worry dear. I'm sure it will be okay. We're so excited to visit Hawaii and see you. We miss you dearly."

"I miss you, too," I said. It had been just over a year since I'd moved here and hadn't seen my parents since. "I'll be working most evenings, but we'll have time during the days to catch up. I'll see you soon then."

"Yes, see you soon, sweetie."

"Okay, bye Mom."

"Bye."

I hung up the phone relieved that Mom was going to smooth this possible problem into a non-issue. Still...I knew my dad would not approve of my dating a Polynesian man. I just hoped he would see how accepted it was here in the islands. But...a man ten years or more my senior and my boss. I hadn't mentioned that part. It would be another hurdle to cross when the time was right. I was hoping that Duke would charm my parents with his Hawaiian hospitality and aloha spirit like he had done with me.

.... **Chapter 18** ....

Happy New Year 1971

I spent the next night, New Year's Eve, with Duke at the Hilton Hawaiian after I finished my shift in the *Makaha* dining room. It felt weird sneaking up the back stairs to his hotel room, but it did add a feeling of suspense and intrigue to our night together. Once again, he charmed me into accepting his invitation by telling me he had ordered a late night plate of *pupus* and a bottle of Pinot Noir, one of my favorite red wines.

Duke had placed a flower lei of white plumeria on the bed. My favorite Hawaiian flower. He remembered that and I was touched. I picked up the lei, admiring its white floral petals with their soft yellow centers. Taking a deep breath, I savored its subtle island sweetness. A note was also on the bed with a pair of lacy white bikini panties.

"Darling Brandi, make yourself comfortable, open the wine, take a bubble bath, or just relax; I'll be up to join you soon for the tail end of the fireworks...and other romantic things! Yours, Duke."

"P.S. I would request that you wear the lei with nothing else on, except the pair of panties."

Whoa, he sure knows how to set the mood and ask for what he wants! Bold and compelling, I thought, with anticipation as I made my way to run a bubble bath and open the bottle of wine.

Duke entered the hotel room. I stood there wearing nothing, except the white flower lei, a pair of white, lacy bikini panties, and holding a glass of wine in my hand.

He stopped in his tracks. "Beautiful, just beautiful. Come here," he demanded, with a heated look in his dark eyes.

He opened his arms wide. I melted into him as he wrapped me in a big *hula* hug. My lips found his. My body hungry for his kisses and touch. He broke the kiss, took my glass of wine, placed it on the nightstand, and maneuvered me to the bed. Before I knew it we were making our own red hot fireworks.

♦♦♦

Later from our hotel balcony, we watched the end of the fireworks display, which the Hilton put on over the lagoon. The brilliant fireworks burst into vibrant circles and shapes that lit up the night sky and left me in awe.

Locals went crazy here on New Year's Eve. Firecrackers would roar throughout the night around the city until you couldn't bear it anymore. Tomorrow, the streets would be littered with a coat of reddish fireworks wrappers, as if it had snowed red overnight. It was a sight to see and a mess for the city to clean up.

♦♦♦

Long into the night, those firecrackers kept exploding while keeping me awake. I lay there in bed with Duke, but dreaming of my far away navy man, Skip. What was he doing this New Year's Eve of 1971 back in New London, Connecticut? Was he at a party? Was Skip celebrating with someone else...doing what I was doing? God, what I would give to be with him right now! I missed his way of loving me.

Inhaling deeply, I tossed and turned, trying to find a more comfortable position and thinking that it was so different being with Duke. It was good, but Duke didn't have my heart. I was beginning to realize the big difference between sex and making love to someone with your whole heart and soul. I ached for that kind of love making that I had with Skip. Would I ever have that again? Would I go through my life without that kind of connection and heartfelt love? It made me sad to dwell on it.

Closing my tired eyes, I started thinking about my mom and dad coming to visit. I needed to talk privately with my mom. Get some advice. I felt lost without Skip. I knew she had gotten her heart broken once, too, but I didn't know the whole story. Maybe she could offer some insight. It would be good to listen to her wisdom.

♦♦♦

My parents had known each other growing up as kids. However, they never dated until after World War II, when my dad came back from overseas and my mom moved home to Seattle from San Diego. Dad had been a B-17 pilot stationed in England and flew thirty plus bombing missions over Germany. Life expectancy for a B-17 plane was six weeks; most didn't make it back home. I don't know how my dad survived, but I was grateful that he did. A handsome, gentle, charismatic man. He had a deep love for the outdoors and a heart of gold is how I would describe him. However, he was also bigoted about certain things.

Lying there listening to more firecrackers going off outside, I couldn't help but think how very different my parents were. Mom, a professional dancer and Dad, an avid fisherman and hunter...to the point of obsession. How in God's name did they end up married to each other? Opposites must attract, I thought, thinking that in two more days I could wrap my arms around them both with a big aloha welcome. Finally, I drifted off to sleep and the firecrackers stopped around 3 a.m.

Chapter 19

Aloha Mama San & Papa San

My parents arrived at Honolulu International Airport looking like typical tourists. Both as lily white as the inside of a coconut. My *papa san* (dad) sporting a big grin, and wearing an aloha shirt and slacks. M*ama san* (mom) trailed behind, dressed in a light blue summer shift, a sweater, sandals, and sunglasses. I waved excitedly as they neared me.

"Aloha!" I cried, and then draped purple and white orchid leis around each of their necks.

"Oh honey, this is so sweet of you!" Mom said, as she hugged me tightly. "It's so good to see you; I've missed you so much."

"I've missed you, too!" I stated with excitement, hugging my dad as well.

"Hey *Sis*," he said, with joy in his voice. My dad always called me *Sis* because I was the middle child of three and the little sister in the family. "You look so tan," he exclaimed, "and your hair; it's so gold from the sun."

I grinned. "Yeah, living in the sun all the time and lying on the beach tends to do that, Dad." I was wearing a short little sundress that showed off my shoulders, arms, and legs.

"Well, you're too tan, honey. You're going to ruin your skin," Mom said with concern. I laughed, thinking that some things never changed; she was always worried about me.

"It looks good on her," Dad said, with a smile as we walked toward the baggage claim area. "I can't wait to go deep sea fishing," he stated, while putting his arm around my shoulder. "Never been fishing for marlin or tuna; bet that will be a story to tell to all my fishing friends," he beamed.

"And I'm sure whatever you catch, Dad, you will expand and exaggerate on the whole story in great detail," I teased. "You being the master fisherman and storyteller that you are," I said, with a nudge in the ribs and he grinned knowingly.

"By the way, I'm working tonight until eleven, so you two are on your own this evening. Once you check into the *Moana* Hotel you can have a mai tai out in the Banyan Court Bar. They have the best mai tais on Waikiki. It will be happy hour about the time you get there and probably some Hawaiian music, too. You're going to love staying there. It's so *groovy* and right on the beach!" I stated with enthusiasm. "And it's such an old historic hotel. It was the first hotel built on Waikiki back in 1901. It's like my very favorite place to have a drink and gaze out at the sparkling ocean."

"That will be lovely, honey. Happy hour right on the beach. George, won't that be nice? We can watch the sunset. How romantic, don't you think, dear?"

"Yes, sweetheart," he patted her bum, with a gleam in his dark brown eyes.

Mom blushed. "Well, we're going to enjoy the beach and the pool tomorrow, rest up for our Pearl Harbor tour the next day. The following day your dad is going fishing. You know your dad...he has to go fishing or he'll be biting at the bit," she cried.

"Of course he does," I smiled, thinking that he never went anywhere unless he could fish or hunt. "That's fine, Mom. You and I can hang out that day until I have to go to work around four," I said with a grin. "And then Duke wants to take us all to dinner later this week, too."

"Perfect, honey. Catch up time with my beautiful daughter, dinner out, and meeting Duke," she beamed. "Won't that be nice, George? We get to meet her local boyfriend, Duke."

My dad frowned. "Sure, whatever you say, Virginia," he responded, with a lack of interest as we picked up their luggage and hailed a taxi into Waikiki.

♦♦♦

My dad's reaction to meeting Duke was swimming through my head. He obviously wasn't happy about me dating a Polynesian man. Would dinner out with Duke change his mind? I certainly hoped so. I just prayed that he would keep his opinionated thoughts to himself. However, knowing my dad, he would probably slip a derogatory comment in somewhere during the course of our dinner. I didn't think it was possible for him not to voice his disapproval of mixed couples dating or worse those that got married.

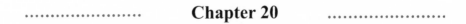

Chapter 20

Beach Day

Two days later, I stood at the entrance of the Waikiki *Moana* Hotel. I was meeting my mom here for our girls' beach day. This grand old hotel built back in 1901 housed beautiful European style architecture, popular at the turn of the century. It always gave me a feeling of stepping back in time. The entire outside of the hotel was painted white with half a dozen Ionic two story columns, which graced the grand front porch area with palm trees lining the circular driveway. On the expansive porch lanai, there were at least ten comfortable wooden rocking chairs where you could just sit, have a drink or watch tourists strolling up and down *Kalakaua* Avenue.

Moving up the entrance stairs, I entered the lobby with its intricate woodwork and detailing throughout the inside structure; it always left me in awe. Glancing around, I noted the wide hallways that were once used to accommodate steamer trucks. Extra high ceilings and cross ventilation windows were used to cool the rooms, long before air conditioning and restorations took place. Still...it harbored a stately lobby with wood floors, large area rugs with breadfruit patterns, Hawaiian pictures, and canoe paddles on the walls. A giant display of colorful tropical flowers with bird-of-paradise, bamboo orchids, plumeria, yellow ginger, and many others were mounted on a large mirrored table, which gave the lobby an air of island elegance.

Outside, there were wide lanais built for oceanside dining in addition to a swimming pool and lounge chairs. In the middle of the courtyard was a beach bar and an entertainment area, accompanied by an enormous banyan tree that was about 75 feet high and 150 feet across, which spanned the area providing much needed shade and a feeling of tranquility.

Standing there in the open-air lobby, the sparkling ocean beckoned beyond; the beach was dotted with multi-colored sun umbrellas, lounge chairs, and people sunbathing. All of it a typical beach setting of splendor, which touched my soul. Did I really live here?

I pushed back a strand of my long golden brown hair, changed arms with my beach bag, and took in a long deep breath. A beach day with Mom while Dad was out deep sea fishing was just what I needed. I was excited to spend time with her. We were going to spring for a beach umbrella and lounge chairs, too.

It was only around 11 a.m., but already the smell of burgers from the beach bar grill wafted in the air. My stomach growled. Today, I was going to treat my mom to a Hawaiian teriyaki hamburger with a slice of pineapple on top. My favorite. But first, some beach time together. We had a year of catch-up stories to share, I thought, as I waved at her coming down the lobby hallway.

She was wearing a colorful blue flowered print muumuu, flip flops, and a straw sun hat. Even in a muumuu, she looked fantastic with her long beautiful dancer legs and curvy Marilyn Monroe body. At fifty-one, she could still turn heads with her dancer's grace, poise, and fluidity in her walk. I couldn't help but hope that when I was her age, I'd look just as good. She made me feel proud. Not many moms looked as attractive as she did and kept their youthful sexy figures.

"Hey Mom, you sure look the part," I laughed.

"I do, don't I?" she snickered, giving a quick twirl and then hugged me.

"Come on, follow me," I said, with a wave of my arm. "We'll get our sun umbrella and beach chairs. Did you and Dad have a good time on the Pearl Harbor tour yesterday?"

"Oh yes, it was fascinating, sobering, and...chilling," she shook her head, as we continued through the lobby. "So many men lost that day, December 7, 1941; it's still embedded in my memory. I will never forget it! I was only twenty-one years old when the Japanese attacked Pearl Harbor; it felt like our safe world ended. I remember feeling so scared. War...it changed our lives forever!" she recollected, as we walked through the lobby.

"Back then, feelings of disbelief, anger, revenge, and honor ran rampant," Mom said with sadness. "Seeing the USS Arizona memorial brought it all back like it was yesterday. I felt sick to my stomach, but also pride and gratefulness for all the young men that enlisted and fought for our country's freedom," she stated quietly, while wiping a tear from her cheek.

"Just like Dad did, right?"

"Yes, he dropped out of college and enlisted like so many thousands of young brave men. I hope you never have to experience that feeling of your country under attack. It just scares the living hell out of you!" she stated, with conviction as we stepped down the stairs leading to the outside courtyard.

"I can't even imagine, Mom," I said, looking out at the peaceful sparkling aqua waters. "And those Japanese carrier-based fighter planes zooming across the sky, zeroing in with their bombs, guns, and torpedoes on an unsuspecting naval facility," I said, shaking my head. I'd seen many documentaries on it growing up. The chaos of exploding bombs, the fires on board ships in the harbor, men running to battle stations trying desperately to defend against the attacking Japanese.

"What really caused Japan to attack us, Mom?" I asked.

She stopped and we stood still. "Well, a lot of things, but mostly in the 1930s our American foreign policy in the Pacific hinged on support for China. It was all political and Japan had been at war with China since 1937. By 1941 Japan occupied all of Indochina. They entered into an alliance with the *Axis powers,* Germany and Italy," she emphasized.

"At that time, the U.S. severed all commercial, economic, and financial relations with them. Japan believed that once the U.S. Pacific Fleet was neutralized, then all of Southeast Asia would be open for their conquest. When the Germans invaded the Soviet Union, it was Japan's chance to occupy more of the Far East, without a threat of attack upon their rear forces by the Russians. It was then, that our negotiations with Japan fizzled out. As a result, Japan had overwhelming hostility toward the U.S., which resulted in the attack on Pearl Harbor," she pursed her lips in disgust.

"And did you know that only six U.S. planes were able to get into the air during the first attack? Then the second attack hit. In less than two hours, 180 aircraft and a dozen ships were destroyed. It was horrific and a devastating loss. But it woke up our country, the *sleeping giant*, and our declaration of war against Japan."

"God Mom, it seems that all wars throughout history were about greed or gaining control of lands or religious beliefs. What a waste of human lives! And this Vietnam mess is all political, too! And it's not even a declared war!" I cried.

"I know, it's such a mess," she agreed, as we started walking again.

"The Pearl Harbor attack killed 1,177 sailors and marines that day," she stated. "Yesterday, I cried reliving it all during the tour as did many other tourists. Even your dad had tears in his eyes."

"I'm not surprised, Mom." We walked in silence for a moment, both of us reflecting on the lives lost until Mom spoke again.

"At the end of the Pearl Harbor tour, we both were emotionally drained and overheated. Coming back to the hotel and dipping into the ocean was a welcomed relief and so were the mai tais," she grinned, while taking a deep breath.

"I can see why you love living here," she glanced around. "It's so beautiful. Gosh, I've missed you, honey!" she took my hand and squeezed it.

"Yeah, I do get homesick sometimes, Mom, but island life has grown on me. I just love it all! The blue skies, the sunshine, and the ocean. I don't think I could ever move back to the mainland," I emphasized. "By the way, I'd like to hear more about when you lived in San Diego. Maybe you can tell me some stories that I haven't heard?"

Mom put her arm around my shoulder. "Hmm...well, I think you're old enough to hear the whole story of my San Diego time. Just don't judge me though, dear. I was young like you and crazy in love with a very handsome marine. Let's swim first, and then I'll tell you the whole story, but...it might take all day," she laughed, as we approached the rental shack to get our beach umbrella and chairs.

God, I loved my mom. She was so easy to talk to. We were so much alike. All those years of driving me to 6 a.m. and 8 p.m. workouts and swim meets. I don't know how she did it! She understood my passion and commitment because she had been a serious professional dancer.

The little that I knew about her San Diego time was that she had gotten her heart broken back then, just like I had with my navy man Skip, here in Hawaii. I didn't know all the fine details and I wondered what had driven her to leave Seattle and move to San Diego, when she was only twenty-one years old. Was she like me just seeking new adventures or was there more to the story? I couldn't wait to stretch out on our lounge chairs, hear more of her San Diego stories, and maybe get some pieces of wisdom that I could draw on.

We settled into our beach spot, adjusted the sun umbrella for more shade, spread out our towels on the lounge chairs, slipped off our cover-ups, and headed into the inviting cool blue ocean. Bobbing around like floating corks, we simply enjoyed the feel of the current and the gentle waves while chatting back and forth. We were like best girlfriends that hadn't seen each other for years.

Once back under our beach umbrella, we stretched out on the lounge chairs, put on our sunglasses, and lathered up our bodies with sunscreen. I had on my little black bikini and Mom had on her jade green one-piece suit that matched her eyes. She also brought along a little ice cooler. We pulled out two cans of Coke and we both said "ah" at the same time after the first swallow and laughed together.

"So, tell me more about San Diego, Mom. I want to hear it all. Why did you move there in the first place?"

Lying down on the lounge chair, Mom crossed her ankles, ran a hand through her short silver streaked hair, and took a deep breath. "When I was just twenty-one years old, I met a very handsome marine officer at a military nightclub in Seattle. He was older than I was and had been married once. He swept me off my feet when we first danced together! Oh God, could he dance! And you know how I love a man that can dance! I fell in love with him during that first slow number, "Only Forever" by Bing Crosby. What a song that was!" she said dreamily.

"I'd never been in love before," she sighed. "It was like magic! I wanted to be with him forever. A month or so later, he was reassigned to San Diego. He begged me to go with him. So...I followed my heart. We told my family that we had gone to the Seattle Courthouse and gotten married, but of course, we really didn't," she gazed out at the ocean lost in memories.

"Oh, Mom! I never knew that. You little devil, you. Here I was thinking that I was not living up to your standards," I teased. "I've been with a few men, but I've never lived with one or pretended to be married. Gosh, in your day that must have been a big deal. Oh, the shame of it, Mama...I'm shocked!" I teased with a laugh, and then took a long refreshing drink of my Coke.

"Yes, well it was scandalous hiding the fact that we were living together and really not married. We drove down together in his car and got an apartment close to the marine base. It was heaven for a while," she admitted, with a blissful smile on her face.

"So what happened? Did he get shipped overseas? Or worse, killed?" I asked, while feeling the gentle breeze wash across my skin.

Mom looked up at the blue sky and the puffy white clouds drifting by. "It was the hardest thing I ever had to do, saying goodbye when he got shipped out to the Philippines. I loved him so deeply and it was so painful not knowing if he would come back alive. All I could do was hang on and hope that he would return. I prayed every day for his safety," she whispered.

"Working full time as a telephone operator helped fill the void. Then, after he'd been there several months, he sent me a letter telling me he married a Filipino woman," she paused and closed her eyes briefly. "He shattered my young foolish heart. I trusted him so much. I put my reputation on the line for him. I gave him everything, including my heart. Looking back, I think being in love like that is really being in lust. Electric chemistry is such a potent draw." She reached over and patted my leg. "Following your heart doesn't always work out. Remember that, honey," she said with conviction. "Trust your gut when it comes to love."

"God Mom, I'm so sorry. I know how you must have felt. I gave my heart and soul to my navy man, Skip, when he was here in Hawaii. I was so in love with him. It was the first time I felt really in love," I confessed. "When I was with him it was total bliss. I think I wrote you and told you that he was in subs?"

"Yes, you did."

"Well, he did two ninety day patrols during our brief time together here. It was like sending him off to war, too. This cold war stuff with Russia now," I shook my head, "their sub, the USS *Kamehameha,* was deep under the ocean doing top secret deterrence patrols; it's scary and dangerous stuff collecting data and spying. I missed him with all my heart when he was gone." I paused and looked out at a catamaran skimming across the waters. Would my heart ever move on?

"I don't know, Mom, there's something about sending your lover off like that, which makes being in love more intense. More desperate passion. I wanted to hold on and not let go. In the end though, Skip broke my heart. He could have stayed here in Hawaii, but he chose to go with the sub back to New London for upgrades and get more naval schooling. He didn't ask me to go with him. He just said *that he would get things set up and see how it goes.*" I breathed in deeply remembering the hurt of it all.

"And here I sit, still madly in love or as you say, in lust with him and hanging onto hope. I got so tired of being alone these last couple of months, I gave up and now I'm seeing Duke, but I'm not in love with Duke. He's much older than I am, at least ten years, but we have a lot of fun. He wines and dines me in expensive places. We snorkel and do open water swimming together; he's just very charming to be with, but he's my boss, too."

"Your boss?" She sat up straighter.

"Yeah."

"Be careful with that, sweetie, that could be trouble," she said, taking a sip of her Coke. "Let me ask you this. Would you go to Skip, if he asked you?"

"I don't know, Mom. You just told me that following your heart doesn't always work out. I don't think he was in love with me as much as I was with him. He's the kind of man that women drool over. I always felt I couldn't compete with that. It was like a roller coaster. He'd pull me in and then he'd pull back."

"Hmm...well, I remember what my mother used to say...*the man you think you are in love with at twenty, you would spit on at thirty,*" she laughed softly. "I can't tell you what to do with Skip. You'll have to figure that out for yourself. I am the last person to judge you, honey."

"Thanks, Mom, for telling me everything. You've got guts, I'll say that," I grinned. "But you stayed on and continued to live in San Diego, right?"

"I did, yes. My best girlfriend, Jane, and I got an apartment. She worked for the phone company, too. Both of us were operators.

It was shortly after that heartache blow that I started dancing at the military bases with a troupe of young girls. We put on stage shows and I was the choreographer for each routine. We sent hundreds of young marines off to the Pacific after the Japanese bombed Pearl Harbor. There's nothing that can compare to dancing in front of a packed house of military men! I used to do a rumba number that drove them wild," she laughed. "But oh my, what an audience! Clapping, hooting, whistling, foot stomping, it was unforgettable!" she said, with a smile and a far away look in her eyes.

"You were unforgettable, Mom. I've seen the beautiful black and white close-up picture of you in that rumba costume and some others with the troupe. Wow! I bet you girls did drive them crazy."

"We did, but what a wonderful feeling to be able to dance like that and send those guys off with those kinds of sweet memories. I remember looking out into the audience and thinking how many of those young brave men wouldn't come back," she said with sadness. "It broke my heart into pieces."

"Well, it makes me so proud of you, Mom." I leaned over and gave her a big hug, before she started reminiscing again.

"Watching a military parade in the forties was such a thrill. I remember it distinctly," she stated with that dreamy look again. "Those parades were thrilling to the core to watch!" She adjusted her bathing suit strap, took in a deep breath, and continued in a voice a decimal higher.

"The stirring, exciting sounds of the U.S. Marine Band in the distance. Hundreds of people standing on the sidewalk while the song, "Halls of Montezuma," drifted in the wind. Platoon after platoon of camouflaged clad marines. Row upon row of hundreds of marching feet stomping in perfect time, as only the marines can do! Young men loaded with backpacks, helmets, boots, rifles, and grim faces," she emphasized.

"Crowds clapping in praise and appreciation. Waves and kisses thrown. It was awe-inspiring, gut-wrenching, and tear-jerking all rolled into one. Tears for those young men leaving for war and tears for those of us whose men were already in combat. And yet, through it all, a wonderful feeling of pride. Pride in those men. Pride in our country. Fierce loyalty beating in our hearts! All of us sending out our love to all those young, eager, yet hesitant men knowing what they were about to face," she paused, inhaled and exhaled deeply. "It was the best of times and the worst of times, as they say, but oh, what a united country were we. Committed and determined to not let our democracy and freedoms be taken away," she stated proudly, gazing out at the horizon.

"Oh Mom," I said, wiping a tear from my eye. "I have goosebumps right now. I can't even imagine that, but you painted a beautiful picture. Thank you. You're really the best. I felt like I was right there with you when you were describing it," I said, before stretching out my body, and then finishing my Coke in silence.

"It's getting hot, Mom. Do you want to dip in again?"

"I sure do, honey, let's go," she said as she got up, took my hand, and we headed down the Waikiki beachfront like two sisters forever linked as one.

.... **Chapter 21** ....

Teriyaki Burgers

It was after 2 p.m. when Mom and I headed off the beach to get some lunch. What a great time we had talking and dipping in and out of the ocean. "Let's go to Duke's Bar and Grill for teriyaki burgers, Mom. It's just next door at the Outrigger Surf Hotel. It's got the best burgers on the Waikiki strip," I declared, while leading the way.

"Sounds wonderful to me, dear," she said, slipping on her beach muumuu, putting on her flip flops, and then following behind me.

Duke's Grill is an open-air patio restaurant that looks out over the sparkling blue ocean and the horizon. The roof is made of fake straw that looks like a grass hut. The wooden walls are covered with tons of Hawaiian surfing memorabilia. Pictures of *Duke Kahanamoku,* the great Hawaiian surfer and Olympic swimmer of the 1920s, were everywhere. Everything about Duke's Grill said, *this is Hawaii,* including several very old canoes hanging from the high ceiling. Used surfboards and canoe paddles were mounted on the walls. Duke's had that unmistakable appearance of a surf shack museum loaded with past island history.

We stood waiting to be seated. The clatter of noise, the hustle of the wait staff, and Hawaiian music played in the background, making the place feel alive. "Two for lunch?" the hostess asked with a big smile.

"Yes please," I replied, as we followed her to a table for two. A huge overhead palm leaf fan provided a cooling breeze as we took our seats. "Mom, you have to try the pineapple teriyaki burger, it's just the best. Oh, and an extra tall *guava* iced tea."

"Okay, I trust you to know what's good," she nodded, putting the menu down as the waitress took our orders. Within a few minutes our large *guava* iced teas were delivered. They were packed with ice cubes, cold to the touch, and beautifully decorated with a purple orchid and a pineapple slice on top of each glass.

"Oh, how pretty this is," Mom said. "And it's good, too."

"I know and it's so refreshing," I said, taking a long swallow.

"By the way," Mom said, "are you still swimming at that outdoor pool you told me about in one of your letters?"

"As often as I can, Mom. I walk from my apartment into Waikiki to the Natatorium pool, usually around lunchtime. It's right on the beach down past *Kapiolani* Park. I can get in a good workout and still have time to lie on the beach, before I head to work around four, unless I am working a dayshift at the Hilton pool cafe. It feels good to push myself again in a workout. Did you know that the Natatorium pool is a World War I memorial pool? It was dedicated to the men and women who served during that war. And get this...after the Pearl Harbor attack, it was taken over by the U.S. Army and used for training during World War II."

"No, I didn't know that. It has quite a history then. You said it was a huge pool, right?" she commented, glancing at the doves that were scrambling on the cement floor looking for crumbs.

"Well, you couldn't use the pool for competition. It's incredibly long. Too long for a regulation meet pool. It spans 100 meters by 40 meters and it's salt water, too. It's great for distance workouts, but not for sprints. It's cheap though and hardly ever used. I'm glad I can train there, instead of just doing ocean water swimming. It keeps me in shape and I love that. God, I do miss those swim team days and training hard for nationals," I admitted with fondness.

Sipping her iced tea, Mom said, "Well, I never thought I'd say this, but I do miss all the swim meets, too. It was my social life and connection to all the swim team parents. Those were such fun times. All those away meets with a car load of girls," she chatted, with happiness in her voice. "But I don't miss those daily 6 a.m. workouts that I had to drive you to for years," she declared. "Or the regular 8.p.m. workouts either. Those really cut into my time, but I did it because I love you and you were a star from the time you were ten years old. I understood your dedication and passion. I was like that with my dancing as well."

"Thanks for always being there for me, Mom. I couldn't have done it without you. Not to change the subject, but your San Diego stories were an eye opener. I know you stayed on after your heartbreak, but why did you move back to Seattle later?"

Mom took another deep breath and stirred her iced tea around with the straw. "Well, there's more to the story that I didn't tell you."

"There is? Do tell," I said with raised eyebrows, while looking at the next table across from us. Their order of fish and chips had just been delivered. My stomach growled and my mouth watered. Those garlic fries smelled heavenly.

"Yes, well, remember my best friend, Jane?" she asked, sipping on her iced tea.

"Yeah, she's still your dearest and best friend. I remember when she came to visit you a couple of years ago from San Diego. What a character she is," I chimed in.

"That she is, but she got in trouble back then," Mom said with hesitation.

"Trouble, what kind of trouble?" I pressed.

Our waitress arrived with our plates brimming full of big sweet Hawaiian bread buns and burgers dressed with a fresh slice of pineapple, cheese, and lettuce, smothered with thick teriyaki sauce. On the side of the plate, Hawaiian garlic fries were piled mountain high.

"Looks delicious!" Mom marveled.

"It is, dig in," I ordered and kept talking. "So what happened to your girlfriend, Jane?"

"She...she got pregnant by a marine," Mom divulged with a tone of soberness.

"Oh God, how sad, and let me guess, the marine didn't want any part of that!" I said, taking a big bite of my yummy burger.

"You got that right."

"So how did you help her?" I questioned, while loving the juicy taste of this teriyaki burger and pineapple.

"Well, he got shipped out to the Pacific. Unfortunately, he didn't come back. Nevertheless, being an unwed mother with a baby on the way was just the worst possible thing that could happen to a girl. I mean...it was so shameful. You were shunned, ostracized, and considered a loose woman with no morals. We were convinced that no man would want you after that." Mom paused and then she took another bite of her burger before continuing.

"Jane's mother wouldn't take her in to help her and basically disowned her. It was so traumatic," she confided. "Jane wasn't alone though; it happened to more young girls than I can count. Most girls did what Jane did and adopted the child out or went to an unwed mothers' home. We didn't have the pill back then. Most of us relied on the rhythm method, condoms or a diaphragm, and prayed that we were safe. I was Jane's best girlfriend. I had to help her," she paused. "Yum, this is so good, honey," she acknowledged, and wiped her lips with a napkin.

"Keep going," I encouraged.

"Well, we were panicked. Jane had little money saved. She couldn't afford an unwed mothers' home. So...I wrote to my mother. My mom said she would take Jane into her home. Jane had already decided to adopt the baby out. So, now you know why we moved back to Seattle. We told everyone, to avoid gossip, that her husband was in the marines and fighting overseas." Mom picked up a couple of fries to eat. "It was such a difficult time for Jane, to say the least."

"God, Mom, that must have been so hard for you both, especially Jane," I said, dipping my fries into some ketchup and popping them into my mouth.

"It was awful, but my mother was an angel. Your grandma was so understanding and so non-judgmental. God bless her. You know, I would do the same for you or any of your friends," she stated with certainty. "Just know that I would never disown you, no matter what. Shit happens when you least expect it."

"Mom!"

"Well, it does and we women pay the price for unexpected pregnancies."

"Yeah, we do. I know you wouldn't disown me, Mom. That's what I love about you." I reached over and patted her arm. "Did Jane go back to San Diego after the baby was born?" I questioned, while a gentle breeze blew through and the waitress poured us more iced tea.

"Yes, she did and still lives there today. She married later and had three kids. Divorced now, but no one knew about the child she adopted out."

"Wow, that's quite a story and so sad. So you stayed in Seattle and Jane moved back to San Diego," I sighed shaking my head. "Then, how did you end up marrying dad?" I questioned, wondering if my dad had swept her off her feet like the marine had done.

"Well, your dad had always been sweet on me when we were growing up together in the same neighborhood. My mother suggested I write to him while he was overseas. As a B-17 pilot, he was stationed in England and making bombing runs over Germany. So we started writing to each other."

"Yeah, he told me that once. But did Dad rock your world like the marine guy?"

Mom took a long swallow of her iced tea. "Your dad is a very handsome man, but no, he wasn't the love of my life, if that is what you're asking. My biological clock was ticking. I wanted a family, a home, and a man to take care of me. I wanted a man that I could trust. Your dad had all those qualities. He lives his life with integrity, has a kind heart, and is devoted to me. He's always been a good man, but..."

"But what?" I asked, taking the last bite of my burger.

"But...I never counted on living with a man that is so obsessed with fly fishing and hunting. It hasn't been easy all these years dealing with that. He's gone a lot. Doing what he loves to do. Having his own business affords him that luxury. I swear he lives to fish and most of the time it takes priority over everything else, including me. I have had to learn to live in his shadow," she said with frustration.

"Yeah, I get that, Mom. He'd fish until the cows came home. So you resent that?"

"I do, but he finds his peace on the rivers. I try to remember that he fought in the war. Who knows how he has learned to live with that and the guilt of bombing missions. However, there are times when I ache for a different kind of man. A man that loves to dance and is a romantic at heart, but you can't have everything in one man. If you think you can, then you're nuts. Happiness comes from within and accepting life as a gift. Finding the good things in a marriage that can sustain you. My close girlfriends, and you children have been my godsend and my lifeline," she acknowledged.

"That's kind of sad, Mom," I replied, finishing off my burger. "I should write your story someday."

"Well, you can, but not until I am dead and gone," she laughed. "Despite it all, your father and I have had a good life together with a lot of friends and fun times. I'm thankful for that and grateful that your dad is so devoted and loving. I didn't marry the love of my life, but I believe you make choices that sometimes turn out for the best," she smiled.

I smiled back. "Yeah, but I had my heart broken, too, just like you did."

"True, but do the things you love to do. The things that give you great joy like your swimming. Be kind and forgive everyone, including yourself. Life has a way of opening doors, if you open your heart."

"Words of wisdom, Mom. Thanks, I'll remember that," I said, eating the last of my fries and finishing my iced tea. "I have to leave soon and get ready for work this evening. What are you two doing tonight?"

"Oh, we thought we would walk around Waikiki and pick a place to eat dinner. Maybe sit poolside later and listen to Hawaiian music. Tomorrow we're going to drive around the island."

"Okay. The following night Duke has invited us all for dinner at the Hilton Hawaiian Village. Reservations are at seven. I'm off that night, so I'll meet you both here at your hotel and we can walk there together."

"Perfect. We'll look forward to it. And don't worry about what your dad may think about you dating Duke. I already asked him to keep his bigoted comments to himself."

"Thanks, Mom," I said, hoping that he would do just that. But would he?

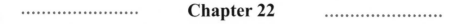

Chapter 22

Meet & Greet

Two nights later, my parents and I strolled down *Kalakaua* Avenue on our way to have dinner at the Hilton Hawaiian Village with Duke. Traffic buzzed by, horns honked, tourists crowded the sidewalks, and military men hovered around night club entrances smoking cigarettes and checking out the girls passing by.

The island of Oahu was the hub for vets on R&R from the Vietnam War and military personnel stationed here at Pearl Harbor. Every time I'd see a good looking navy man in uniform with sandy blond hair, my thoughts would return to those steamy, hot magical nights with Skip. Perhaps dating other people would eventually bring us together again in the months to come. I continued to hope that maybe, just maybe, he was still in love with me like I was with him. However, once again, I stuffed that thought and the deep longing ache, into the back of my mind, as my parents and I continued towards our destination.

Mom was wearing a pretty, soft pink, sleeveless shift with white sandals. Dad was clad in a bright blue and white aloha shirt with beige slacks. His face and arms looked somewhat sunburned from his deep sea fishing excursion of two days ago. Both had big aloha smiles on their faces, as we entered the Hilton Hawaiian Village.

"Oh, honey, this is stunning! The open-air lobby is magnificent. Oh, and the flower displays are so colorful and beautiful!" Mom said with emphasis.

"It is a pretty place," I agreed. "Dad, you have to see the koi fish ponds; they are brimming with brightly colored koi," I said, knowing that anything to do with fish would get his immediate attention.

"Show me the way, *Sis*," he grinned and put his arm around my shoulder. *Sis*. I loved the fact that he always called me *Sis*. My nickname, which he had given me as a little girl. It made me feel special. "Right this way, Dad," I replied, leading them to a little outside grotto area with a small bridge, which you could stand on and look down at the koi swimming in the pond below. "Unique, aren't they?" I said.

"Oh my, they're so big and the colors!" Mom said. "Orange, black, gold, and white spots; they look like giant goldfish."

"Well, dear, there are many colored varieties of koi," Dad clarified. "They're a carp fish, not real good for eating though. Their varieties are distinguished by coloration, patterning, and scalation. The *Japs* were the first to breed them for color in the 1800s," Dad said, while I cringed at his use of the word *Japs*.

I could tell Dad not to use that word, but then he would probably not talk to me for the rest of the week or worse repeat those horrific stories of atrocities committed by the Japanese during World II. I grew up hearing about those Japanese war crimes, like the rape of Nanking, the capital of Nationalist China that took place in 1937. That conflict between Japan and China eventually became the Pacific branch of World War II.

What was Dad saying now? "The POWs from World War II in Asia included 27,000 Americans. They suffered deplorable conditions, starvation, torture, diseases, and executions. Rice was the only food provided. Vitamin B deficiency and paralysis ran rampant. Forty percent of the prisoners died in Japanese internment camps and only four percent of the 93,000 POWs died in European camps," he declared.

"Wow, I didn't know that statistic, Dad." How could I judge my dad knowing all this? I hadn't walked in his shoes. God only knows how the men that fight in a war find the strength to go on and not be prejudiced. The Japanese were *Japs* and the Germans were *Krauts* in his book. That would never change. I had learned that it wasn't worth arguing about, as he switched topics from the war to koi fish.

"They're a cold water fish and they adapt to many climates and water conditions, which give them a high survival rate. The *Japs* use them in garden ponds for displays like this one here," Dad stated, with a wave of his arm.

"Well, they're sure colorful," Mom said with a smile.

"Yeah, and they let the kids here at the hotel feed them. Did you know that they're symbols of love and friendship in Japan?" I added, pointing to a huge orange and white one that came to the surface, mouthing for food, as we continued across the beautiful Hilton grounds.

◆◆◆

The sky was turning a pretty coral color and the sun was sinking below the horizon. Dusk here in the islands was a magical display of beauty. A gentle breeze kissed my bare shoulders and I felt an anxiousness seep into my gut, knowing that in moments I'd be introducing Duke to my parents. Duke wasn't Japanese, but he did have slanted eyes and dark brown Polynesian skin. Would my dad be okay with that? Or would he read me the riot act about dating someone of a different race? All I could do was trust that Duke would charm my dad like he had me over the past month.

◆◆◆

As soon as we entered the *Makaha* dining room, Duke greeted us at the door. "Aloha, I'm Duke Haku," he beamed. "You must be Virginia? I see where your daughter gets her good looks," he flattered her. Then he leaned in closer, placing a delicate lei of small white ginger buds around her neck and a kiss on her cheek. Mom blushed like a teenager and lovingly fingered the lei. "Thank you, Duke. It smells heavenly like a subtle perfume."

"Here in the islands, it's our way of showing hospitality and affection. I'm glad you like it," Duke replied. "It's white ginger. One of my favorites."

Duke looked very handsome in black slacks and a white aloha shirt, which was accented with a black kukui nut lei around his neck. Not to mention his thick black hair and those dark mysterious eyes that were captivating. I knew Mom was thinking, what a handsome, exotic looking man. Charming and cultured. My Mom was always a sucker for a striking man or a man in uniform. She nudged me lightly in the ribs with a look of curiosity.

"And Brandi, my *love*, you look stunning tonight." I was wearing that little red mini halter dress that was backless. Duke leaned in and placed a quick kiss on my cheek.

"And you must be George?" Duke looked my dad straight in the eyes and they shook hands. "I've heard a lot about your fishing achievements. A world record steelhead you caught on a dry fly that you tied yourself. Pretty impressive. I love to fish, too," Duke revealed. "I'd love to hear you're fishing stories over dinner, George."

Oh great, I thought, more fish stories. Lucky us. Yahoo. However, it was better than my dad's war stories, which I had asked Duke not to bring up. Plus, I didn't want Duke to talk about his pilot days in Vietnam. I wasn't sure if all that was true. It seemed far-fetched. Some things Duke said just didn't add up and that was one of them.

Nevertheless, Duke had worked his charm; my dad was beaming like a *tiki* torch. "I do love to fish. I went deep sea fishing yesterday and man oh man; I landed a king-sized marlin, too. What a fight that was! Took me half an hour to land it. Weighed over two hundred pounds and was six feet long!" Dad boasted, with a silly grin on his face.

"Well, that's great, George. Glad you had a good time. Follow me, folks, and I'll take us to our table. By the way, I took the liberty of ordering something special from our head chef tonight, starting with some *pupus* and a couple bottles of wine that will pair nicely with the meal I have planned," Duke assured them.

"Sounds good to me," Dad said, placing his hand on my mom's lower back and directing her forward into the busy dining room.

◆◆◆

The wonderful aromas of garlic, grilling meats, and flaming desserts wafted in the air. Even though I worked here, I had never had the privilege of dining here. I simply couldn't afford it, but I had tasted most everything.

White tablecloths on every table and folded gold cloth napkins gave the room a touch of class. Soft lighting with small glass candles on all the tables created a romantic atmosphere. However, most impressive were the oversized front windows that looked out over the ocean and horizon, and of course, Duke had reserved a window table.

Graciously, Duke pulled out my mother's chair and our waiter, Koa, pulled my chair out for me. Adjacent to our table was a silver ice bucket with a bottle of white Albariño wine. I had already told my folks that Duke had a lot of pull being the food and beverage director here.

Once seated, our waiter poured a taste of wine for Duke's approval. He went through the taste and swirl test. "Perfect," he said and spoke to my dad. "Brandi tells me that you love raw oysters, George. We're having *kumanoto* oysters on crushed ice first. This wine will complement them perfectly," he stated, while the waiter poured for the ladies first.

Yeah, like my parents would know a good wine from a cheap wine, I mused. My dad would probably have preferred a shot of whiskey, but then Duke was in command.

"Virginia, Brandi says you don't care for oysters, nor does she, so I ordered fresh big island prawns for you ladies instead," Duke said, with a sparkling smile.

Mom grinned and clapped her hands. "Oh, bless you, Duke. Oysters are not my thing, but this wine is lovely; I love a dry white wine," she marveled.

"It is at that, Virginia. It's made from white wine grapes from northwest Spain and Portugal. It pairs beautifully with simple shellfish like prawns and oysters," Duke assured her.

I leaned over and gave Duke a peck on the cheek. "Thanks, love, you remembered that I don't like oysters," I purred.

Meanwhile, my dad turned the conversation back to fish stories that I'd heard a hundred times, but Duke seemed to love it.

During our appetizers, the conversation turned to Duke. "Did you grow up here in the islands?" Mom asked, taking a bite of prawns plated on a bed of lettuce.

Duke slipped an oyster into his mouth and swallowed it. "No, I didn't grow up here, Virginia. I'm mostly *Maori,* the indigenous people of New Zealand. I was an orphan there and lived in an orphanage most of my childhood," he shared.

I just about choked on my wine! What? I thought he grew up on the big island! Wasn't that what he had told me? I could have sworn he said there was even some royal Hawaiian bloodline in the family. *Maori* and from New Zealand? What was going on? Conflicting stories, but this wasn't the time to challenge him. I took a giant gulp of my wine and stared at him with question marks in my eyes. I'd ask him later when we were alone to explain this story.

◆◆◆

We were totally spoiled throughout dinner. *Ahi* fish and scallops, spiced sake-braised big island spinach, and lemon grass jasmine rice, followed by macadamia nut pie for dessert. Duke wanted to order after dinner drinks for us all, but we were on our third bottle of wine and declined. Instead, we just had decaf coffee. All in all, it was a memorable evening and I know my parents were impressed. Duke wrote everything off on his hotel expense account.

Later though, my dad made a point of pulling me aside after we left Duke and the restaurant. "He's a charismatic man, *Sis.* I like him, but don't bring him home!" he commanded with authority.

Wow! That was blunt. I didn't tell him that I had no intention of bringing Duke home, but that wasn't his business to know or was it? Two more days and they would be gone and I wouldn't feel like I was under my dad's watchful eyes anymore. Independence from his critical views gave me a sense of freedom, not being under his roof anymore. It was one of the reasons I loved living here. I promised myself to never be that judgmental, as I said goodbye to them and went outside to think. I wanted to get to the bottom of Duke's conflicting stories before he took me to bed.

.... **Chapter 23** ....

Lusty Night

My parents walked back to their hotel and I strolled around the Hilton grounds thinking about some of the things Duke had said during dinner. Things that just didn't make sense to me.

I sat down on the beachfront pier and took off my heels. The night air was warm and tropical. The moon was full and bright casting a silver glow across the ocean waters. Hawaiian music from an outside bar echoed in the background and the croaking of area frogs sang out like a concert of baritone instruments. It was peaceful, but it did little to quell my growing concerns of Duke's conflicting childhood stories.

Sitting there on the rock pier and dangling my bare legs, I took a deep breath admiring the beauty of the moon's glow. My thoughts turned to my heart throb, Skip. What was my navy man doing tonight? God, I missed him. His sweet sexy smile. His Midwestern drawl. The way he kissed with so much passion. How much I loved going to bed with him and how he always made me feel so beautiful.

It made me sad to think that my folks didn't get to meet Skip. They would have adored him. With Duke, they had their reservations. My mom telling me that Duke was too old for me, and my dad's objections to dating a man of another race and culture.

I looked up into the dark clear sky, which was abundant with ribbons and ribbons of thousands of stars. Stars that seemed to speak to my heart. It was like looking far into the future, but not knowing what that would hold. Where would I be in ten years? Would I be with Skip or someone else? Would I have a family and be happy? Questions that I didn't have the answers for. My mom's words of wisdom filtered through my muddled thoughts, *following your heart doesn't always work out.*

The gentle lapping of the waves hitting the beach reminded me that it was getting late. Duke would be making his rounds to the bars and checking on things before retiring to his suite. I wanted to ask him a few questions about his orphan story before we ended up in bed together. Rising, I brushed off a bit of sand from my dress, ran a hand through my long hair, picked up my heels and purse, and walked barefoot back to the Hilton grounds.

◆◆◆

"There you are," Duke said, as I entered his hotel suite. He was wearing only a brown and black *tapa* print sarong wrapped around his waist that reached his ankles. My breath caught in my throat. That dark brown skin, his bare muscular chest and arms, damp wet hair from a recent shower, and his magnetic smile made me melt. He was like a chocolate dessert. In that native *tapa* sarong, he reminded me of a Hawaiian prince. Bold, sexy, and so very tempting.

"I loved meeting your parents tonight," he affirmed.

"Yeah, it was so nice of you to do that," I responded, with a sincere smile. "But, I wanted to ask you..."

"Come here, girl, so I can love on you," he interrupted, and held his arms out wide with a big inviting grin. God, he was getting too hooked on her, he thought. Most of his ladies he would be with a few times and move on, but this one...she was athletic and so very sexy. He was beginning to love spending time with her and not just in bed. Remember, he told himself, enjoy the ride, but you will eventually want someone new.

Oh God, I thought, he was so appealing. I dropped my heels and purse. I couldn't help myself. I floated into his outstretched arms. He smelled fresh and clean, a subtle earthy scent that teased my senses. He wrapped me in a big aloha hug and held me tight against his pelvis, swaying together. *Hula* motions I called them. His signature move. It left my body on fire.

Placing his hands on my hips, he pressed himself even closer. He kissed me deeply, exploring, tasting, and teasing me with his tongue. All thoughts of asking him about those conflicting stories evaporated with the blaze within me. My body overpowering me with lust. Oh God, I needed this and wanted him.

When his kisses ended, he held me close and looked into my brown eyes. "You know that I really adore you, Brandi. I don't usually get this attached to any one woman, but you are so damn lovable and so different. I like that you don't wear a lot of makeup or perfume. I like that you don't mind hanging out at the beach and getting your hair wet. And that beautiful swimmer's body of yours, it's incredible!" he said, with hunger in his dark black eyes.

Reaching up, he ran his hand through my long hair. "I love your golden hair, too. You're mine!" he claimed, before his hands gently lifted my halter dress over my head.

I stood there with only my black bikini panties on. Red hot heat sizzled through me. He undid his sarong. It dropped to the floor. His magnificent body ready in all its glory. He took me right there, on the carpeted floor, as the night slipped away like a shooting star.

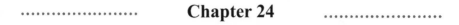

Chapter 24

Davy Jones Locker

My parents and I were seated at Davy Jones Locker, a bar located underground at the Outrigger Surf Hotel. It was dark inside like a cave. This unusual bar boasted a giant sized six by five foot window behind the bar station.

Through the bar window, patrons could view the hotel swimming pool above ground. It was a one-way window, where we could see in, but swimmers in the pool couldn't see us. It made for comical conversations while drinking and watching people swim around uninhibited. Outstretched legs, flailing arms, funny faces, and butts pressed against the window created lively laughter and sometimes crude comments.

Sitting at the bar, we ordered three mai tais. My friend, Sneaker, was bartending. We called him that because he would sneak extra booze into your drinks, if he knew you. We watched him mix our mai tais. Large rock glasses packed with ice, then light rum, some lime juice, orange Curacao liqueur, and orgeat syrup followed by a hefty floater of dark rum. I knew from experience that his mai tais could knock your butt on the floor.

"There you are, Brandi. Just the way you like them," he grinned, placing the drinks in front of the three of us. There's nothing like a really well made mai tai, I thought, that's not too sweet with plenty of rum, a skewer of sliced pineapple, and a cherry on top.

"Drink them slow, folks. They're potent," Sneaker said turning to my dad.

Mom stirred the rum around and took a sip. "Oh my, yes, they are strong. Be careful, George," she laughed. "I'll have to do a Hawaiian dinner when we get back to Seattle and serve mai tais," she licked her lips with a grin.

"Yeah, Dad," I echoed. "Sneaker makes them pretty powerful."

My dad waved his hand like no big deal and drank a hefty swallow. "Really good, I like the dark rum," he grinned and raised one eyebrow. "You do that, dear! A Hawaiian dinner party would be fun and these mai tais would be a big hit, too. I'll make the mai tais and everyone can wear aloha shirts and muumuus," he announced.

"Okay, dear, I'll arrange it when we get back home," Mom offered.

"That sounds like fun, guys," I added. "Are you hungry? I'll order us some *pupus*. Maybe some teriyaki chicken wings and some tempura shrimp?"

"Sure, that would be great, *Sis*," Dad responded, pointing to the window and laughing at someone's big fat *okole* pressed up against the glass. All of a sudden, all of us were laughing our heads off.

Mom stirred her drink with the swizzle stick. "I love these mai tais," she stated. "I'll be sad to leave the islands. It was sure nice of Duke to cover that dinner last night. It must have cost him a small fortune," she stated.

I turned sideways facing her. "Mom, he wrote it all off on his hotel expense account. He has a lot of perks there," I said, sipping my drink.

"He's certainly charming; sad that he was an orphan and didn't know his real parents," Mom said.

"Yeah, I didn't know all of that. He told me he grew up on the big island. I intended to ask him about all that last night, but I forgot," I said, remembering our lusty night together.

Dad leaned his arms on the bar counter. "Well, you know the *Japs* forced 200,000 Asian women into prostitution during the war.

They were known as the comfort women. Most were Korean sex slaves, but many were from East Asia. The *Japs* invaded many of those remote Pacific islands, including New Zealand. Duke could have been a result of that," he surmised. "There were thousands of orphans born of mixed races during that time and no one wanted them. Hell, he could be half *Jap* and *Maori* for all you know."

I raised my eyebrows. "I didn't know that, Dad, but that is a possibility."

"George," Mom said, "it doesn't matter; he's a very nice man."

Dad shifted his position. "The hell it doesn't," he raised his voice. "It's one thing to be dating him here, but back on the mainland," he shook his head, "you'd be crossing the line, *Sis*. I'll say it again. Don't bring him home!"

I swallowed hard. The rum in the mai tai was giving me courage to speak my mind. "Dad, if you must know, I don't intend to move back to the mainland anytime soon. Duke is a lot of fun, but I don't intend to bring him home. And Dad, you don't get to tell me who I can date either!" I said strongly. "I'm twenty-one and not a kid anymore. I make my own choices and take responsibility for them," I added, feeling confident and a little fearful. Dad always ruled the roost in our house and you didn't question his authority.

Dad's body language tensed. His nostrils flared. I could tell he was pissed that I had the gall to stand up to him. It was the first time I had ever done that. My pulse jumped a notch.

Mom intervened as usual, always the smoother-over person in our family. "Now, let's not argue about this. We're here to have a good time."

Just then, Sneaker placed a large plate of chicken wings, dripping with thick teriyaki sauce and sesame seeds in front of us, along with a plate of sautéed shrimp, all of it smelling heavenly.

"Now, pass me a chicken wing and let's talk about something else," Mom smiled, breaking the tension.

"Sure, Mom," I replied, passing her the plate of wings.

"Tomorrow, we're going to the Polynesian Cultural Center for a *luau,* and then we fly out the following day. Have you been there, honey?" she asked.

"No, but I hear it's really cool. It's on the northern shore of the island located by the little town of *Laie*. Did you know that *Laie* is a big center for the Mormons? They have a Latter-day-Saints temple there and they own and operate the Polynesian Cultural Center," I said.

"I wasn't aware of that," Mom replied.

"Yeah, they have eight simulated tropical villages and performances of various dances along with arts and crafts from Polynesia. Duke told me that it was originally a commercial venture to fund employment and scholarships for BYU-Hawaii students. It opened in 1963. Be sure you see the fire and knife dances when you're there. It's done with blazing swords of fire; it's captivating. The *hula* girls will blow your mind with the way they move their hips, Dad," I teased.

"Your mother does a mean *hula*, too, what with her dance background," he grinned and Mom wiggled in her seat with glee.

"The *luau* part you will love. Lots of authentic food and dances. Have fun," I said.

"We will. Are you able to come to the airport to see us off the following day?" Mom asked, taking a bite of a chicken wing and licking her fingers.

"No, I'm working at the poolside bar and grill that day. So, this will probably be the last time I see you both before you leave. I'm glad you came and we had a really good time. Dad, your fishing trip was a winner," I chirped. "Did you ship the fish home?" I asked.

Dad grinned and reached for a couple of shrimp. "No, I donated the marlin to the fish market. I guess they use them to help feed the needy here or send to the canneries."

"That's cool, Dad. What a nice thing to do," I smiled and patted his hand, as we continued to drink our mai tais and indulge in the *pupus*.

Someone put some coins in the jukebox that was over in the corner. One of my favorite songs by the Stones came on, "I Can't Get No Satisfaction." I started singing along. Mom tapped her foot keeping time and Dad grumbled. "Rock and roll; I don't know what you see in that kind of music, *Sis*."

I just laughed. "Oh Dad, you are so out of it. But then, you are old, aren't you," I teased.

He put his arm around my shoulder. "If I didn't feel so damn good right now, I'd swat you one. This is the best mai tai I've had this whole trip. Sneaker, another round if you will, please. I've got to hit the head, excuse me ladies, I'll be right back."

I leaned over and whispered, "Thanks, Mom, for calming Dad down."

"Yes, well he is adamant about mixed couples. If you don't want all hell to break loose, you better do as he says. Besides, Duke is a little too old for you, don't you think?"

I tapped my fingers on the bar counter. "Yeah, but he's a lot of fun. He's leaving the Hilton at the end of January. I guess he's got a food and beverage position at the Coco Palms on Kauai. I don't know why he wants to leave; he's got it pretty good here. He wants me to come visit him often," I said wearily. "I don't know if that will happen or if I can afford it. I keep hoping that Skip and I will be together again some day," I sighed deeply.

Mom patted my hand. "Sweetheart, if you are not in love with Duke, don't feel obligated to him. Listen to your gut. It will always tell you what to do."

"More words of wisdom, Mom?" I asked with a slight smile.

"Yes, and remember that. Here comes your dad. Change the subject quick."

Dad scooted onto his bar stool.

"You know what I miss about living here?" I said.

"No, what?" Dad questioned.

"I miss being at Oso on the river in the summer." Oso was our family's privately owned riverfront property along the Stillaguamish River, sixty miles north of Seattle.

"Yeah, we missed not having you there last summer. I hooked and landed several steelhead and cooked them at our annual Labor Day barbeque. What a party that was! Plenty of sunshine and it didn't rain the whole weekend," he crowed.

I nodded, remembering those fun times, campfires, swimming and floating the river, and family dinners. However, nothing was going to pull me away from the islands, unless Skip called from the naval base in New London, Connecticut and asked me to marry him. But what were the odds of that?

.... **Chapter 25** ....

Call of Aloha

My parents had left two weeks ago. Duke and I had spent many nights together at his Hilton hotel suite engaging in late night dinners, drinks, and sweet romance. He had given his notice and last week had moved over to Kauai. His new position as food and beverage director at the Coco Palms Resort started on February 1st.

A beach house provided, an expense account for entertaining guests, and plenty of hotel perks like his laundry washed and pressed. It all seemed too good to be true. It was impressive, but I still couldn't understand why he wanted to give up the Hilton prestige. He'd said he just wanted to get off Oahu; it was getting too crowded.

Duke had asked me to come visit him on Kauai. We agreed to that and he would pay my airfare. But would he follow through with that promise?

◆◆◆

I was hanging around my apartment listening to my transistor radio and singing along with the song, "Kind of a Drag" by the Buckinghams. It was a drag without Duke around, I admitted. I missed our rendezvous nights, his charismatic personality, our beach times, snorkeling together, and especially being wined and dined.

Tomorrow, I was headed to Kauai to spend three glorious days with Duke. My roommates, Donna and Sherry, tumbled into the apartment, tired from working all day. I was in the kitchen cooking dinner for them. Onions and garlic sautéed in butter permeated the air.

"Hey, smells good," Sherry said. "What are you cooking?"

"Soy chicken and stir-fry vegetables," I grinned. "I have an hour before my cocktailing shift tonight. I thought dinner together would be nice before I head to Kauai tomorrow."

"That's really nice of you, Brandi," Donna said, dropping her purse on the sofa and reaching for some plates and silverware. "Are you excited to see Duke?"

I added the sliced chicken breasts to the stir-fry and some pasta to a pan of boiling water. "I am excited. I've never been to Kauai and Duke has promised to show me around the island," I said, waving a wooden spoon in the air.

"That's cool. Does he have a car over there?"

"Well, he was going to ship his red Ford Galaxy over, but it was mysteriously towed away right before he left. I saw the tow truck at the Hilton parking lot and asked the truck driver why he was towing it."

"And why was it being towed?" Sherry asked, with a raised eyebrow.

I continued to stir the chicken mixture. "The driver told me that the bank repossessed it. That the owner didn't make payments. I asked Duke about it, but he said the bank was crazy. He said he paid cash for the car six months ago. Then, he said that he would buy something new on Kauai."

"Hmm, that sounds kind of fishy, don't you think, Brandi?" Donna stated, while setting the table. "His two roommates kicked him out because he didn't pay his rent for two months. You're not sure how old he really is or what his childhood story is all about. Oh, and then, let's not forget the flying F105s in Vietnam story. Honestly, I really like him, but I think he makes stuff up," Donna said. "But Brandi, you know he's not your future, so it's not your problem how he lives his life. Just be aware of some of his lame excuses."

"Yeah, but he's still fun to be with, and he treats me like a queen," I smiled, trying to ignore those concerns, as I stirred the chicken around in the fry pan and added a half a cup of soy sauce.

"He is charming, I'll give him that," Sherry remarked.

Both my roommates had dinner and drinks, several weeks ago, at the poolside bar and grill. I introduced them to Duke, who in turn chatted with them, and then he wrote their entire meal and drinks off. They were impressed, to say the least. Later, they said he was very handsome, irresistibly charming, and charismatic, I remembered, just as our phone rang.

Sherry picked it up. "Aloha," she said and paused to listen. "Yeah, she's here. Is that you, Skip?"

My ears perked up. My heart leaped! Skip? Was Skip calling me? Sherry handed me the phone smiling from ear-to-ear. "Guess who?"

Oh my God! I was shaking with excitement and nervousness. I hadn't heard his voice in over three months. "Aloha," I squeaked out.

"Aloha, my beautiful *island girl.*"

"Skip! Skip, is that you?" I turned away from my roommates. Our landline had a long extension cord, so I walked down the hallway for some privacy.

"It's me babe. I've been missing you so much. I really made a mess of things with us," he said, with longing in his voice.

Oh God, just hearing his soft Midwestern drawl left me breathless! I could just picture him in a pair of Levi jeans and a T-shirt with a seductive, boyish grin on his face. That vision was making me remember the first time I had met him a year ago here in Hawaii. Back then, I had thought that he was out of my league and way too good looking to be with me.

I pressed the phone closer to my ear. Deafening music and muffled voices blared in the background. I heard the words of the song, "Working my Way Back to You" by the Four Seasons, playing loudly. Somehow, I felt sure that he was working his way back to me. He must be at a party, I thought. It sure sounded like it. Five o'clock here meant that it was around ten o'clock back on the east coast. My mind was spinning with questions. Why was he calling me out of the blue?

"God, I've missed you so much, Skip and everything about you!" I gushed.

"Are you seeing someone these days?"

"Ah...sort of, yes, but he's not you, Skip."

I heard him tell some people to "hush up" before he spoke again. "Girl, I don't care, just know that I can't go on without you." I heard him take a deep breath. "Will you marry me?"

"What? Did...did you just ask me to marry you?" I gasped, trying to contain my disbelief and excitement.

"I did. I love you so much! Will you marry me?" he asked enthusiastically .

"Oh my God! Yes!" I promised, stunned beyond reason.

"She said, *'Yes,'*" he hollered to everyone. A cheer went up and he was laughing and getting congratulations from the crowd. He raised his voice a notch. "When do you think you can fly out here?" he asked.

"I'll have to give my two weeks notice and save up some money for airfare," I explained, hoping that he would offer to pay my way, but he didn't.

Instead, I heard him say, "We'll live together first and if it doesn't work out, then don't worry. I'll pay your airfare back home. God, I can't believe you said, *'yes'*! I'll call you next week and I'll look for an apartment for us, too. Well, babe, this call is costing me a butt load of money, so until next week, sleep tight and dream of me. I can't wait to have you in my arms again. I love you. Bye, my *island girl.*"

"I love you, too! Bye, Skip," I whispered and hung up the receiver. Standing there in a daze, I caught my breath. My mind a jumble of mixed thoughts and emotions. All of a sudden, I felt a pang of doubt buzzing through me. I walked back into the kitchen while staring into the anxious faces of my roommates.

"You look excited and bewildered, Brandi. What did Skip want?" Sherry questioned, with eyes full of expectation.

I took a really deep breath and placed my hands on the sides of my face. "Oh God, he asked me to marry him! I said, *'yes'*!" I answered with a big smile, and then I bit my lower lip.

"What?" Donna questioned. "Are you sure, Brandi?"

"I was...until he said something at the end. Now I'm doubting him again. He was at a party and I think he'd been drinking, too."

"What did he say at the end?" Sherry asked, placing her arm around my shoulder as we sat down on the sofa.

"He said we would live together first and if it didn't work out, he would pay my airfare back home. Geez, what kind of a marriage proposal is that?" I tossed my arms up in the air. "Is he already thinking that it might not work? And how long would we live together? I don't want to just live together on a trial basis," I stammered.

"Hmm, you'll need to ask him that. I wasn't going to tell you this, Brandi, but now I have to," Sherry said. "Last week I ran into Scottie, Skip's old navy buddy. Scottie told me that Skip took leave over New Year's and went back home to Nebraska. Some of Skip's old friends set him up with his high school girlfriend, Linda. The one that shattered his heart. I guess they spent some time together. According to Scottie, that didn't work out either. Sounds to me like Skip still doesn't know what he wants," Sherry said with a sigh.

"Yeah, sounds that way to me, too," Donna concurred. "Better think twice about this, Brandi."

"Why didn't you tell me sooner, Sherry?" I asked.

"I've been waiting for the right time, but I think now is the right time."

"Geez, what am I going to do? I already said, 'yes.' I really have doubts now." My mother's words of wisdom crept back into my thoughts...*listen to your gut. Following your heart doesn't always work out.*

"Sleep on it and let's have a stiff drink together before dinner," Sherry said.

"I can't. I have to go to work shortly."

"Here's my advice," Donna interjected. "Go to Kauai. Have fun. Let Duke spoil you, then decide when you get back. If Skip was with Linda, then you can certainly be with Duke. If however, you decide to go to Skip, then you need to tell Duke face-to-face. It's the right thing to do."

"Yeah, it is. God, I'm so confused right now. I always thought that if Skip asked me to marry him, I would be ecstatic. And I am... but now...what if I go back there and he gets tired of me like he probably did with Linda?"

I stood up and looked out the lanai window. Palm trees rustled in the breeze and our neighborhood was alive with people coming home from work. I could hear children playing in the yard across the street and the smell of meats on barbeques. It all reminded me of how much I loved living here in Hawaii.

"You guys have dinner without me. I'm going to walk to work. I need some fresh air. I'll see you both when I get back from Kauai. Hopefully by then, I will have reached a final decision," I said, slipping on my flip flops.

◆◆◆

Leaving the apartment, I couldn't help but think about all this new information that Sherry told me. Skip hadn't mentioned getting back with Linda. Was I willing to take another risk with him and move five thousand miles away and possibly get the boot like Linda did? Was I really ready to leave my beloved Hawaii? And what about Duke? Was he worth a continued relationship with? Could I even trust his off-the-wall stories?

Traffic buzzed by me. The sun was dropping low on the horizon as I headed down the street. A three mile walk to work would help. My mind shifted to a song that I'd heard many times since it came out in 1966 by the Lovin' Spoonful, "Did You Ever Have to Make up

Your Mind?" Those lyrics drifted in and out of my confused brain. Just like the song, I was faced with choosing one over the other. I felt like I was being sucked by an undertow of currents and didn't know which way was up or down. What had I gotten myself into? And what would I decide to do?

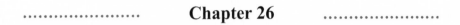

Chapter 26

Garden Isle

The following morning, I was standing at the Honolulu inter-island airport counter where I checked in and proceeded to the departure gate. Once on the tarmac, a balmy breeze blew my long golden hair around. Slipping on my sunglasses, I wondered how this trip with Duke would turn out. It was so cool, even though I had conflicted feelings about him. And now, Skip was back in the picture and messing with my heart with a marriage proposal. My bruised soul had just started to learn to live without him these past months.

Here I was flying off to Kauai and into another man's arms. I felt very guilty about the whole thing. Saying yes to one and then being with another. Duke would no doubt spoil me and treat me like his queen. If there was one thing Duke was really good at, it was that. Dinners out, cocktail parties, and dancing under the moonlight; he had promised all those things. Just thinking about it put my imagination and excitement into overdrive. However, I was acutely aware of the thin line I was walking and my imminent circumstances.

Dressed in a soft, slinky, navy shift and silver flip flops, I walked up the outside stairs and boarded the small prop plane, glad to be out of the glaring sunshine. Taking my seat, I glanced out the window, watching as more people boarded the plane. I sat back, adjusted my seat, and pulled out a flight magazine, which showed our air route to Kauai. From wheels up to wheels down at *Lihue* Airport, it was a whopping twenty-three minute flight. Having never been to Kauai, I was looking forward to becoming acquainted with the garden isle, known for its vast, rich, colorful array of tropical flowers that thrive throughout the island. Plentiful rainfall made Kauai the wettest place on earth. However, sun and heat are just a breath away after a daily dose of rain.

An older lady sat down next to me. We greeted each other as the propellers turned over. The stewardess went through the safety drills. Shortly thereafter, we taxied down the runway and picked up speed.

Up, up, and away. Oahu and its blue aqua waters and reefs disappeared from view as my thoughts drifted to Duke. Recently, I had questioned him about his conflicting childhood stories. He did reconfirm that he was a *Maori* orphan from New Zealand, but he had been adopted when he was ten by a couple on the big island of Hawaii. The royal bloodline remark, he claimed he never made. Did he just forget what he said? It did confuse me.

I replayed our conversations about his so-called pilot days in Vietnam and his car being towed away, too. I didn't know what to believe anymore. Now I had to tell him about Skip's marriage proposal. It rattled me with uncertainty. I had to be honest with Duke, even if I didn't leave Hawaii or go to Skip.

Before I knew it, the garden isle of Kauai was visible from the air. My first thought was how strikingly beautiful the island was. Breathtaking cliffs, thousands of feet high, lush green valleys, towering waterfalls, and spectacular beaches and coastlines that seemed to go on as far as the eye could see. In a matter of a few minutes, we landed at the *Lihue* Airport. It's a very small inter-island airstrip just like I had imagined. Exiting from the plane was a portable stairway that led onto the tarmac.

Duke was waiting for me about six feet from the stairs. He held his arms out wide with a great big Hawaiian smile. Oh God, he looked good, I thought. Aviator sunglasses, jet black hair, dark chocolate skin, and his athletic body; it was enough to make me forget about Skip. I smiled back and floated into his arms. I had missed him these last two weeks, I admitted. Missed those strong arms around me and our romantic nights together.

He stepped back, admiring me. "God, you look delicious, *love*. I've missed you, especially in my bed," he teased. It had surprised him just how much he thought about her and missed her these two weeks apart. Looking at her now, he felt his blood flame with heated desire. She was under his skin in a way that no other woman had been, but could he stick to just one woman? It wasn't who he was and he doubted that.

Duke slipped his arms around me and kissed me deeply. My body tingled and my pulse shot up. Geez, what was I going to do? He broke the kiss. I slipped on my sunglasses and took a deep breath. I'd forgotten how powerful his kisses could be.

"Wait until you see the Coco Palms Resort. It's magnificent!" Duke boasted, as he picked up my suitcase and we headed down the tarmac. "My beach house is a dream! It's just a block from the beach. You're going to love being here and I intend to spoil you with all my attentions." He placed his hand on my *okole* with a sweet little pat. "My car is just over there," he pointed to a hardtop coupe Datsun 240Z sports car.

I stopped with surprise. "That's your car? The midnight blue 240Z?"

"Pretty, isn't it? She's last year's model, a 1970. I got a real good deal on it. Talked them down to $3,200 from the original sticker price of $3,500. Paid cash, too. Perfect for island driving, don't you think?"

"Yeah, it's very cool. Where'd you get the money?" I questioned, thinking that just weeks ago his Ford Galaxy had been repossessed on Oahu. My red flags went up again.

"Oh, I sold some stock. I have a lot of investments, Brandi," he clarified. "My stockbroker wired me the cash." He opened up the hatchback lid and placed my suitcase inside. "Hop in, *love*. It's only about a fifteen minute ride up to *Wailua* where the Coco Palms Resort is," he stated.

Slipping into the driver's seat, he turned the ignition on. "Let's Live for Today" by the Grass Roots blared loudly from the radio. Was that what I was doing, living for today? Trying to coast along without a care? If it was, it wasn't working. The impending cloud of doubt was looming over my heart, making me question my motives and integrity.

◆◆◆

We drove inland from the airport on Highway 50. Dark ominous rain clouds hung low over the island mountains, which were fertile with thick vegetation covering them like a velvet jade moss. The surrounding earth and hills were rich with red-rust dirt that had a fresh wet look, probably from an early morning rainfall. Pineapple and sugarcane fields were plentiful, some with burning stalks that filled the air with smoke and a sweet sickly smell. I took it all in, noting how much more rural Kauai seemed compared to Oahu. There were no high-rise hotels or business buildings like on Oahu, nothing over three stories.

A couple of minutes later, we turned onto Highway 56 heading north on the eastern shores of the island. Here, I could see the ocean sparkling with brilliant sunshine and white sand beaches that seemed to span for miles against a stark backdrop of steep, lush, emerald green mountain cliffs, hugging the island like a protective shield. It was similar to Oahu, but much more vivid, rugged, and breathtaking.

"It's so pretty," I said, admiring bushes of tropical flowers, which painted the landscape with a natural beauty of vibrant purples, reds, yellows, and oranges.

"Yes, it is," Duke agreed. "There's a reason it's called the garden isle. It's like a blooming bouquet all year long," he laughed, as he turned his head to look at me. "By the way, the Coco Palms Resort rests on ancient Hawaiian royal property. It's a popular wedding getaway place. Did you know the Elvis Presley movie, *Blue Hawaii*, was filmed there?"

I turned to smile at him. "I didn't know that. I've never seen the movie."

"Really? It's a love story with a Hawaiian wedding scene. It was a hit back in 1961. Ever since the movie, the resort has made a big business out of Hawaiian-style weddings. We had four this last weekend."

"Wow, how romantic!" I said, dreaming about a Hawaiian wedding day of my own and how incredible it could be under the stars here in paradise. Only question was with whom and when?

I rolled my window down thinking once again about Skip and what I was doing. A warm tropical breeze drifted in cooling my damp skin. The humidity was a bit higher than Oahu, making the air almost like a wet sauna. I turned my attentions back to Duke.

"The Coco Palms is also known for their true Hawaiian torch lighting ceremony. If you thought the one at the Royal Hawaiian Hotel was cool, where we had our first dinner date, this one will blow your mind."

"Why's that, Duke?" I asked, admiring the sleekness of this new 240Z sports car, the black leather bucket seats, the stick shift, and the available leg room it had. I loved this car. It made me feel like a rich jet-setter. Classy. I wondered if he really paid cash for it.

"Well, because their torch lighting ceremony is much more dramatic. There are at least half a dozen local men dressed in traditional *malo* wear."

"What's *malo* wear?"

"You know, it's a piece of loincloth made from *kapa*, a barkcloth fabric made from plant fibers."

"Oh, so you mean just their butts and private parts are covered?" I grinned.

He laughed. "Yeah, to put it bluntly. It drives the ladies wild. It's primal to the core. They chant and dance to the beat of a drum, very suggestive and sensual until the loud call of the *conch* shell is sounded. Once it's sounded, the call is answered by one man, in *malo* wear, running across the huge coconut grove, lighting dozens of torches the entire way to the resort's lagoon," he said shifting gears. "It represents the Hawaiians' call to their dinner ceremony and the Coco Palms does it first class. You're going to love it!" he said, reaching over and running his hand along the back of my neck.

"I can't wait to see it then." I bubbled with anticipation while the heat from his touch set my skin on fire.

"Well, you are going to see it tonight. In fact, you, my lady, will be accompanying me to a formal cocktail party and dinner under the stars. My boss, the hotel manager, will be there, too. I want him to meet you."

"Oh, I didn't bring anything real dressy," I said with concern.

"Not a problem, I'll buy you a cocktail dress. We have a splendid boutique on site and I'll pick it out. I want you to be ravishingly beautiful by my side this evening," he declared, dropping his hand from my neck to stroke my bare thigh. "God, I've missed those legs and everything else, too," he grinned.

My pulse jumped. A rush of heat jetted through me. "Keep that up and I'll be in no shape for dinner tonight," I teased.

He grinned wickedly. "Just testing the waters," he laughed. "It will have to wait though," he said, returning his hand to the steering wheel. "I've got to get back to work and do some things before tonight. So I'll take you to my beach house first. You can unpack and then walk down to the resort. Have the front desk page me when you get there and we'll have a quick lunch and go shopping. I know just the dress I want you to wear. I intend to show off my sexy girl to my staff and guests tonight."

"Uh...okay," I replied, thinking that I had never had a man buy me a dress, let alone pick one out for me. It's a rare man that has a good sense of fashion and what looks good on a woman. I had no doubt that he would dress me to the nines, but was I willing to let him do that? I had paid my own airfare over. So far he didn't pony up for that. I sat back into the bucket seat, crossed my legs, and took a deep breath debating about this. Was I going to have to shell out more money I didn't have for a cocktail dress, too?"

Chapter 27

Kauai Beach House

Duke pulled his car into the driveway. This cute little beach house took my breath away. It was tucked back among several palm trees, bamboo trees, and two plumeria bushes in full bloom. Strategically nestled in the shade with surrounding green grass and exotic blooming flowers everywhere, it stood out like a fairy tale cottage.

We got out of the car. The sweet scent of plumeria was a welcoming aloha to me. I couldn't help but pick one off the bush. Taking in a deep breath, I drank in its intoxicating aroma and put it behind my right ear. A sign in Hawaii that meant I was available, not married. "This place is adorable, Duke," I raved.

"It is pretty nice. Here's the key to the front door. Make yourself at home and then come on down to the resort. I'll show you around before lunch," he said, handing me the key. "See you later, *love,*" he hollered, getting back into the car and driving away.

Wow, I thought, standing there admiring the cottage. It was painted in a light shade of teal blue with an expanded front porch and a veranda roof that wrapped around the entire front of the house. A place to just sit and admire the scenery or doze off. Very cool, I thought, as I walked up the four steps to the double windowed front door. Turning the key, I felt at home even before I stepped inside.

Bamboo floors throughout, a medium sized palm plant in one corner, and a large area rug of light green and white triangle patterns adorned the front room. Three large bay windows graced the main living area providing an abundance of light. A rattan framed pillow sofa and two similar chairs added to the beach cottage mood that made me feel relaxed. Simple and charmingly delightful.

Down the hallway, I peeked into one of the bedrooms. There was a queen sized bed, and two nightstands, each with a small bed lamp. The bedspread pattern was so cute, a cream color background with a pineapple design, which matched the window curtains and lampshades.

My eyes lingered on the long stem red rose placed on the pillow and a note next to it. I put down my suitcase, entered the room, and picked up the rose while smelling its subtle perfume. I smiled thinking that of course Duke would do this. We had missed being together last week for Valentine's Day. I unfolded his note and smiled warmly.

Brandi, thinking of you sharing my bed tonight leaves me wanting you even more.

Yours, Duke.

He's such a charmer, I thought, ignoring all of my doubts. I unpacked and hung up a few items of clothing before changing into a pair of white shorts and a red tank top. Glancing around one more time, I admired the large beach picture hanging above the bed. A beautiful sunny blue ocean scene and the back of two white Adirondack chairs sitting on a sandy deserted beach. A groovy Hawaiian theme. It added a dreamy touch to the whole room. It reminded me that the beach was just down the street.

Unpacking my suitcase, I hung up the two sundresses I'd brought. In the closet was an empty shelf that I laid the rest of my clothes on, a couple of T-shirts, a pair of jeans, my bikini, beach cover-up, and a dressy pair of flip flops. Done, I thought, as I left the bedroom feeling exuberant to be here.

The bathroom was down the hall, so I gathered my toiletries and found space for them on the counter. Strange, there appeared to be some female skin care products on the counter. Hmm...I opened the medicine cabinet. A tube of lipstick caught my eye. Duke had only been here two weeks. Did he already have a female roommate? He'd never mentioned anything about it, but then he always said he lived with girls, rather than guys. I would definitely ask him about this at lunch.

Curiosity made me peek into the second bedroom as I made my way through the house. Two single beds with one dresser and a nightstand. Simply decorated with a beach theme. Each of the beds was unmade as if two girls shared this room. Well, no surprise there. Knowing Duke, he was probably charging them rent and pocketing it. Sneaky, I thought, since he gets this place for free. I walked out shaking my head in disbelief. Why didn't he have any guy friends like Skip did? Maybe because he moved around a lot. In the short time that I'd known him, two and a half months, he had gone from the Outrigger Hotel to the Hilton and now the Coco Palms. That just didn't make much sense to me.

Heading into the kitchen, I opened the refrigerator surprised to find a six pack of Cokes and other food. I popped a Coke, thinking that after lunch, I would hit the beach for some sunbathing and bodysurfing. I had the whole afternoon to myself until the cocktail reception tonight. Strolling onto the front porch, I stretched out on a lounge chair while drinking my Coke and admiring the yard.

Four palm trees blew gracefully in the breeze. I loved to watch their green fronds sway back and forth like a *hula* in the wind. Their gentle motion was as if they were talking to me. Off in the near distance, I could hear the sounds of the pounding ocean waves breaking. A handful of little white doves skittered on the grass, pecking for seeds, while the sun shone brightly with puffy white clouds against the cobalt blue sky.

Sitting there, I decided that I wasn't going to let Duke pay for an evening dress. I would cover the cost myself if it wasn't too expensive. However, hotel boutique shops tended to be pricey. Duke had expensive taste. I swallowed hard. My bank account was pretty skimpy after just paying my airfare and rent. I lived from paycheck to paycheck and counted on tips to make ends meet. Would Duke be offended if I didn't let him pay for a dress? Would he even understand that I didn't want to feel like a kept woman? Probably not, I thought, as I finished off my Coke and headed out to meet him with some pending questions and concerns.

I made my way down the secluded side street. One long block away was the Coco Palms Resort. Spanning more than thirty acres were hundreds of palm trees known as coconut groves. The resort was a brown cottage style lodge, three-stories high that boasted over ninety-six rooms.

Stopping at the entrance of the registration office, I read the display about the Coco Palms. As Duke had told me, the grounds were at the mouth of the *Wailua* River, an ancient Hawaiian site of royalty and hospitality. I learned also that many legends and events of historical, cultural, and religious significance took place here.

What I didn't know was the dramatic torch lighting ceremony originated at the Coco Palms and later other hotels in the islands started doing it. Today, the vast coconut groves along the coastline are referred to as the *Coconut Coast* of Kauai. In 1810 Kauai became part of King *Kamehameha's* new Kingdom of Hawaii. So much history right here where I was standing and I could just picture how primitive it was back then.

With a satisfied smile, I entered the open-air lobby. Impressive, I reflected. Wooden floors and Hawaiian sculptures along with paintings of Hawaiian royalty, which adorned the walls behind the reception desk. Off to the side, a beautiful enormous display of many tropical bird-of-paradise plants stood out with their bright orange bird-like heads and long green stems. They really did look like exotic birds, instead of flowers, I marveled.

Approaching the reception desk, I smiled at the pretty young girl behind the counter. She was dressed in a colorful muumuu and a bright red hibiscus flower tucked behind her ear. Long flowing blond hair and blue eyes, she looked like a typical California girl.

"Aloha," I greeted her.

"Aloha, how can I help you?" she smiled sweetly.

"Could you please page Duke Haku for me? He's expecting me."

"Certainly," she said, with a sweet smile. "You must be Brandi?"

"Yeah, I am. How'd you know?" I asked with surprise.

She picked up the intercom and paged him. "Oh, Duke told me about you coming to visit. I live at his beach cottage. I'm Mindy, by the way. My girlfriend, Chrissy, lives there, too. We both were looking for a cheap place to live and well, Duke offered.

He's certainly made an impression on all of us here at the Coco Palms," she stated. "And he's so good looking and so much fun to live with!" she emphasized as Duke strolled in and stood next to me.

"Hey *love*, did you get settled in okay?" he leaned over and gave me a quick kiss on the cheek. "I see you've met Mindy. She's one of my roommates," he smiled at her. Mindy smiled sweetly back at him with an adoring look in her eyes that I didn't miss. Was she enamored with him?

"Yes, I met her," I responded with a fretful tone, thinking that she did have obvious designs on him. Mindy was a knockout. Petite, long blond hair, and probably around my age of twenty-one. Even in the employee provided muumuu there was no mistaking the abundance of her oversized breasts. An uneasy feeling swam through me as I turned my attentions back to Duke.

"Thank you for the rose and the note...you are very tempting, Mr. Haku," I teased, with a sly smile.

"Good, that's what I want." He reached for my hand and gently squeezed it. "Come on, let's have a little lunch," he coaxed, as we drifted hand-in-hand out past the reception area and down the path to an outside cafe.

"See you later, Duke!" Mindy called out a little too sweetly.

"For sure, Mindy." He waved goodbye with a wink.

"You didn't tell me you had two girls for roommates," I said.

"They just moved in last week. They needed a place to live, so I offered. It's no big deal. Both are really great girls from California and a lot of fun so far."

"Mindy is very sexy. I think she has eyes for you."

"Are you jealous, *love*?"

"I don't have any room to be jealous," I said, thinking that I had accepted a marriage proposal from Skip just yesterday. Later tonight I would put it all out there. Would Duke be jealous? Would he try to convince me to stay in Hawaii? I had butterflies in my stomach like before a swim meet. Anxious, nervous, unsure, and scared.

Once seated, Duke ordered for both of us. He didn't even look at a menu, just told the waitress to bring us the lunch special of teriyaki beef sandwiches with Maui onions and a side of *poke* salad to share along with two iced teas. I have to admit that it was kind of a turn-on when he took control and did the ordering. I felt like such a spoiled girl when I was with him.

We had a talkative lunch catching up on the last two weeks apart. Duke telling me all about the resort and his responsibilities as food and beverage director. I shared with him stories about my roommates, Donna and Sherry. Nothing much new, except that Donna was thinking of moving back to California in the spring. Sherry was still without a boyfriend, but Donna was going to set her up with a friend of hers. I avoided the conversation about Skip. It wasn't the right time. For now, I was Duke's as we left the cafe and strolled through the grounds until we came to the boutique shop.

Pearl Boutique

The Pearl Boutique was a small specialty shop with the finest evening and aloha wear. I took a deep breath as we entered. Looking around, I knew there was no way I could afford any of these elegant cocktail dresses. I hadn't even looked at the price tag on any of them yet!

"Mona, this is my girlfriend, Brandi," Duke said to the clerk.

"Nice to meet you, Brandi," she said. "Mr. Haku has picked out a few things for you." She motioned for me to follow her to the dressing room.

Duke grinned at me. "Choose one of the three that I selected, Brandi. Surprise me later. Come back to the reception area at six o'clock and I'll meet you there," he said, as he turned to leave.

"Hey, don't you need to come back to the beach house to change later, too?" I asked.

"No, I've got a change of clothes here." he stated, with a wave and disappeared out the door.

"This way," Mona directed. "Let me know if you need any help," she said, closing the door to the dressing room.

I reached up and touched the first evening dress. I flipped over the price tag. Whoa! $125.00! That was more than my monthly rent! I doubted that Duke would pay me back. It would take me forever to pay off any of these dresses. I only made $4.25 an hour as a waitress and hostess. It was a good thing I made great tips because it was cash in my pocket and it covered all my other living expenses, but geez, these prices were for the rich and famous.

Trying on all three dresses, I decided on the first one. It was stunning with a black stretch curve-sculpting fabric consisting of 86% rayon, 12% nylon, and 2% spandex with a bustier design that hugged my breasts and showed off my slim waistline. It had a short hemline above the knees, accented with a two inch, sexy, lacy hemline.

I modeled it for Mona, the sales clerk. "Oh, it's beautiful on you, dear. Just beautiful! I wish I could wear something as form fitting as that. You certainly have the figure for it."

"Thank you," I smiled.

"Let's get you a pair of heels to go with it," she declared.

Mona picked out a pair of black, dressy, suede heels, open on the sides with a black converter strap around the ankles. I had to admit, it showed off my long, tan legs, but the price! Thirty dollars, yikes! I twirled around looking in the full length mirror. The shoes and the dress were perfect. I felt like a Hollywood celebrity in it as I slipped it off and changed back into my shorts and tank top.

"Mona, I do love it." I said, as I stepped up to the sales counter.

"Well, you enjoy yourself tonight," she grinned knowingly. "By the way, you picked Mr. Haku's favorite one. He'll be pleased."

"Yes, I'm sure he will be," I said, and wrote out a check that my account would barely cover. I'd have to pick up extra hours and tips. I was broke now.

◆◆◆

The walk back to the cottage made me sweaty and hot. I hung up my cocktail dress, changed into my black bikini with a pair of surfer shorts, and slipped on my beach flip flops. It was 2 p.m. and I had time for a little sunbathing. Grabbing a towel, my transistor radio, sunscreen, and a beach mat, I headed down the street again, excited to catch a few waves and get a catnap on the beach.

The *Wailua* Beach took my breath away. Spanning about a half mile, it's a wind-swept, spectacular white sand beach. With no reefs to protect it against open ocean swells, it was known as a popular surfing spot for locals and tourists. However, Duke had told me that because of the *Wailua* River emptying into the ocean, it created strong rip currents and powerful shore breaks, making for poor swimming and dangerous conditions.

Finding a spot partially in the shade, I laid out my beach mat, put on some Coppertone sun lotion, and admired the beautiful setting. The surf was up. Several red flags were visible along the beach shore warning people of a high risk factor. Nevertheless, a handful of surfers and boogie boarders were scattered across the rough waters waiting for the perfect waves.

Stretching out, I turned on my transistor radio. "Mama Told Me (Not to Come)" by Three Dog Night had me humming along. I loved that song with its catchy lyrics and beat. Ah...so nice to let the sunshine warm my conflicted heart.

It wasn't long before my eyes closed. I dozed off thinking about that beautiful cocktail dress and how it made me feel. Elegant and classy. I'd never been to an elaborate cocktail party. I guess I was stepping up in the world. It made me feel older than I really was and sophisticated beyond my years. I sighed deeply as another song, "Foxy Lady" by Jimmy Hendrix tickled my brain.

Tonight, I would bask in the whole experience and be Duke's foxy lady. With that, I rose deciding to dip into the water, but not do any body surfing. The breaking waves and riptide looked too strong and intimidating. Kind of like Duke could be, too strong and intimidating.

.... **Chapter 29** ....

Starstruck

No one was home when I came back to the beach cottage. Duke's two roommates must still be working, I thought. At 4 p.m. I had two hours to shower and get ready. Taking the cocktail dress off the hanger, I laid it on the bed along with the heels before I jumped into the shower. Time to shampoo my hair and rinse the sand off my body.

Later, I slipped on one of Duke's *tapa* print sarongs and tied it around my chest letting it drape to my knees. Perfect to wear while I dried my hair and did my nails and makeup. Barefoot, I stepped out onto the front lanai with a towel around my head.

Toweling off, I ran my hands through my hair, fluffing it up, letting the sunshine and warm breeze cascade through it. I smiled, thinking that it was so much easier these days using a blow dryer than those old bonnet hair dryers we had as teenagers. However, I did miss sitting under the stationary hair dryers, the heat lulling me to sleep. It seemed like I was always under one, since my hair was wet so much of the time from swim workouts. I had loved my chosen sport, but never liked wet hair and no makeup at meets. It wasn't a glamour sport, but I always had long hair and pierced earrings to try and look feminine, I remembered with a grin.

With no time to waste, I went back into the cottage, plugged in my blow dryer, and went to work. My beautiful, golden brown hair turned out perfectly. Full and flowing softly to my shoulders. I admired myself in the mirror. I loved my long hair, my tan skin, and even being tall. I didn't always like being the tallest girl around, but now as a young woman living here in Hawaii, I had become comfortable and proud of my height and slim body.

Next on my list, I did my nails while watching the local Hawaiian news. Bright red nail color, perfect with the black, sexy, cocktail dress, I surmised, while listening to the news commentary. It was all about South Vietnamese forces that invaded Laos on February 8th, and the return of 200,000 American soldiers coming home. What a relief. President Nixon had unleashed the Christmas bombings on North Vietnam, the most massive bombardment ever. Would this mess ever end? "Get all our boys home!" I yelled. "Stop this war!" I turned the channel.

At least this other station wasn't about the Vietnam War. The Eisenhower silver dollar was being put into circulation. I remembered growing up under President (Ike) Eisenhower. My dad loved him because he was a military man. A five-star general and supreme commander of the allied forces in Europe during World War II, he had made a name for himself. He was our 34th president from 1953-1961. Cool, I thought, a real silver dollar with his face on the front side.

I was just about to go out front and read a magazine, when Chrissy, I guessed, walked in. "Hi, I'm Brandi."

"Oh yeah, Duke said you were coming to visit. I'm Chrissy. Nice to meet you. We love living here and Duke, he's so charming," she stated sincerely.

"Yes, he is at that," I replied. Chrissy was a blond, too. She was a little taller than Mindy with an hour glass figure and cute as well.

"I hope you made yourself at home?"

"I did, thank you. I'm meeting Duke at the resort at six for a cocktail party."

"Yeah, he told us about that. You'll have a really great time. I wish I got to go to those private functions, but woe is me, I'm just a poor waitress," she sighed.

"Oh, I do that, too, on Oahu. I love the tips," I smiled.

"Yeah, they do come in handy. Luckily with Duke, our rent is half of what we used to pay, so that's a big help. I'd love to stay and chat, Brandi, but I have a date. I need to shower and get ready. If you need anything, just holler, okay?"

"Okay," I replied, liking Chrissy instantly and feeling no threat.

♦♦♦

I entered the Coco Palms resort reception area as dusk was showing its face. Mindy wasn't working; someone else was. Good, I reflected, thinking once again that she seemed enamored with Duke. Would she make a play for him when I was back on Oahu? Duke and I didn't really have an exclusive relationship; at least we hadn't talked about that. He was a player and a charmer. That I knew for sure. It was probably the perfect setup for him. I would never know what he was doing or with whom. I wondered if I would continue to visit him or fly off to Skip. This weekend would be very telling.

Glancing around, I admitted that I loved this open-air lobby and the warm evenings. Imagine, the third week of February and still so tropical at night. Standing there waiting for Duke, I looked out over the vast coconut groves and a garden area, where dozens of white lights were strung designating a gathering place. Duke was there talking to some employees as they finished setting up portable bars, dozens of circular cocktail tables about chest high, buffet tables with a variety of delicious looking *pupus*, and colorful, tropical floral displays as centerpieces.

People started to gather for the cocktail function. Duke looked up and saw me. With a wave, he strolled over to me looking very sexy in a white aloha shirt, white slacks, and white shoes. My pulse jumped a beat. He looked so classy, sophisticated, and in command of all the proceedings underway.

"There you are," Duke commented, as he came up the stairs into the lobby. I did a little twirl. "Wow! You look gorgeous in that dress!" he beamed. "I was hoping you would pick that one," he said, with a sparkle in his dark brown eyes.

I smiled flirtatiously. "Why thank you, Mr. Haku, I'm glad you approve."

My beautiful evening dress made me feel elegant, feminine, and very sexy as did Duke's comment. I had never ever owned or bought a dress this expensive. I felt like I was in a world that I had never before experienced. It was like a taste of fine wine, which tempted me to want to live in this kind of ambiance and environment for the rest of my life.

"I most certainly do approve," he marveled. Reaching out his arms, Duke pulled me close and gave me a quick kiss on the lips. "You amaze me, Brandi," he said. "Come, let me introduce you to the Paramount executives who are hosting this event."

Paramount film executives, wow, I thought. Could I hold my own hobnobbing with people from the entertainment world? Influential, elite, Hollywood people that were much older and more affluent than I was? A world I knew nothing about, but was going to experience tonight.

Taking a deep breath, I felt unnerved. However, Duke took my hand. Being with this older man, who was the food and beverage director here, gave me confidence and settled my nerves. I felt a sense of pride to be his date tonight. He wouldn't have invited me if he felt that I couldn't hold my own with this elite group, I reassured myself.

◆◆◆

The cocktail reception was lively, noisy, and entertaining. Duke introduced me to the big shots as his "lady." Never in my life had I felt so prestigious or glamorous. I moved throughout the crowd making small talk, everyone so envious that I lived here in Hawaii.

Duke made a point of making sure that I met his boss, Mr. Jackson, the hotel manager. He was from the mainland, Caucasian, and probably in his late forties. We shook hands and he placed a white and yellow plumeria lei around my neck. "Aloha, Brandi.

It's nice to meet you," he said, as Duke drifted away to greet other guests.

"It's nice to meet you, too, Mr. Jackson."

"Please call me Ron," he stated with a smile.

"Okay, Ron. The Coco Palms is sure an enchanting resort."

"It is indeed. We are very pleased to have Duke. In the short time he's been here, he has made a huge impression. He's very charismatic and able to charm our guests and staff. Of course, being of *Maori* heritage adds to his allure. He's very knowledgeable and proficient in his field and he's always here working."

"That's so nice that you are happy with him," I responded.

"Yes, and I see that I am needed elsewhere. Please excuse me, Brandi. Enjoy your evening," he said, leaving with a quick stride.

I turned around with my cocktail in hand and was talking to a couple from New York, when the thunderous sound of a *conch* shell being blown made everyone stop what they were doing. Its booming sound, a reverberating echo of times long past.

Darkness filled the entire coconut grove and a million stars sparkled overhead. Duke was holding my hand. The makeshift wooden stage was set. "Get ready, *love*. Watch the *conch* blower. When he's done, his *malo* dressed warriors will perform a dance with the pounding drums in the background," he stated, while placing a quick kiss on my cheek. "By the way, you have made quite an impression on the men here tonight, especially in that dress with your beautiful long legs," he gushed. "Some have asked me if you are available for a paid evening."

"What!" I cried with surprise. "Well, I hope you told them that I'm not that kind of girl?"

"I did, but it doesn't stop men from asking or dreaming," he chuckled, as the *conch* blower ended his Hawaiian call to dinner and then six men joined him on stage.

◆◆◆

For the next few minutes, I was mesmerized by the warriors' various movements. Bare flesh everywhere, except for the small piece of loincloth that covered their private parts, along with elaborate tattoo designs on their muscular arms, legs, and chests. A *Maori* tradition, a symbol of sacredness.

"This dance they are doing now is called the *haka*. It's from my *Maori* culture. Watch as they begin stomping their feet along with rhythmic shouting," Duke emphasized. "See the one with the tattoo on his face? It's called a *moko*. That's the most sacred part of the body, according to my culture. It's a declaration of who you are," he declared with pride.

And just like that, the place was transformed into a traditional ancient battle-ground, where male warriors danced for war preparations. My heart was beating so fast. Their rich, deep war cries touched the core of my being with a primal stirring. The shadowy dim lights and their dark skin left my imagination swimming in a state of pure lust, reminding me that Duke looked just like them. Sexy, sensuous, and physically masculine in every way.

"Penny for your thoughts," he said, with a grin and placed his hand on my lower back.

"Hmm...they look as good as you do...naked," I answered, with the primal beat of the drums continuing to stir my senses into a frenzy. Duke's hand rested on my lower back, creating a gentle circular massage, which caused my pulse to spike even higher.

When the *haka* dance ended, one man began his sprint through the coconut grove carrying a torch of fire. One after another, dozens of *tiki* lanterns were lit as the area became a glowing field of fire and light.

"God, it's spectacular! It's everything you said it would be, Duke, and more. I'm totally in awe!"

"I told you," he said with a big grin. "My people know how to ignite the soul."

"You can say that again, wow! I've never seen anything like this before or felt this kind of heartfelt connection to Mother Earth."

At the conclusion of the *haka* dancing and the torch lighting ceremony, the reception party ended and people disappeared into the sweetness of the magical star-filled night.

◆◆◆

"Come on, *love*. It's time you and I have dinner...alone," Duke whispered. He took my hand and led me across the grounds to one of the finer dining rooms.

Situated towards the opposite end of the hotel, facing oceanside, Duke and I strolled in and were immediately seated at a private table for two. White lights hung loosely from the rafters surrounding the entire patio restaurant. Small palm tree candles dressed the tables. Bamboo beam structures, like an open-air carport, along with a *tiki* hut stage up front, gave way to a small dance floor. Three local entertainers were setting up their equipment when our waiter, Paco, arrived.

"We'll have a bottle of Pinot Grigio and the smoked Hawaiian swordfish with the sake braised spinach, the prosciutto wrapped mushrooms, and saffron rice, Paco," Duke said with a nod.

"Very good, Mr. Haku," he replied and disappeared.

"It's enchanting here, Duke," I said, as warmth filled me with elation.

"It is at that. You're enchanting, too," he pointed out, as Paco returned with our wine.

"Oh...thank you, Duke. You make me feel so...so alive and tonight at the reception I felt so sophisticated and grown up!"

He laughed softly. "Brandi, you were a hit. Every woman there was jealous of you. I was honored to have you by my side," he raised his glass of wine. "To you, *love*,"

I smiled back feeling the magic of his words. I raised my glass and we toasted together. The chilled wine tasted refreshing and sharpened my appetite for an evening of more enchantment.

◆◆◆

Across the street from the resort, the dark ocean waters glistened like sequins in the moonlight and the breaking of the waves created its own soft music. A full golden moon hung high in the sky accenting a billion bright stars. The balmy breeze was like a cozy fire. It kept my spirits aglow with romantic expectancy.

I turned my attentions back to Duke. He looked so handsome, so alive, so animated. There was something about dating a much older man that was definitely different than someone closer to my age. Maturity perhaps, inner self confidence, and knowing the key to making a young girl feel enamored, adored, and on top of the world. Taking a deep breath, I wondered how I could tell Duke about Skip's marriage proposal. This evening had been extraordinary and impressive. I was absolutely starstruck!

We would talk during an after dinner drink, I decided, as the musicians began singing "Now Is the Hour" and playing their endearing ukuleles, adding another layer to my already growing infatuation for Kauai and...Duke.

Chapter 30

Kauai All Night Long

Dinner was fantastic and the Hawaiian music captivating. I was soaring on a wave of ecstasy, but would it come crashing down on me once I told Duke about Skip's marriage proposal? I shifted in my chair, dreading my coming confession.

Paco, our waiter, approached us. "Can I get you both an after dinner drink?"

"Yes, how about two Courvoisiers?" Duke requested, while looking into my eyes with want and desire.

"Very well, Mr. Haku."

"Courvoisier, what's that?" I asked.

Duke smiled broadly. "You have a lot to learn, my *love*. It's a fine cognac served in a heated snifter glass. You'll love it, trust me."

"I guess I do have a lot to learn about fine dining and liqueurs," I offered, while pushing a strand of my long hair behind one ear.

Moments later our heated snifters of Courvoisier arrived. A rich, copper colored liquid that was pretty just to look at.

"Now, Brandi, take the snifter and hold it, palm up between your middle finger and ring finger, so that your palm is against the bottom of the snifter. The heat from your hand will keep it warm," Duke said.

"Okay," I replied, and picked up my snifter holding it like he was doing.

"This is all about the experience, *love*. Now swirl it around, gently."

I smiled with pleasure at what Duke was teaching me. I never knew there were such things like this ritual.

"Now, hold your snifter at chin level and inhale the vapors. Let the fumes sweep through your sinuses. Concentrate on identifying flowers and spicy notes. The aroma is called the nose. The vapors enhance the flavor and the experience," Duke said, and then he inhaled its vapors with a dreamy look of pure delight on his face.

I did as instructed. "Oh, wow!" I said. A strong aromatic aroma streamed into my sinuses.

"Okay, now place your nose into the snifter as you take your first sip. Breathe in through your nose as you taste it."

Once again, I did as he said. Inhaling its vapors and then sipping slowly. My taste buds burst alive as the Courvoisier slid down my throat with a smooth, warm, mellowing effect. Its heat spreading deliciously through my body.

"It's very potent, but oh, so smooth. I can feel its warmth all the way down to my toes. I think I love it!" I smiled with complete satisfaction and awe. Holding the snifter out in front of me, I once again admired its rich copper color.

"It's to be savored. Drink it leisurely," Duke advised.

"Okay," I said.

Duke leaned back in his chair looking very comfortable and relaxed. "Did you know legend has it that Napoleon loved his Courvoisier so much, he took hundreds of bottles with him during his years in exile from France?" he said, taking another sip.

"I didn't know that, Duke, but I can see why. It's extraordinary... like you, Duke. Thank you for teaching me this," I said, sitting up straighter, knowing that I couldn't delay my conversation about Skip any longer. I cleared my throat. "Duke, there's something I need to tell you," I said with great hesitation.

"Oh and what would that be?" he said looking intrigued.

From across the table, I leaned in closer. Ukulele music drifted in the background, soft and alluring. It was the "Hawaiian Wedding Song," so tender and sweet. I felt a lump form in my throat. I didn't want to hurt Duke, but I had to tell him. I took a deep breath.

"Duke, I...I got a call from Skip. He asked me to marry him," I said softly, pausing for his reaction.

He raised his eyebrows and sat straighter. "And what did you say, Brandi?" he asked, as his deep brown eyes widened.

"I said, *'Yes'*, but...I have doubts," I replied softly.

Duke took a slow swallow of his Courvoisier, studied me, and then reached for my hand. "Brandi, my sweet Brandi, you are way too young at twenty-one to get married. You're the type of woman that needs to be shown off. Pampered, if you will, like we've done tonight." He stroked my hand lovingly. His tenderness touched my heart.

"I know you think you are still in love with this navy guy, but honey, do you really want to get married and be saddled with playing house, cleaning, laundry, cooking, taking care of a man, and possibly a handful of kids? I don't think you'd be happy living that way, at least not yet, being that you are so young. Are you willing to leave me and all this behind, too?" he gave a wave with his hand indicating this place and setting.

I didn't answer, but just stared into my glass not wanting to look into his questioning eyes.

"Brandi, look at me."

I raised my head slowly and saw deep concern written in his eyes. "I know you love living here in Hawaii. You've only been here a little over a year. Don't throw it all away. Stay with me. I'll fly you over here as often as you want," he implored with conviction. "I'm curious though, what did Skip say when he asked you?"

I took another sip of my drink. "He said, *'Will you marry me?'* And then he said, *we'd live together first and if it didn't work out, then he would pay my airfare home*," I replied in a regretful tone.

"That doesn't sound like he's serious to me. I'd say he has some doubts as well."

"I know; the last part of what he said has me wondering, too. He's been gone for over five months and I had pretty much decided to move on, especially since meeting you."

Duke was thoughtful for a moment before he spoke. "Brandi, you know I'm not the marrying kind, but we have so much fun together and I love spoiling you and introducing you to things you've never done before," he said sincerely. "Don't run off to him. Keep having fun while you're young."

Rising from his chair, he came over to me. Reaching out his hand, he said, "Come, let me dance with you and make it all better again."

Pulling out my chair, he took my hand in his. "Brandi, Brandi, what am I going to do with you?" he whispered, as we reached the dance floor. He pressed his body close into mine.

What was he to do with her? He didn't want to lose her. She had touched his heart in the short time he had known her. It hurt that she was even considering leaving and marrying that navy guy. If he had to, he would try to be exclusively hers. Later tonight in bed, he would tell her that, and make love to her all night long, until she begged him to stop.

♦♦♦

A slow number, "Some Enchanted Evening," played. As we danced in each other's arms, the lyrics lingered in my brain. I wanted that kind of love, like the Frenchman and the navy woman in the movie, *South Pacific*. A love that was true, passionate, and lasting. Would I have that with Skip, if I did go to him?

I knew that I didn't have a long term future with Duke, but we did have so much fun together and I loved being wined and dined, spoiled like a goddess. Plus, he was so much older and worldly, and I had to admit, he was very passionate in bed. He definitely knew how to rock my boat, I thought, as he held me tighter.

His fiery touch heated my skin. His cologne and his sensuous slow *hula* movements left me melting into him as we became one with the song. I simply let the music float through me, casting its spell of desire and need.

Right then, I knew deep in my gut that I couldn't leave these beautiful, enchanted islands...not yet anyway. Duke was right, I was far too young to run off and get married. I just couldn't take the risk. My heart was here in Hawaii, not five thousand miles away with a navy man, who had chosen to leave me behind.

◆◆◆

Walking back to the beach cottage, hand-in-hand, Duke was whispering soft love notes into my ear. "You're so beautiful. I loved having you by my side tonight. You just make me feel so alive."

I nestled into him and he put his arm around my shoulder. The warm midnight air lifted my spirits as did Duke's words. With darkness all around us and a full moon that lit our way down the street, it was magnificent. Soft blowing palms that echoed in the background, the alluring sound of waves breaking on the nearby beach, our romantic dinner, and dancing under the stars. It was a fairy tale evening.

I felt a calmness settle within me about my decision to stay in Hawaii and keep visiting Duke. Coming to Kauai had opened my eyes to a life that I wanted to continue to experience. I had just stepped into a world of glamour and intrigue.

When I get back to Oahu, I would call Skip and tell him I wasn't leaving Hawaii. Tonight, I was Duke's I conceded, as we entered the cottage and quietly slipped into his bedroom.

◆◆◆

Duke's roommates had long since gone to bed. The gentle wind blew through the open bedroom window creating softness in the air, kissing my bare skin as Duke was doing. His tender kisses touched every part of my body as we stood together in the darkness of his room. Swaying together, naked, and filled with desire.

"I'll be exclusive with you, Brandi, if that keeps you here with me," Duke whispered. "I never thought I'd say that, but I will if that's what you want."

"Oh, Duke," I whispered back, "I'm not going to leave. Hawaii has my heart. You've been very convincing tonight."

"Good," he said, with a smile looking into my eyes. "Visiting me here every two weeks will keep it exciting and new all the time. I promise you that I will treat you like the princess that you are," he said, as he moved me towards the bed.

Never had he made that kind of verbal commitment before to any woman. He wondered if he really could do that and for how long? Sweet Brandi. He loved that she was so gullible. She would never even know if he did sleep around. Living here on Kauai would create that freedom which he needed. It would be the best of both worlds, he admitted to himself as her body once again became his.

It was a night to remember. Sweet loving words of Duke's commitment to me furthered my trust in him. All my previous red flags evaporated in waves of heated, passionate lust long into the Kauaiian night. I felt sure, I persuaded myself while listening to the early morning Kauaiian rains, that all my doubts had been washed away.

Chapter 31

240Z Travel Time

Fresh rains added to the humid morning air. A steamy mist rose in the yard as Duke and I sat side-by-side, on the front porch, enjoying our morning *Kona* coffee. Puffy white clouds, in the brilliant blue sky moved quickly overhead. The warmth of the sunshine uplifting my spent body.

Dressed only in one of Duke's large sized T-shirts, I crossed my legs sitting back with a satisfied smile on my face, content just to sit and admire the scenery...and Duke. He had on a pair of red surfer shorts and flip flops and was bare from the waist up. My God, his body was so muscular and defined, I couldn't help but marvel at it.

"It's my first day off in two weeks, Brandi. I thought we would take the 240Z and drive the island, maybe go see the *Waimea* Canyon. I haven't had an opportunity to explore yet. Are you up to it?" Duke grinned and patted my bare leg.

I took another swallow of my coffee, letting the caffeine help wake me up. "After last night, Duke, I think I could use a little driving and relaxing time," I said, breathing in deeply and relishing the clean fresh ocean air. "God, it's so beautiful here, so quiet compared to Waikiki."

"Without all the traffic and street noise, it is quiet," he agreed. "So, my *love*, let's take a shower together and have a little breakfast, too, before we hit the road," he said, with a seductive hint in his voice.

"A shower together?" I questioned with surprise.

"Yes, a shower together, one for the road," he laughed, and took my hand leading me back into the cottage.

"Where do you get your energy, Duke?" I joked, with a toss of my head.

"It comes from just looking at you!" he teased back.

◆◆◆

Later, we settled into his new midnight blue 240Z eager to spend the day sightseeing. We were content, refreshed, and well fed with a breakfast of minced ham, scrambled eggs, jelly toast, and orange juice. We loaded up the car with a cooler of iced drinks, cold cuts, and our snorkeling gear.

Heading south along Highway 56, we traveled towards *Lihue* Airport and then cut inland on Highway 50. Both our windows were rolled down. I loved letting the warm air blow my ponytail around. I leaned forward and turned on the radio to a local rock and roll station. "Signed, Sealed, Delivered I'm Yours" by Stevie Wonder, played loudly. Its lyrics reminding me of Duke's decision to be exclusively with me for now.

"Waimea Canyon is all the way on the west side of the island," Duke commented. "It's worth the drive; I've heard it's spectacular. It's dubbed the Grand Canyon of the Pacific, ten miles long, one mile wide, and more than 3,500 feet deep. The earth and canyon walls are an incredible reddish color from the erosion of the canyon's red soil," he stated, as we passed the inland town of *Pohi.*

"I've never seen the Grand Canyon except for pictures. This will be so cool to see something similar, Duke!"

"It's not as vast, but it is supposed to be incredible. Lots of lookout points we can stop at and take it all in," he grinned, while adjusting his aviator sunglasses. Turning up the volume on the radio, he said, "Oh, I love this song." He hummed along to "Make it With You" by Bread. "This song is how I felt about you, when I first saw you on the beach in that black bikini, Brandi. I knew I wanted to be with you," he admitted. "I wanted to nail you right then!"

"You did, did you? So you pursued me?" I asked lifting my eyebrows.

"That I did," he grinned. "Just like the song says."

Laughing, I said, "It's one of my favorite songs, too." I started singing while loving this little road trip. The sleek feel and power of the 240Z as Duke let it rip. I was on a racetrack with an older, sophisticated man that never slowed down. Blue skies, sunshine, a new sports car, a gorgeous dark skinned prince by my side, who had admitted that he wanted to be exclusively mine, and seeing the island of Kauai. Did it get any better than this?

◆◆◆

Waimea Canyon was breathtaking to see. I was in awe of its natural beauty and amazing rich colors of earth, canyon walls, and stunning green vegetation surrounding the hills. We were standing at *Pu'u ka Pele* lookout and Duke was rattling off historical facts.

"The canyon was formed by the steady process of erosion, but also by a catastrophic collapse of the volcano that created the island. Kauai is the top of an enormous volcano, which rose from the ocean floor roughly four million years ago. Pretty amazing, isn't it?"

"Yeah, totally amazing," I said, standing next to Duke at the lookout point. The wind kicked up, the sun was blazing down, and stretched out before us was the magnificent *Waimea* Canyon. A creation beyond words. It left me feeling small in its vastness and pure wild beauty.

◆◆◆

Later, we drove to the *Na Pali* Coast State Park. The coastline is a rugged sixteen miles on the northwest side of the island with high cliffs along the shoreline, which rise as much as 4,000 feet above the Pacific Ocean. It's inaccessible to vehicles, but hiking, kayaking, and helicopter rides offer spectacular views.

Duke and I didn't hike, but we did enjoy a picnic lunch at the *Na Pali* lookout overlooking the vegetation of the *Kalalau* Valley, where the state park was formed to protect the lush uninhabited terrain. Once again, I found myself enthralled by its natural, stunning, and mystic beauty. There was something beyond this earthly plain here in the islands. A sense of spiritualism. A God force that spoke to me from the land itself. A history of its people with a connection to Mother Earth.

◆◆◆

On our way back, we stopped at *Poipu* Beach and did a little snorkeling and exploring of the tide pools. It was a perfect day with Duke and another romantic evening coming, too. Dinner at the resort, dancing in the starlight, and a repeat of the previous night back at the beach cottage; all of it would hold me until my next visit in two weeks. I was filled with bliss, but could I afford the airfare again? Would Duke spring for that? So far, he hadn't reimbursed me for anything.

Tomorrow, I was returning to Oahu and back to another reality. I was dreading calling Skip and telling him that I was not coming back east to marry him. It was time to let Skip go, even though he would always have my heart. Would I regret this decision in the months or years to come? Most likely, but I was too young to run off and get married. My heart was not ready to leave beautiful Hawaii behind or the enchantment of Duke's world.

◆◆◆

The following morning on the plane ride back, I couldn't help but wonder if Skip would hang up on me and never talk to me again, when I told him of my change of plans. I didn't want to hurt him, but I knew it would, especially when I let him know that I was seeing someone else. No man wants to hear those words. In truth, I felt that Skip and I both had too many doubts. Neither one of us was really ready to get married. At least not yet, I believed. Skip once told me that he would never get married until he was twenty-nine or thirty. Right now he was only twenty-five.

I glanced out the plane's window admiring the clouds below us and the aqua blue ocean waters. Oahu came into view. The island where I had met and fallen in love with Skip. In my mind, I would always be his *island girl*, no matter what. Would telling Skip I wasn't coming back to him close our island door forever?

Secretly, I hoped that somehow we would continue to correspond and be a part of each other's lives. Was that even possible after my change of heart? Probably not, I thought, with a deep sadness.

◆◆◆

The prop plane landed at the Honolulu International Airport. I was suddenly struck with the heart wrenching goodbye that had taken place here five months ago with Skip. No promises had been made. He said something like *he would get things set up and see how things went.* My heart had closed after that, but the scar was still there. I never wanted to experience that kind of hurt, loss, and disappointment again. My spirit was still tender and bruised, afraid to venture into that kind of all consuming love again. My mother had once told me that *following your heart doesn't always work out.*

Another door had opened now with Duke. It was safer to be his lady while I lived in Hawaii. Wasn't it? At least, I had convinced myself of that after my Kauai visit. Duke was just so charming, so sophisticated. My young heart was protected with a guarded wall around it. Oh God, why did young love have to be so hard and complicated?

Chapter 32

Navy Blues

I felt like I was struggling in the middle of a riptide being pulled from two different directions. One part of me wanted to rush off to Skip and spend the rest of my life with him, but the other part wanted to stay in Hawaii and be spoiled by Duke. I couldn't believe that I was going to tell Skip that I wasn't coming back east to marry him. He still had my heart and probably always would. In truth, I wasn't sure I had complete trust and faith in us as a couple. What if I ended up being an anchor that Skip would tire of? I just couldn't take that risk based on how our Hawaiian time together had been so off and on.

Picking up the phone, I paused before dialing his number. Taking a deep breath, I glanced around our apartment front room. The white curtains blew lazily from the open lanai door and the warm breeze felt suddenly feverish against my skin. No one was home, my roommates both at work. My stomach churned. My mouth dry as sand.

There was going to be nothing pleasant about this phone call, but there was no escaping that. My pulse raced. I ached with dread. My first year here in Hawaii, I had loved Skip with all my heart and soul. The only man I had ever been in love with. How could I do this?

Stalling, I noted how much I loved this apartment. Tropical print cushions on the rattan sofa and chairs. Our spectacular view of the *Ko'olau* (windward) mountain range. The foothills were packed with residential neighborhoods alive with twinkling white lights at night. Off to the leeward side were the high-rise hotels of Waikiki. All of it had charmed me when I had first moved here from Seattle a year ago. I had fallen in love with Hawaii. The constant sunshine, the blue skies, the aqua ocean, all of it touched my soul and adventurous spirit. What I did know for sure was that I wasn't ready to leave it all behind. I was making the right decision, wasn't I?

Picking up the phone, I started to dial Skip's long distance number. It was around 2 p.m. Hawaiian time, so back east it would be around 7 p.m. Dear God, this was going to be so hard. Momentarily chickening out, I put the phone back on the cradle. I stepped away and just stared blankly at the phone.

Stalling again, I was trying to build up my confidence. Trying to muster the courage to tell him of my change of heart. Suddenly, the phone rang. I jumped nervously at the unexpected sound. Picking it up, I answered, "Aloha."

"Aloha, baby, it's me, Skip."

I swallowed hard. "Skip, I was just about to call you," I said, tentatively without much enthusiasm.

"Really? That's great. Have you got your airlines reservation booked yet?"

"Skip, I'm...I'm not coming back there. I've...I've been seeing someone else this past month. God, I'm so sorry," I said, taking a deep breath and wanting to crawl into the woodwork like a cockroach and disappear. I felt like such an awful person.

"What? Jesus, Brandi, I don't know what to say."

"I'm so sorry, Skip. I...I just have too many doubts. I'm not ready to leave Hawaii yet." A prolonged silence hung in the air. Dead air that passed between us. Suffocating. I could hear him inhale and exhale deeply. I pictured him standing there stunned at my confession.

"God, Brandi, I guess there isn't much more to say then, except that you're the best thing that ever happened to me. I blew it. I waited too long. I should have known that a girl like you wouldn't be alone for long. I'm sorry, too. I should never have left you behind like I did," he confessed, with sadness and pain in his voice.

Tears sprang from my eyes. "I'm sorry, too, Skip," I mumbled while crying. "I'm just not ready to leave Hawaii or commit to getting married to anyone right now. You will always have my heart, no matter what," I said with conviction. More silence.

"Can I still write you?"

"Yes, of course. I'd love that. I'm so sorry, Skip," I said again, with deep grief in my heart. "Please forgive me?" I begged.

"There's nothing to forgive, Brandi. It's my fault. Be good and take care of yourself," he said with sorrow. "You will always be my *island girl.*"

The phone went silent. My heart felt empty and drained. I sank to my knees. Unrestrained tears ran down my face. Oh God, I had hurt him so much. Would he ever forgive me or write me again? Or would he just move on and forget all about me? Sadness, shame, guilt, and a deep sense of loss engulfed me as I hung up the phone, knowing that my life would never be the same. This was one of those crossroad decisions in my young life that would probably haunt me for a lifetime. I doubted that any man would ever steal my heart away again like Skip had done, and now...I had to learn to live with that.

◆◆◆

Well, this just sucks! Skip hung up the phone in total disbelief. His heart swallowed up with emotions he couldn't even name. Hurt, rage, madness, grief, and a deep sense of loss streamed into his thoughts.

"God damn it!" Brandi had said yes she would marry him and then she'd changed her mind in less than a week! He just couldn't believe it! He didn't know who he was most mad at...her or himself. "Jesus, I should have never left her alone in Hawaii." He grabbed his coat and car keys, heading out the door to the nearest bar.

Riddled with questions and seething at his stupidity, Skip opened the car door and sank into the driver's seat. Rain belted the windows. The wind howled like a banshee. He banged his hand against the steering wheel. "Shit!" As mad and as shocked as he was, he knew in his heart that he wouldn't give up on Brandi, at least not yet. He lit up a cigarette and stared blankly out the clouded car window. Let her have some fun while she still lived in Hawaii, he thought. God knows, he'd had his share of women since he'd enlisted in the navy five years ago. She'd said she was seeing someone, but she didn't say she was in love with him, so he'd keep writing to her.

He wondered if somehow Brandi had found out about his reconnecting with his high school girlfriend, Linda. Sleeping with her and then calling it quits last month. If so, he couldn't blame Brandi for her change of mind. Nothing was confidential in the navy, everyone knew your business. It was a small world, even though he was five thousand miles away. There was still hope, he rationalized, as he puffed on his smoke determined to win her back. God, he was so in love with her. She was everything to him. Tears stung his eyes; he gave into the moment and cried for the first time in his adult life, not knowing if he could muster the strength or will to move.

Chapter 33

Unexpected Waves

Three weeks had passed since my gut-wrenching conversation with Skip. I didn't expect a letter and there wasn't one. I had heard from his navy buddy, Scottie, that he was partying hard. He would probably be doing another ninety day patrol across the Atlantic in a couple of months. I still thought about him all the time because I was still in love with him, but our timing had been all wrong.

After that phone conversation, I kept myself busy taking on extra hours at work. Without Duke working at the Hilton Hawaiian Village, I had few distractions. The additional income would help pay back my exhausted bank account for that expensive cocktail dress, shoes, and airfare. Duke must have forgotten about that since he never offered to reimburse me.

My roommates, Donna and Sherry, were invited to come to Kauai with me this weekend. Duke had offered to put them up at the Coco Palms and write off their rooms on his expense account. With a glass of red wine in our hands, the three of us stood together in the kitchen toasting our good fortune.

"Here's to Kauai," I said with enthusiasm.

"Yeah, here's to Kauai," Sherry beamed. "This is so sweet of Duke to offer us a free hotel room! What a guy! I'm so excited. I've never been to Kauai before Brandi," she stated, while taking a swallow of her wine.

"You're both going to love it! The Coco Palms Resort is just the coolest place. Oh, and the *Wailua* Beach right there is magnificent. Dinner under the stars and the torch lighting ceremony with the *huka* dancers is like so cool! Those local Polynesian guys, wearing only a loincloth during the presentation, they will set your hormones on fire!"

"Here's to the local boys!" Sherry cheered.

"Cheers!" Sherry and I said together.

Donna smiled weakly with a blank expression. "Let's get packed," she said dully, making her way down the hallway into her bedroom.

I glanced at Sherry. "I thought Donna would be excited."

"She's been acting very strange this last month," Sherry said. "Kind of subdued like she's preoccupied or something. You've been working a lot of hours so you haven't seen her much. I heard her throwing up yesterday morning," Sherry shared. "She just hasn't been her usual happy self lately."

"Hmm...maybe she ate something that didn't agree with her."

"No, I think it's more than that," Sherry said with puzzlement. We both put our glasses of wine on the counter and headed down the hallway.

"I'm not taking much, just two sundresses, a couple of T-shirts, cutoffs, and my bikini," Donna yelled from her room.

"Yeah, keep it light," I hollered back. "You won't need much."

"Do we need to rent a car?" Sherry asked, as she stood behind me in our bedroom.

"Yeah, Duke's sports car only seats two," I replied, picking out a beach cover-up, a pair of surfer shorts, a tank top, and two halter top dresses. "We can rent a car at the airport; it won't cost much with the three of us pitching in. Duke is working, so he'll meet us tonight at dinner."

"Okay, by the way again, it's so nice of Duke to do this," Sherry countered. "He sure knows how to spoil you, Brandi," she said, with envy in her voice. "I'm not sure about some of his stories, but I'll take a free hotel in Kauai any day."

"Yeah, me too," Donna cried out. "I really need some beach time to sort some things out."

"Yeah, like what kind of things?" I questioned. "I thought you were pretty content with your life, especially now that you broke up with your boyfriend, Tom."

Donna came out of her room and stood by the entrance of our bedroom. "Well, for starters, I am glad I broke it off with Tom. He just has no direction, no ambition at all. I think that's why he enlisted in the navy. He likes being on that aircraft carrier and being told what to do. The military life isn't for me. Besides, I'm just not that crazy about him anymore. I'm glad he's out to sea for six months and that their ship is going to San Diego on return, instead of back here at Pearl," she said with relief.

"You are?" I questioned, standing close to her.

"Yeah, I am. But there is one big problem still," she said tightly.

"Oh, what's that?" I asked with concern.

Donna stood facing me. Her eyes searching mine...for what? Reassurance? Her shoulders slumped. She looked away for a moment. When she looked at me again her eyes were filled with tears and what I thought was fear.

"I'm...I'm over a month and a half late," she said softly. "I've never been late before. I screwed up on my birth control pills last month right before breaking up with Tom." She took a deep breath and pursed her lips. "I'm pregnant!" she cried, with a tone of desperation."

"Oh, Donna, are you sure?" I questioned with shock.

"Yes, I've been having some morning sickness and I just feel so tired. God, I'm so scared," she gasped.

"It'll be okay!" I tried to reassure her. "The three of us will come up with a plan, right, Sherry?"

Sherry came forward hugging Donna. "Right! We'll help you, no matter what!"

"Yeah, well, it's such a disgrace to be unmarried and pregnant. I don't know what to do," she said doubtfully, with tears streaming down her face.

"Donna, you are a strong, confident, accomplished woman. You make an incredible income. Together we'll work it out!" I insisted. "You're not the first unwed woman who has had to face this. There are choices, but it won't be easy. Whatever you decide, just know that we are here for you!"

"Oh God!" Donna yelled in desperation. "I won't have an abortion and I won't marry Tom just to save face," she replied with conviction. "I don't believe that's always the best decision."

"Neither do I, Donna," I said, feeling despondent and shaken for her. "Will you tell Tom?"

"No! It would never work with him. I don't want him to know. Oh God, I'm old enough to know better at twenty-nine," she wailed. "I can't believe I could have been so stupid to have missed two days of my birth control pills!"

"Okay, okay, calm down, Donna," Sherry said, with an arm around her shoulder.

"Yeah, take a deep breath. Steady yourself for a minute," I chimed in. "We'll work this out, but first we have to finish packing and get to the airport. We'll find a solution this weekend on Kauai. That's our goal, okay?"

"Okay," Donna nodded with a brief look of relief. "You two are the best, thanks for being willing to help me," she sniffled.

"We're here for you, Donna," I said. "You don't have to go through this by yourself. Later, I'll tell you my mother's story about her best girlfriend, who was unmarried and pregnant during World War II and how they handled it."

"It happened to your mother's girlfriend?" Donna's eyes widened with surprise.

"Yeah, way back in 1942. They stuck together and so will we. It's not the end of the world, although it may feel like it right now. We'll get you through this," I promised, as the three of us hugged and Donna cried in our arms.

◆◆◆

So far, this month of March was blowing in like a grand tsunami, throwing high pitched waves at me from every angle. Our girl time in Kauai now had some added complications to address. In my heart, I knew whatever Donna decided to do, the three of us were there for each other. No judgments, just sincere friendship, love, and support.

On the drive to the airport, I couldn't help but wonder what Donna's mom and dad would say. Would they disown her like my mom's girlfriend's mother had done? Donna's parents were divorced, I remembered. She had a tight, close relationship with her dad, but not her mom.

Suddenly, my problems with Skip and Duke paled next to what Donna was facing. Maybe this was another reason why I was meant to stay and live here in Hawaii. I would fight for Donna and be that strong shoulder to lean on, just like my mom had done for her best girlfriend some thirty years ago.

Chapter 34

Kauai Time

An hour later, we girls took the bus into Waikiki and then the shuttle to the airport. Our Friday afternoon flight would get us to Kauai around 4 p.m. The shuttle was packed. We were not sitting together on the bus or the flight over to Kauai. However, we had made an agreement to discuss Donna's situation over dinner at the Coco Palms.

Happy hour at six and dinner at seven was what Duke had informed us prior to our arrival. "I'll meet you both in the lobby about 5:45," I said. "We can get an outside table for happy hour and enjoy a mai tai or two. Duke will meet us there, but he's managing a banquet tonight. He'll be popping in and out throughout the evening," I explained, as Donna and Sherry dropped me off at the beach cottage. "You two go check into the resort and get unpacked. Stroll around and check it out. I'll see you in an hour."

"Okay," Sherry smiled. "It sure is quiet here and pretty, too," she said, with a goodbye wave and drove the rental car out of the driveway. I headed inside to take a quick shower, wash my hair, and put on fresh makeup. Three weeks without seeing Duke. I was excited to be with him again; in fact, I was buzzing with anticipation. He had called me a couple of times telling me how much he missed me and couldn't wait to have me in his arms again.

Stepping into the cottage, I noticed a dozen long stem red roses in a vase sitting on the coffee table. Were these from Duke? I bent down to smell their perfumed fragrance and picked up the card placed within them. It read:

Brandi, you are the rose of my heart.

Yours, Duke.

"Oh wow!" I gasped. He sure does know how to charm me. Touched with delight, and feeling like one of those beautiful roses, I made my way down the hallway and into his bedroom. Pausing in the doorway, I stood there captivated. Stirring memories of our Kauai romance roused my senses. Expectation for our time in that queen size bed tonight left me lightheaded. His dark skin. That muscled body. That million dollar smile. His charming convincing ways. What a turn-on he was. I couldn't wait to be with him later this evening, I mused, as my pulse quickened.

Once unpacked, I took a quick shower, washed and dried my hair, and redid my makeup. Slipping on my red cotton halter dress and dressy silver flip flops, I twirled in front of the full length mirror. Perfect. Duke loved this little number on me. He'd be putty in my hands tonight, but then I would be putty in his hands, too.

On my way out, I stopped to smell the bouquet of roses again and reflected on Duke's thoughtfulness and romanticism. I was feeling spoiled already.

The sunset was gloriously warm and the palm trees swayed effortlessly in the gentle breeze. I picked a plumeria off one of the trees and placed it behind my right ear before heading down the street to the resort. Donna and Sherry were waiting for me in the open-air lobby.

"This place is incredible," Sherry marveled. "Our room looks right out onto the grotto garden. It's just beautiful," she beamed.

"Yeah, and it's so peaceful here," Donna chimed in. "Just what I needed," she said, placing her arm around my shoulder.

"Oh good, and by the way, you both look very pretty in your sundresses," I commented.

"Yeah, a real change from my usual around-the-house muumuu," Sherry chuckled.

"I'll say, but you look good. Come on, let's go to the Catamaran Bar and have a mai tai," I grinned. "Maybe before Duke joins us, we can talk about what you are going to do, Donna, about your pregnancy.

"Yeah, let's do that," Donna sighed loudly. "I need to talk things out before coming to a final decision. Just being with you two here on Kauai is comforting and will help me to put things into perspective."

With that, we left the lobby and headed to the outside Catamaran Bar. It was that time of evening when tourists packed the bar for "buy one get one free" mai tais. We had just sat down at the table when Duke strolled in. "Hey ladies, welcome to my island home," he said, with a twinkle in his dark brown eyes and a hundred-watt smile. "You look gorgeous, Brandi." He bent forward and gently brushed my lips. "God, I've missed you."

I smiled up at him. "I've missed you, too. Thank you for the beautiful roses, Duke. You spoil me way too much," I sang.

"You got roses?" Sherry questioned, as our mai tais arrived topped with a pineapple wedge, a cherry, and a purple and white orchid flower.

"I did. A dozen of them from this romantic man." I beamed at everyone and reached for Duke's hand and gently squeezed it.

"Do you have a brother, Duke?" Sherry asked with a chuckle.

"No, sorry I don't, but I intend to spoil all three of you ladies while you're here. Order whatever you'd like for drinks and dinner. My staff knows to put it on my expense account," he boasted. "I'll try to join you later, but right now I've got a banquet to manage, so enjoy yourselves," he said leaving us.

My eyes stayed glued to his backside as he sauntered away. Those perfect fitting pants with his tight, sexy *okole* left me panting. Wow! He could be a male *huka* dancer. Tonight though, he was my *huka* man, every delicious part of him. And I intended to dance the night away in his arms to lovely Hawaiian music, and then later make our own music in his Kauai beach cottage bedroom.

◆◆◆

"Don't you just love a good mai tai?" Sherry asked, sipping hers and bringing me back to the present moment. "These are just perfect, not too sweet with a hefty dark rum floater. Yum, yum," she said and the three of us laughed in agreement.

The sun was casting shadows across the grotto garden area where colorful tropical flowers lined the walkways. A balmy breeze kissed the air with a gentle softness, which helped create a warm bond among us girls as did the alcohol infused mai tais.

Donna leaned forward, lit up a cigarette, and inhaled like it was her last breath. Exhaling slowly, she stared up into the darkening sky. "I never thought I would find myself in this situation," she confessed.

"Shit happens," Sherry stated. "So Donna, what are you going to do?"

"Yeah, I know you've been thinking about that," I interjected, feeling thankful that I wasn't facing this kind of crisis. Thank God for birth control pills, I thought, but nothing was one hundred percent foolproof. Donna had missed two days of her pills and look what happened.

"I haven't thought of anything else since I found out!" Donna said with turmoil.

"Well, you could have the baby and adopt it out. That's what my mom's friend did," I said quietly, as we huddled closer together in confidence.

"Yeah, I could," Donna replied. "However, I know I could never give this baby up in the end. It would just kill me. I'm going to call my dad when we get back to our apartment. He's my rock. We're very close. He won't disown me. At twenty-nine years old, I may never get married or have another chance to have a child. And I think my dad would love to have his first grandchild, even if I'm not married." She paused, flicked her smoke in the ashtray and took another drink of her mai tai. "Are you both shocked that I want to keep this baby?"

I placed my hand on hers. "God no, not at all, Donna." I replied sincerely. "You have a college degree. You make a great income. You're a strong willful woman. If anyone can be a single mom, it's you. You're pioneering for all of the girls of our generation."

"Yeah, well, be ready to be shunned and whispered about," Sherry said. "You have guts, Donna, I'll say that much. I'd go to an unwed mothers' home, hide there, and then adopt the baby out, but that's just me. My family would disown me and be so ashamed. They wouldn't want anyone to know and I think that is so sad."

"It is sad," I agreed. "We could put a wedding band on your left hand and people that don't know you won't even question it. There's a jewelry store here on the premises."

"That's a really good idea," Donna agreed. "The people I work with will know though, but frankly I don't give a damn! By the way, I went to the library last week and did a little research. Get this, last year in 1970 there were over 175,000 babies from unwed mothers adopted out in the U.S. alone! And because their conformist parents were horrified of the reflection it put on them, most girls were sent off to unwed mothers' homes."

"That's horrible," I wailed.

"Yeah, it is," Donna confirmed. "Daughters that get pregnant, you know, are considered promiscuous or low-class," she said, shaking her head. "I mean to tell you, I am neither promiscuous nor low-class! I made a dumb mistake, but I won't be bullied into doing what society thinks is the right thing to do. I take responsibility for that and I do have a choice," she jested.

"Yes, you do, and I love and respect you for it, Donna," I added. "You're the director of recreation there at the Y, so bully for them and society if they have a problem with it."

"Yeah, maybe someday it won't be such a shameful thing to have a baby out of wedlock," Sherry said.

"That'll be the day!" I cried. "It's a pity that our culture has such unforgiving rules, where all the blame is put on the woman, but encouraging the sexual adventures of men is okay," I said. "Heck, most of us had very little sex education, if any. I read somewhere that thousands of girls get pregnant the first time they have sex, mostly because they are so naive about conception." I shook my head in disbelief. "Geez, why is it always the woman who has to be the one to practice birth control most of the time? I sure wish I didn't have to take birth control pills," I said adamantly, "but I'm glad they're available for us today. Still...doctors chastise you if they know you are single when giving out birth control prescriptions."

"Well, it goes against my Catholic religion to practice birth control," Sherry stated, while flicking an ash from her smoke into the ashtray. "But then, I don't even have a boyfriend these days, so I don't know why I take them. I guess, just in case I do have sex again someday. Like that's going to happen to this chubby lady," she sighed deeply, and then waved to our waiter ordering another round of mai tais.

"Oh Sherry, you'll find someone nice, I'm sure of it. Why does it have to be so shameful to bring a new life into this world if you're unwed?" We all stared at each other. We reached for each other's hands. We held on as if it were our lifeline. Tears filled our eyes as understanding and compassion dawned. We were in this together, no matter what.

Still...I couldn't help but think about that revelation of unwed mothers. Imagine 175,000 babies adopted out last year alone. It was hard to fathom and so sad, I thought, for all of those young unwed girls. Its toll would undoubtedly last a lifetime for all of them, trying to forgive themselves or make peace, never knowing their babies. It filled my heart with grief and sadness just thinking of it.

◆◆◆

Soft ukulele music strummed in the background as we listened in silence. Adjacent to our table was a tiny makeshift stage where three local boys sang in unison. A keyboardist, a drummer, and a ukulele player soothed our troubled minds with their mellow voices and the island's magical, hypnotic lure. Everything would be all right, wouldn't it?

Chapter 35

Kauai Secrets

With Donna's decision to keep her baby, we girls felt we had cemented a sisterly bond. Nothing would keep us from sticking together through this. Sherry and I had even agreed to help Donna financially, if needed. How lucky I was to have such caring, loving roommates.

Dinner under the stars was perfect, just what we girls needed. Caesar salads followed by coconut shrimp, fried rice, and stir-fry mixed vegetables. Duke joined us for dessert and after dinner drinks. "I hope you ladies enjoyed your dinner and the music?" he asked.

"Oh yes, thanks, Duke, it's been so cool," Sherry replied. "The seafood was out of this world," she gushed. "I feel so spoiled by you. Thank you for covering it all."

"It has been my pleasure, ladies," he grinned, while indulging in an after dinner drink of Courvoisier. "Did you like the torch lighting ceremony?"

"Oh God, it was incredible," Donna cried. "I loved the male *huka* dancers, the drum music, and the *tiki* torches being lit. It was really something to watch!"

"It is at that," Duke agreed. "The Coco Palms really does it right. I'm glad you enjoyed it. If you will excuse us please, I'd like to dance with my beautiful Brandi before the night ends."

"Of course, Duke," Sherry said. "We're tired anyway and ready to hit the hay, so have fun you two. We'll see you for breakfast, Brandi, around 8 a.m. if that's okay?"

"That's perfect. I'll meet you here at the outdoor cafe," I said as they both left.

"They're great roommates, Brandi, and good friends. I'm glad they could come here with you."

"It was much needed time together," I responded, thinking of Donna and her decision to keep her baby. In my eyes, she was so brave, I contemplated, while looking up at the dark sky filled with a billion bright stars.

Sweet, soft, aloha music played in the background. The musicians were strumming their songs of romance and desire making me feel melancholy. My thoughts drifted back to Skip. Oh Skip, I was still in love with him, even though I turned down his marriage proposal. As if sensing my distance, Duke took my hand. "Shall we dance, *love?*"

"Yes, let's dance," I answered, feeling a little sad and my thoughts shifted once again back to the present moment and to Duke.

He led me to the dance floor. White lights were strung around the entire outside dining area. So romantic. Duke pressed his body close against mine. The scent of his after shave lotion was earthy and intoxicating. Alone on the dance floor, we moved slowly together in our own private dance. Duke's sensual *hula* movements stirring every fiber in my body making me forget the past and...momentarily Skip. He sure knew how to set my hormones on fire. Later, we walked back to his beach cottage. Back to where we could make our own sweet Hawaiian music together, during the rest of this Kauaiian night.

The next morning it was another beautiful sunny day with the wind and surf up. Strolling down the street past the resort, I took a detour to the beach. Barefoot, I walked leisurely along the shoreline wading in and out of the water. I had a half an hour before meeting Donna and Sherry for breakfast at eight.

The morning sunshine washed my face with warmth while the breeze blew my ponytail around. Time slipped by as I became lost in reflection. Somehow, everything fell into place this morning. Donna's situation having been decided last night lifted my spirits. The beauty of the sparkling aqua water and the sun shining helped to block my scattered thoughts. I'd made my decision to continue to live here in Hawaii, I told myself as this morning slipped away like the swell of a wave.

Turning, I headed to meet the girls for breakfast and later spend the day on the beach or by the pool. One last evening of dining with the girls, dancing under the stars with Duke, sweet romance, and then heading back to Oahu tomorrow morning.

Our last evening was just as romantic and fun as the first night had been, and this morning we were headed home.

Donna and Sherry had their suitcases in hand as they waited in the lobby of the resort. "This was such a cool little trip coming over here and Duke paying for everything. Too bad we have to leave this morning," Sherry jabbered.

"It sure was! And I feel good about my decision to have this baby and keeping it," Donna smiled. "Now I just need to call my dad tonight. He'll probably want me to move back home with him."

"Would you do that?" Sherry asked.

"I don't know. It would make it easier. We'll see," Donna said glancing around. "Hey, isn't that Duke over there?" She pointed to a partially screened darkened alcove behind a hallway.

"Yeah, who's the pretty blond he's got his arms around?" Sherry questioned.

"I don't know, but she looks like she's been crying. I can't really tell with Duke's back facing me," Donna stated.

"What's he doing?" Sherry whispered, as they watched Duke lean in and kiss the blond gently on the lips. His hand rose as he touched her face before he strolled away.

"Well, that was an intimate kiss and touch, if I ever saw one," Sherry murmured.

"Do you think he's seeing her as well as Brandi?" Donna jeered.

"Sure looks like something is going on. Do we tell Brandi what we just saw?" Sherry asked.

"We have to!" Donna waved her hand. "You know, Duke is a lot of fun and very generous, but I've never really trusted him. I think he's a player with a lot of secrets."

Sherry sighed, "Yeah, I get that feeling, too. God, this will set Brandi on fire. She's been too trusting with Duke, but he does spoil her like a queen."

"It's a good cover, isn't it? Living here on Kauai and Brandi having no idea what goes on when she's gone." Donna shook her head. "Men!" she cried, as Brandi came into view and their voices hushed in an awkward silence.

The blond stepped up behind the registration check-in desk and proceeded to answer a phone call.

"Hey Brandi, you all ready?" Donna asked.

"Yep, all packed. Duke and I said our goodbyes this morning. Where's the car parked?"

"Oh, it's out in the front lot," Sherry answered. "But we need to tell you something before we leave," Sherry frowned.

"What's wrong?" I asked, noticing Sherry's grim expression.

"Well, we saw Duke moments ago with that blond girl at the registration desk," Sherry stated.

"Oh, that's Mindy, one of his roommates," I said, glancing over at her with a quick wave. She smiled, but it seemed forced for some reason like she was upset.

"Yeah, well, Duke was in the back corner with her. His hands were wrapped around her waist and he kissed her," Donna said. "On the lips! I hate to be the bearer of bad news, but I think there might be something going on between the two of them. They looked pretty cozy with each other."

I stared at my roommates. I didn't doubt what they saw. They wouldn't make something up like this. I trusted them more than I trusted Duke. His words of promises to be exclusively mine crashed into my trusting self. Was he just telling me what I wanted to hear when I was with him? Was there something going on with Mindy, too? How would I know when I didn't live here? Had I been played?

"Brandi, go over there and ask her what's going on," Donna demanded. "Be a strong woman."

I shook my head. "No!"

"Go or I will!" Donna cried.

"Okay, okay." I said, as disbelief soared through me. "You two stay here. I'll be right back." I marched over to Mindy. I sucked in a deep brave breath. Mindy lowered her gaze and wouldn't look at me.

"Mindy, my girlfriends saw Duke kiss you moments ago back in the corner. Are...are you seeing Duke? And don't lie to me. Just tell me the truth," I pleaded, hoping it wasn't what my roommates thought.

She looked up at me and exhaled deeply. Tears shown in her eyes. "We...we have a thing going on. But I...I disappear when you visit. I...I have feelings for him, too, but I have to share him with you!" she jeered.

"What!" I wailed.

"I'm sorry," she said. "I wish he felt about me the way he feels about you!" she blurted out with jealous eyes. "It's just sex for him, but not for me. I'm in love with him."

"Well, that makes me feel a whole lot better." I huffed while turning and walking away, hurt beyond belief. What was it he had promised? *That he would be exclusively mine.*

Well...Duke could kiss my sweet *okole* goodbye.

.... Chapter 36 ....

Back on Oahu

It was good to be home at our apartment this evening. Donna called her dad shortly after we got in from our Kauai trip. The three of us sat around in the front room discussing her phone call.

"Are you going to move back to your dad's house like he asked?" I questioned, while sprawled out on the sofa drinking an iced tea and munching on freshly popped popcorn, which permeated the front room with that yummy enticing smell.

Sherry was sitting on the floor propped up with a couple of pillows behind her back. Donna sat Indian style in one of the rattan chairs. Both were enjoying a smoke and iced teas as well. Our radio was on and the song, "People Got to Be Free" by the Rascals played. Its lyrics seemed to speak to me of a need to be free...of Duke.

"Well, I don't know if I will move back to my dad's place. It's sweet of him to offer and I am touched that he is so supportive of my decision to keep the baby," Donna said, reaching for a handful of popcorn.

"Was he surprised when you told him?" Sherry asked.

"Oh yeah, shell-shocked is more like it. We talked it out and he loves me, no matter what. God, I'm lucky to have such an understanding father, unlike my mother who will be appalled when I tell her," Donna admitted. "My dad has always wanted to be a grandpa, but probably not this way," she laughed.

"A dad like that, wow!" I reinforced. "You're very lucky, my friend. My dad would come unglued. My mom would be there for me, but it would cause a lot of family problems. So you will stay here in Hawaii?"

"Well, I'll work another couple of months. I'll see how things go before committing to moving back to California," she said, munching on popcorn. "Speaking of decisions, Brandi, what have you decided to do about the Duke thing?"

Pursing my lips, I closed my eyes briefly, took a deep breath, and exhaled loudly. "I'm sure I'll hear from him when he discovers that I know he's also sleeping with Mindy. I won't be seeing him again. I'm done with Duke. He took advantage of the situation and of me. It sucks, but I'm not in love with him. I don't trust him," I said with conviction. "I guess it's good that he lives on Kauai and not here on Oahu," I admitted, stuffing my mouth full of popcorn and savoring the buttery taste by licking my fingers.

"It makes me so mad that Duke cheated on me. I loved being spoiled by him and all the wining and dining. Oh, and his irresistible charm. He was fun, but I'm writing men off for a while," I said, with conviction and took a sip of my iced tea.

"Oh, that'll be the day," Sherry teased. "You draw them in like the island trade winds," she laughed, while blowing smoke into the air. "I'll bet you'll have another guy knocking on your door within a month."

"Will not!" I yelled. "I'm serious."

Sherry got up and opened the front door. "I'm going to get the mail," she said, with a shake of her blond head of hair and left.

"Seriously, Sherry, I'm taking a break. I'll pick up more work hours and get back into the pool again," I hollered after her.

Donna blew a smoke ring toward the ceiling and leaned comfortably back in the chair, stretching. "Taking a man break would be really good for you. Besides, Brandi, I think you're still stuck on Skip."

"Yeah, you're right. It's weird, I still think about him and miss him all the time, even when I was with Duke."

"I know you do. Here's my advice. Duke spoiled you and was very charming, but your heart still belongs to Skip, right?"

"Yeah, it does, but I blew it when I changed my mind on his marriage proposal three weeks ago. I don't think I'll ever hear from him again," I said with deep regret. "There's nothing I can do anymore, but try to move on."

"Don't bank on that. You never know what might happen. Skip did say he was going to keep in touch, didn't he?" Donna asked, as she crushed out her smoke in the ashtray.

"Yeah, but I'm not counting on anything. He's probably trying to forget me and I don't blame him, but damn, I miss him so much. I sure made a mess of things. Why didn't I listen to my heart, Donna? If Skip had been here, instead of five thousand miles away when he proposed, it would have been different. I would have married him," I confessed.

Sherry meandered back into the apartment carrying a few envelopes in her hand. "Mostly junk mail," she claimed, "except for this letter...from Skip," she said, handing it to me with a big grin.

"Oh my God, really?" I reached out taking the letter as if it were gold plated. My heart pounding like turbulent surf. A feeling of hope raced through me like a warm blanket and then...a feeling of fear and trepidation. I had hurt Skip deeply. Was this his way of truly saying goodbye forever? Slowly, I opened the letter.

Dear Brandi,   *March 10th*

I miss you, my beautiful island girl! You are in my thoughts constantly. Even though I have been deeply saddened that you decided not to marry me, I have decided not to give up on you. In my heart, I believe we are destined to be together again. I have never loved a lady like I love you. I've never been in love like this...ever! Your spirit shines and you make me feel alive and complete. To me you are the most beautiful woman I have ever been with. You have my heart! I should never have left you alone in Hawaii. I was scared of how much in love with you I was. And so, I ran away putting distance between us. That's why I don't blame you for changing your mind about marrying me, but I'm hopeful that the Hawaiian gods are still in our favor. And that, your heart still feels as mine does. There are so many things I need to tell you, to say in person that I never did, if I get that chance?

Love Always,

Skip

P.S. I am applying for officer training school in Virginia Beach. If I get in, I will have some R &R time before it begins. I intend to return to Hawaii and win you back, if you'll have me? I believe anything is possible as long as you are with me. Until then, stay the sweet beautiful island girl that I love.

♦♦♦

Tears sprang from my eyes as I finished reading Skip's letter. My heart's rapid heartbeats lifted me in a suspended feeling of disbelief. Hope buoyed me. I had been such a fool falling for Duke's charming, but deceptive ways. Nothing could replace what my heart truly felt for Skip. It was so simple. I was in love with Skip and no one else.

Out of breath, I stood up and told my roommates what Skip had written. It was time to pour my heart out to Skip. To say all the things I was never bold enough to say. I desperately wanted a second chance to be with him once again.

"If you both will excuse me, I'm going to make a long distance phone call to Skip," I said, with a surge of adrenalin. Picking up the phone, I headed to the privacy of my bedroom.

Chapter 37

Aloha my *Kumu* (Sweetheart)

With my heart in my hand, I dialed Skip's phone number. It rang three times before I heard his sweet Midwestern drawl say, "Hello."

"Aloha," I said softly. A sense of relief swept through me hearing his voice. A warm soft afternoon breeze floated across my bedroom from the open lanai door. The palm tree fronds outside danced lazily in the wind. I held my breath waiting. Suspended in time.

"Brandi?"

"Yeah, it's me, Skip."

"God, it's...it's good to hear your sweet voice. Did you get my letter?" he asked anxiously.

"I did. You sound tired, Skip, are you okay?"

"I am now! It's been rough without you in my life."

"Oh, Skip, can you ever forgive me? I've been such a stupid fool. I should have jumped on the first plane to be with you when you asked me to marry you. There's no one that compares to you. I thought I could replace you with someone else, but there's such a huge difference between sleeping with someone and sleeping with someone you're in love with. And I'm still in love with you!" I blurted out, while picturing him with those deep blue eyes, sandy blond hair, handsome face, and that boyish grin.

"Honey, you just made me the happiest man alive," he said with enthusiasm. "I don't want to go through my life without you."

"You've always had my heart, Skip," I confessed.

"And you've always had my heart, too. I'm lost without you, girl. Are you willing to give me a second chance to do right by you?"

Elation swam through me as swift as a strong current. "Yes, are you willing to give me a second chance, too?"

"There isn't anything in the world that I want more right now," he said with a big sigh. "Listen, I got accepted to officer training school in Virginia Beach. It will be a couple of months before I can return to Hawaii on some much needed R & R and be with you," he drawled.

"I'll wait, Skip!" I cried, feeling like my heart would burst with excitement.

"I don't want to leave Hawaii without you this time, Brandi. I don't want to screw it up again with you...ever!"

"Oh Skip, I've messed things up so much, too. I got all caught up with this older man that wined and dined me. It was a world that I had never been introduced to before. It was exciting and fun, but it wasn't real love like it is with you!" I confessed.

"Well, honey, I've done my share of messin' things up, too," he laughed. "I've been with a handful of women since you, including Linda from high school, but no one measures up. As far as I'm concerned, there's nothing to forgive. Can we start over?"

"Yes," I answered quickly.

"Well, hold tight then. I'll be heading your way as soon as I can."

"I'll be true to you, Skip. I swear."

"And I'll be true to you, too. Write me as often as you can until I can get there, okay?" he insisted. "It's whatever's written in our hearts darlin' that really matters. Let's promise to always speak from our hearts from now on, okay?"

"Okay, and you are so right. It's what's in our hearts that matters the most," I said, with sunshine in my voice and feeling drugged with happiness. "Well, Skip, I better get off the phone; this call will be costing me a lot. Write to me everyday if you want!"

"You got it, girl. I'll be dreaming of you each night until I have you in my arms once again. God, I love you so much. Bye, my beautiful *island girl.*"

"I love you, too! Bye, Skip," I sang out, as I hung up the phone smiling from the inside out.

Truly, there were some Hawaiian gods watching over me, I thought, feeling the spirit of aloha, love, and hope surfing through my soul.

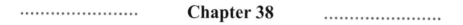

Chapter 38

Calm Seas

Over the next two months, I kept myself as busy as I could, picking up extra shift hours at the Hilton Hawaiian Village. It was a grind, but I had a purpose and was saving my money for future needs, like airfare to Virginia Beach, in case Skip's finances were running low. I wasn't sure when he'd arrive, but I was counting down the days, knowing it would be soon.

As for Duke, he was history. I had told him to stuff it. I wasn't interested in seeing him again. I wished him the best. He'd said he was sorry about the Mindy thing, but that it just wasn't in his nature to be with one woman for long, even though he said he loved being with me and would miss me. Lesson learned, I thought.

What was it my mom had always told me? Oh yeah, *there was a gift in every challenge, if you looked for it.* With Duke, he had filled a need and introduced me to elegant dining and a circle of higher society, which I had never experienced before. The confidence and grace I developed with him would stay with me throughout my life; I felt sure of that. However, the shadier side of Duke heightened my awareness of how one can be duped by simple manipulation and a charming personality.

It was the first of May today. I'd heard through the island grapevine that Duke had been fired from the Coco Palms. He'd been writing off exorbitant expenses for visiting friends and tourists that were above and beyond his expense account. His 240Z sports car had been repossessed by the bank, too. Apparently, he didn't pay cash for it and he never made a payment in the past four months. None of it surprised me. Living a life like he had money, but probably didn't.

He opened my eyes, that's for sure. I didn't want his lifestyle now or someone that was a womanizer.

Skip may not have known his true heart when he ran from me the first time, but he did have integrity. Everything about Skip was real. He was honest and down to earth. We both had grown and recognized what was in our hearts during the past months apart. Love is a testament of being true to yourself. No longer was I afraid to follow my heart.

Today, I got a letter from Skip telling me that he would be flying into Hawaii on May 15th. Dizzy with anticipation, I was counting down the days and dreaming of our reunion. Would he ask me to marry him again? If so, was a beach wedding possible? Floating on hope, I wasn't going to leave Hawaii without being his wife!

.... **Chapter 39** ....

Sailor on Board

Tonight Skip would be here in Hawaii! It had been almost two months since that last phone call with him, but we had written each other weekly. I couldn't believe that in a matter of hours I would see him again. Buzzing around my apartment like a honey bee on a mission, I showered, washed my hair, shaved my legs, did my makeup, and was dressed two hours before I needed to head to the airport. It was May 15th and I had planned ahead by taking this Saturday night off and Sunday, too. Nothing was going to keep me from meeting Skip's plane.

"You look beautiful, Brandi," Donna stated, tidying up the apartment and rearranging some throw pillows. "Isn't that the little red halter dress that Skip loves you in?"

"Yeah, it is. Do you think he'll remember it?" I asked doing a little twirl.

"Oh yeah, he'll remember it for sure," Sherry said, with a big grin while sitting on the sofa having a smoke. "What time does his flight get in again?"

I looked at my watch. "In less than four hours, arrives at 1:50 p.m. I know it's early, but I can't sit here any longer. Donna, can you drive me to the airport now?"

"Sure thing. Let me get my purse and we can go. Are you sure you don't want us to be there with you?" she asked.

"I'm sure, just drop me off. I probably won't be home until tomorrow afternoon sometime," I chirped.

Sherry grinned. "Oh, and why is that, Brandi?"

"You know perfectly well, Sherry," I laughed, and danced around the room.

"Yeah, pretty cool that Skip booked a hotel room at the Waikiki Reef Hotel," Donna said, patting her growing tummy. "This baby is already moving around like it's on roller skates," she laughed. "Five months along and I'm starting to feel like a blimp already."

"I think you have that glow about you, Donna," I commented as we headed out the door to her car. "See you later, Sherry," I yelled.

"Have fun, Brandi. Give Skip a big hug for me. See you tomorrow sometime."

"Okay," I hollered back, closing the door behind us.

The mid-morning heat assaulted me as we took the flight of stairs down to the parking area. "It's a hot one today, so glad you have air conditioning in your car, Donna." It was only eleven, but the temperature this morning was already a blistering ninety degrees with little or no trade winds.

"Are you good with moving back home next month to live with your dad until the baby is born?" I asked.

"I'm more than good with it. He's so happy with my decision and excited for this baby. Things have a way of working out, just like it has for you and Skip. I'm jealous, but happy for you both. And I'm glad that Sherry has a teacher friend that she's going to share a house with," Donna claimed, as we approached her car and got in.

"Yeah, things have worked out, but not without some hard lessons," I admitted. I was also glad that Duke wasn't in my life anymore. What a lesson that had been. A much older man than what I had thought. My friend Puna, the musician, had told me that Duke was thirty-six, not thirty-two. Duke had never been in the military either, I guess he made a habit of making up stories. Apparently, Puna knew his parents on the big island. No time to dwell on past mistakes, I mused. Besides, today I was ecstatic about Skip returning to Hawaii. Would he ask me again to marry him? I wouldn't hesitate for a minute, nor would I let him leave Hawaii without me this time. Perhaps, I would end up having that beach wedding of my dreams, barefoot in the sand. Anything was possible, wasn't it?

◆◆◆

The Braniff airliner jet landed on the Honolulu International Airport runway. It taxied to the gate and stopped. Inside the gated waiting area, I stood with my heart pounding hard and fast.

Within minutes, the passengers began to depart the plane onto the sunny tarmac. My eyes were glued to the exit door...waiting... waiting...longing to see that familiar handsome face. Would I recognize him from this distance? It had been nine long months since I had last seen him, back in September.

A dozen or so people stepped down the portable stairs. And then more people departed. No Skip, this was his flight, wasn't it? Suddenly, I saw a glimpse of someone in white slip around the exit door. Navy *dress whites!* Oh my God, it was him! Sailor on board! Skip was wearing his *dress whites* and he didn't have to. It was his choice, but he'd remembered how much of a uniform fetish I had. He looked as drop dead gorgeous as I remembered him! My heart exploded in a rush of emotions. Tears sprang to my eyes. My body was shaking with anticipation as I followed his every move.

He sauntered off the tarmac with that easy, sexy walk of his. His eyes locked onto mine. I ran to him. He dropped his duffle bag. He reached out for me. I collapsed into his eager arms. Oh God! I clung to him like a lifeline. Feelings of happiness, love, and relief surged through me.

"My Brandi," he said, looking down into my eyes.

"My Skip," I whispered with passion. He lowered his lips to mine in a magical, heartfelt kiss. A kiss that spoke volumes. It was like in the movies. Two lovers once again joined together after so much time apart. Home in each other's arms.

When he broke the kiss, he looked into my eyes once again. "I'm going to ask you one more time. Will you marry me?"

I looked up at him beaming with happiness. I said, "Yes!"

"Good, because I've been carrying this ring around with me for months," he grinned. Bending down, he pulled a little black velvet box out of his duffle bag. "I'm not leaving this island without you, girl," he stated. Then, he placed the gold band on my finger and kissed me passionately once again.

People around us began to clap and cheer. I didn't even realize they had been watching us. Smiling, we walked hand-in-hand out of the airport headed to the Reef Hotel on the Waikiki Beach. It was going to be a night of reunions and white hot love, that I knew for sure.

◆◆◆

Our hotel room was simple, clean, and air conditioned. An ocean view that swept me into Skip's arms like a rushing riptide. Lost in the bliss of him. His body pressed close to mine, swaying to our own sweet aloha music in the gentle afternoon sunlight. Flesh against flesh. Ravishing kisses that deepened our commitment and hunger for each other.

"My beautiful *island girl,"* he whispered. "I'm so in love with you."

"My Skip, you have my heart always."

"Brandi," he said with a raspy voice, as he took me right then in a frenzy of hurried passion.

◆◆◆

Later, we lay naked together talking, reminiscing, and making wedding plans. I reached over and touched the necklace around his neck. "You still have the St. Christopher medal I gave you when you first left," I said, with eyes filled with wonder.

"I never took it off. I can't tell you how many times I read the inscription on the back. *Beautiful moments with you.* It always gave me hope that we would be together again," he beamed, reaching for my body once again to make more beautiful moments.

Chapter 40

Hawaiian Wedding Song

Skip and I had a blissful late Saturday evening at the Reef Hotel filled with mai tais, a beach walk in the moonlight, dinner under the stars, and a night of loving each other. Sunday we did *Makapu* Beach with my roommates and some of Skip's navy buddies. On Monday, we went to the Honolulu Courthouse and got our marriage license. We only had until Saturday before Skip had to return stateside for officer training at Virginia Beach. On Tuesday, I quit my job and went shopping for a simple beach wedding dress.

Skip was staying at my apartment through the week. We were stretched out poolside. He leaned over and kissed me. "I talked to the base chaplain and he is willing to marry us Thursday evening, right on Waikiki Beach, in front of the *Moana* Hotel!"

Grinning from ear-to-ear, I reached for his hand. "Oh Skip, that would be perfect. Barefoot in the sand, gentle waves on the shore, hopefully a glorious sunset, and a simple wedding ceremony. I can't think of anything I'd rather have...except of course, you as my husband," I beamed.

"You've got that, babe and a lifetime with me," he said, in that adorable sweet Midwestern drawl that I so loved. He played with my long golden hair, as he settled back into the lounge chair, sporting a grin as big and wide as the Pacific Ocean.

"I talked with my old friend, Puna. He's the musician that plays the ukulele at the Hilton Hawaiian Village. He's off this Thursday evening and is honored to play the "Hawaiian Wedding Song" for us at our beach ceremony," I grinned, thinking that song was my favorite Hawaiian song and perfect for us. "He's also very pleased that I ditched Duke a couple of months ago. He said he was a con-man and a player among other things. He was very happy that I was following my heart and marrying you."

"He did...did he?" Skip teased.

"Yes, he did," I responded, knowing that everything had fallen into place just like it was meant to be. I was following my heart and so was Skip. The Hawaiian gods were with us and our timing was right this time.

◆◆◆

Thursday evening was finally here. Skip and I walked into the grand old *Moana* Hotel holding hands. The late afternoon sunshine glistened on the aqua blue ocean waters. The sky was awash with brilliant oranges and pinks as the sun dipped low on the horizon. The base chaplain met us at the *Moana* Hotel outdoor Banyan Court Bar at 6 p.m. We ordered mai tais and then signed our wedding license in front of him. Sherry, Donna, Puna, and Skip's best man, Ranger, joined us for a before wedding drink, too.

The outdoor Banyan Court Bar was packed with happy hour tourists and live ukulele music playing in the background, along with a lovely young lady doing a *hula*. Watching the *hula* always made me feel so in love with Hawaii. I would miss living here, but what a perfect place to say our vows to each other.

My dream of a Hawaiian beach wedding. My dream of marrying my navy man, Skip. It was all coming true. And I always wanted to live the military lifestyle. The bonds and friendships we would have throughout the years to come lifted my spirits like a ray of sunshine. I wondered where our lives would take us as I left to change into my wedding dress.

◆◆◆

Dressed in a short, lacy, white halter dress, I slipped off my flip flops and walked barefoot onto the beach. I had one white gardenia tucked behind my left ear. A symbol that I was married. I carried a simple bouquet of white ginger and baby's breath as I made my way down the beachfront. My heart overflowing with happiness and love.

Our small wedding party stood at shore's end, watching as I made my way towards them. The sunset cast a soft magnificent pinkish glow across the horizon. A warm evening breeze kissed my bare skin making me feel beautiful. Skip was wearing a white aloha shirt, white cotton bell bottom pants, and was barefoot, too. He looked dreamy to me as he stood next to Ranger, his best man.

Sherry and Donna stood next to Puna and the chaplain in front of us. A few people strolled down the beach. Some stopped, realizing what was going to take place.

◆◆◆

Brandi took Skip's breath away. My God, she was stunning. She had a grace about her that left him wondering how he had gotten so damn lucky. The woman of his dreams. Watching her near him, he knew that this was the best decision he had ever made. A life with Brandi was what was written in his heart.

He reached for her hand as she came and stood next to him. "You look so beautiful!" he whispered, with tears in his eyes.

"And you look so sexy," I replied, as Puna began to play the "Hawaiian Wedding Song" on his ukulele. The magic of his voice and its lyrics brought tears to everyone's eyes. The colorful sunset spread across the sky creating ribbons of light that mirrored the love in my heart. The soft trade winds blew across the blue waters lapping gently against the shore. When the song ended, the ceremony began. We spoke words of love, commitment, and promises before the chaplain continued.

"Do you, Skip, take this woman to be your loving wife?" the chaplain asked.

"I do!" he said, smiling into my eyes while we held hands.

"Do you, Brandi, take this man to be your loving husband?"

"I do!" I said with enthusiasm, gazing into Skip's blue eyes with promises that I knew we would always keep.

"I now pronounce you man and wife," the chaplain declared boldly.

"My wife," Skip said, and then he kissed me passionately on the lips. Everyone clapped and cheered as we held each other in a long endearing kiss.

Later, as we strolled down the beach hand-in-hand, I knew wherever our journey would take us, our island love story would be forever written in the sands of Sweet Hawaii.

The End.

Mahalo.

Made in the USA
Monee, IL
18 February 2020

21925051R00134